A VIKING NOVEL
OF
MYSTERY
AND
SUSPENSE

POST-MORTEM EFFECTS

ALSO BY THOMAS BOYLE

The Cold Stove League
Only the Dead Know Brooklyn

POST-MORTEM
EFFECTS

Thomas Boyle

VIKING

VIKING
Viking Penguin Inc., 40 West 23rd Street,
New York, New York 10010, U.S.A.
Penguin Books Ltd, 27 Wrights Lane, London W8 5TZ
(Publishing & Editorial) and Harmondsworth, Middlesex,
England (Distribution & Warehouse)
Penguin Books Australia Ltd, Ringwood,
Victoria, Australia
Penguin Books Canada Limited, 2801 John Street,
Markham, Ontario, Canada L3R 1B4
Penguin Books (N.Z.) Ltd, 182–190 Wairau Road,
Auckland 10, New Zealand

First published in 1987 by Viking Penguin Inc.
Published simultaneously in Canada

Grateful acknowledgment is made for permission to reprint excerpts from the
following copyrighted material:
The Serpent and the Rainbow by Wade Davis, published by
Simon & Schuster, Inc.
"Herman Melville's 'Moby Dick' " from *Studies in Classic American Literature* by
D. H. Lawrence. Copyright 1923, 1951 by Frieda Lawrence; Copyright © 1961 by
The Estate of Mrs. Frieda Lawrence. Reprinted by permission of Viking Penguin Inc.
"Buffalo Soldier" lyrics and music by Noel Williams. © 1983 Kenemo Music, Inc. (BMI).
All rights administered by Bob Marley Music Ltd. Irving Music, Inc.
(BMI) administers on behalf of Bob Marley Music Ltd. for the World excluding the
Caribbean. All rights reserved. International copyright secured.
"Redemption Song" lyrics and music by Bob Marley. © 1980 Bob Marley
Music Ltd. (ASCAP). All rights administered by Almo Music Corp. (ASCAP) for the
world excluding the Caribbean. All rights reserved. International copyright secured.
"Exodus" lyrics and music by Bob Marley. © 1977 Bob Marley Music Ltd. (ASCAP).
All rights administered by Almo Music Corp. (ASCAP) for the world excluding the
Caribbean. All rights reserved. International copyright secured.
"Ghostbusters" words and music by Ray Parker, Jr. © 1984 by Golden Torch
Music Corp. and Raydiola Music. Used by permission. All rights reserved.

LIBRARY OF CONGRESS CATALOGING IN PUBLICATION DATA
Boyle, Thomas, 1939–
Post-mortem effects.
I. Title.
PS3552.0933P67 1987   813'.54   87-40024
ISBN 0-670-81325-7

Printed in the United States of America by
Arcata Graphics, Fairfield, Pennsylvania
Set in Times Roman
Design by Ellen S. Levine

To the memory of my father,

Thomas J. Boyle (1906–1947);

and his sister, my aunt,

Ruth M. Boyle (1903–1970).

In Haiti, the fear is not of being harmed by zombis; it is fear of becoming one.

—Wade Davis, *The Serpent and the Rainbow*, 1985

Hot blooded, sea-born Moby Dick. Hunted by monomaniacs of the idea. . . .

The *Pequod* went down. And the *Pequod* was the ship of the white American soul. She sank, taking with her negro and Indian and Polynesian, Asiatic and Quaker and good, businesslike Yankees and Ishmael: she sank all the lot of them.

Boom! as Vachel Lindsay would say.

To use the words of Jesus, IT IS FINISHED.

Consummatum est!

But *Moby Dick* was first published in 1851. If the Great White Whale sank the ship of the Great White Soul in 1851, what's been happening ever since?

Post-mortem effects, presumably.

—D. H. Lawrence, *Studies in Classic American Literature*, 1923

POST-MORTEM EFFECTS

CHAPTER 1

IT WAS TOO ROUTINE, too harmonious, an afternoon for such calamity.

There was the pale hush of Indian summer. Young lovers, truants and dropouts from the tenements and projects south and east of the park, lay on the grass, dark faces raised to the sun. Stout Polish women propped themselves against shopping bags on the benches. An old Russian, wearing a brown suit and dark, aereated shoes, paced the pavement on Lorimer where it separated the ball fields on one side from the disused recreation center on the other. Children in the blazers and tartan skirts of nearby parochial schools played ball, swung on pipes, darted in and out of the myriad gaps in the wire fencing that surrounded the obsolete playground and the condemned, empty swimming pool. More sinister figures, dealers perhaps, hovered on the fringe. Through all this a solitary man in a black raincoat wandered, head bent and bobbing, as if he were taking, and assenting to, orders from the earth itself. To the west, the onion dome of the Byzantine church endowed a measure of Old World civility, but the horizon was dominated by the bright eerie shoulders of the Chrysler building and the boxlike Twin Towers across the river. The shadows cast by these sections of Manhattan skyline made deeper and deeper incursions into the borough of churches, dulling the already lusterless façades of the warehouses and auto-body shops. The lovers became obliged to turn their attentions to one another.

There was a sense that the grass was dying, one blade at a time, in McCarren Park, Greenpoint, Brooklyn.

The daycare group had established itself on the lushest grassy area west of Lorimer, near the backstop of a baseball diamond, where a pickup softball game was in progress. It had been one of those afternoons. Kate and Rebecca had held hands and talked about babies until Rebecca had tried to con her friend out of a new bracelet and each went off to complain about the other to her doll. Julian and Simon were warned repeatedly about going near the street. Liam was scapegoated by seven children in a row. Noah screamed bloody murder when he wasn't allowed to swing on the yellow swings in the old playground because the ground there was covered with broken bottles. Sarah said to Kirsten: "My mommy has a hair dryer. Daddy says it costs too much electric."

"My daddy has a rash," Kirsten replied.

Susan, the caretaker of the group, held the C section of the *Times* under her nose, keeping one eye on the activity, until Eric, her bearded young assistant, had to invade the dugout of one of the softball teams to extricate Julian and Simon from the ground beneath the bench where they were pulling at the players' feet and giggling. As Susan put the paper down, a fight broke out: "I'll punch you in the ear," Liam threatened.

"I'll hit you in the eye," replied James with conviction.

"James is coming to my house tonight," interjected Rebecca, who had dropped her doll in a puddle.

"You can come to my house and eat lunch dinner, you can eat my head," said Liam. Liam had a stick.

Carlos approached and tried to wrest the stick from Liam. Liam threw a punch. James pulled Liam's hair. Alyssa and

Alexandra sucked their thumbs as they sat on the grass, opening and closing their legs, revealing bright underpants. A tipped foul ball spun into the area between the backstop and the dugout. It skipped in the dirt and caught Simon in the back of his head. Simon began to wail, desperately pulling away from Eric's firm grasp.

Susan separated the embattled trio, put her two pinkies in her mouth, and whistled shrilly. "Gametime!" she called, making her hands into a T. "Food and rest! Back to the house. C'mon, guys, let's get in a line."

A strange child had wandered into the group. He had olive skin and a shock of coal-black hair. He picked up Rebecca's doll from the puddle and held it covetously. Rebecca screamed. The outsider's mother rushed over from the pavement where she had been talking to friends. She was a heavyset woman, with her shirt hanging out and old acne scars on her cheeks. She grabbed the boy by the arm with her right hand, lifting him clean into the air, and stripped him of the doll with the other. Then she slapped him full in the face. "How many time I tellya, keep the fuckin' hands off of other people's t'ings?" She shook him mightily. "How many *times!*"

Eric and Susan winced in unison at the percussion of the blow and the child's answering whimper as they marshaled up their own charges. They looked at one another in pained disapproval. Parents and group leaders in the PlaySpace Co-op did not strike children.

Nor did they have Brooklyn accents.

Only old Mrs. Kosciolek kept her eye on the man in the black raincoat. He loitered for a while in the shadow of the old rec building where the kids used to change into swimsuits and maybe play some Ping-Pong but where the windows and doors now were sealed with cinderblock. He did a kind of weave through the hooky players on the grass, then stared for a while at the kids who had sneaked through the fence and were swinging on the swings or climbing the bars. Then he huddled on a bench not far from where the Russian was taking his daily walk. There was something about this stranger, something out of place, that suggested to her that he was not American, not like *her* kind of immigrant American or the American American of the kids of these new people. These new people left their kids from the day they were born in the hands of babysitters so both husband and wife could work big jobs in the city, make lots of bucks, buy and fix up the old row houses. Drive the poor local people out of their homes. She stared at the skyscrapers, wicked source of all this disruption, with venom. Then a sadness came into her eyes. The thought of the stranger had taken her far away, back to Warsaw. Before they came to get the Jews and *everybody* then had to leave. She could smell cabbage boiling in the tiny flat, taste the sausage in the soup as she sat at the little table with the linoleum cloth. Her first husband, Lech, was sitting across from her in this vision, with his muscles and sparse hair and blackened fingernails, ripping bread from the loaf to dip in the soup, and she knew she was thinking about poverty. And being a greenhorn, a Hunkie, a Polack, whatever they wanted to call it. She wondered what was worse, being poor or being alone? They had gotten off the boat and then Lech passed away. But she met Stanley, who was foreman at the Navy Yard, and things were okay. Not great, just okay. Stanley would eat kielbasi and drink 7 and 7s until he fell asleep in front of the TV instead of coming to bed with her. Now Stanley was gone too and her three kids, whom she had never let out of her sight at the swimming pool until they got their lifesaver's badges, had long since left Greenpoint to be real Americans, to Houston, San Jose, Atlanta. So they made lots of money, lived in nice suburban houses, sent her checks. But no visits, no love! Now her kids should see these new people who were coming *to* Greenpoint to be real American Americans! She wondered where they came from, where they had left mothers, grandmothers, behind and alone. America had made the Koscioleks well off and had driven them apart: her own grandchildren probably never even thought what it meant to be Polack. They didn't even go to church. Her eyes blurred. She knew she was an embarrassment to them. There were entire weeks when her every thought was tinged by the fear that she would never see her children, or *their* children, again.

The children from the PlaySpace Co-op assembled, each clutching a strand of rope, which was, in turn, attached to a central spine of thicker cord held at head and tail by Eric and Susan. The effect suggested a large ungainly insect making drunken but determined progress to some unspecified goal. Except for a couple of the little girls—who wore jumpers and saddle shoes—the kids all wore running shoes and Oshkosh coveralls over superhero T-shirts.

"Hold it, hold it," called Eric.

"Body count," piped Susan, cheerfully, cupping her hands at her lips. Then she extended a paint-stained finger and went through the counting process aloud. "Twelve," she breathed. "I'm losing it. Thank God Camille is taking Aftercare today."

"No," said Eric, "I get twelve, too."

"Noah isn't here," Kate announced, pulling a ribbon from her hair.

"He isn't?" Susan was momentarily stunned; then she ran to the baseball diamond, scanned the faces in the dugout and on the field. Nothing. She scrambled aimlessly around the benches near the pavement.

"He's always trying to get across the street to the swings," said Eric.

"No!" Susan raced across the street and made her way through a hole that looked like it had been blown through the fence by a bazooka. She checked the swings and the jungle gym, kicking broken glass out of her path. Nothing. She ran back and clutched her end of the rope. Eric kept looking around in a circle, not moving. Tears gushed to Susan's eyes. She started to count again. She threw the rope into the air. She yelled, "Jesus fucking Christ; we've lost Noah!"

Mrs. Kosciolek came out of her reverie.

"Who's lost?" she called from her bench.

"A little boy, one of these."

"With bears on his shoes?"

"Right! You saw him?" Relief began to seep back into Susan's voice, but there were lines on her face that had not been apparent a few minutes before.

"Saw him?" Mrs. Kosciolek sniffed. " 'Course I saw him. He went off with the Jew. Black coat and hat, head bowed like he's praying." She sounded very weary. "Over to the pool. Where it used to be a pool." She turned and looked back toward the city. The fading sun struck the top of the World Trade Center at an angle that seemed to send light skipping across the river and rooftops like a stone, flat and golden. She made a face, an expression of profound distaste. She muttered to herself, nodding her head for emphasis, "In the old country they stole the babies to drink their blood. The Jews."

CHAPTER 2

DESALES SAT, BROODING over his cup of black coffee, in the diner on Manhattan Avenue. The blond waitress had recognized him from the television news and kept trying to start a conversation as she hoisted steaming platters of stuffed cabbage or moussaka past him to the other tables.

"It's a shame," she said once, snapping her chewing gum. "I seen the kid lotsa times with his old man on Sundays gettin' the paper. The *Times*," she added with disdain. "They din't come in here. These people eat different. Ya think the Jews did it?"

DeSales shrugged, looking for an ashtray. There was none, so he tapped the ashes into his saucer.

The waitress quickly provided a receptacle from another table. "There's gonna be hell to pay if they did," she went on. "People around here's had enough. When I was a kid we din't even lock the doors." She raised a dark, sharply penciled eyebrow. "It useta be, you knew who your neighbor was, right?" She tapped him meaningfully on the arm. "Everybody was like family, right?"

DeSales gave her a wan smile. This appeared to please her immensely. She skipped across the room to pour coffee. What

DeSales had wanted to say was that either she was older, a lot older, than he was; or that she had come from a particularly stupid family. Greenpoint—or Green*pernt* as they had said it in the old days—had never exactly been the Sunnybrook Farm of the Five Boroughs. And there had never been a time in *his* lifetime that doors had been deliberately left unlocked for the convenience of light-fingered or heavy-hitting characters from the docks and slums that surrounded the neighborhood. Instead he had made nice, and now he was relieved to see Kavanaugh attempting to squeeze his fat ass into the booth. The waitress came back, brandishing one of those menus that are about three feet long and appear to have been manufactured out of used vinyl car seats. Kavanaugh glanced briefly at the handwritten list of daily specials and ordered fresh ham and red cabbage. With a side of mashed, lots of gravy. And a Diet Pepsi. He held a brown butcher's bag aloft: "Pirogis. You can't hardly get them no more. Peg can throw them in the microwave for supper." He gave DeSales a look. *"If* I ever get home on time."

The waitress delivered the soda. She eyeballed all of Kavanaugh as if he resembled John Travolta in tight pants. "Sarge, I seen you on channel eleven once. When you caught the guy in Bushwick was rapin' old ladies and chokin' them with their girdles? Hey, tell me: Is it true if you don't have a girdle on he won't touch you?"

Kavanaugh looked self-satisfied. "True."

"Now I got one more's been botherin' me."

"Shoot, one more."

"Those Negroes that said they were Jews? Last year? They beat their kids with bamboo rods and poured hot sauce on the wounds."

"Yeah. Sure I remember. The Black Hebrew Israelites, they called themselves. What's the question?"

"What kinda sauce was it? What brand?"

Kavanaugh shrugged. "That was in Queens." He waved his hand dismissively. "Out of our jurisdiction."

She thought about that for a moment.

"Well how about this kid here? Any clues?"

Kavanaugh sucked in his red cheeks and duplicated her breathy tone: "Not yet." He winked. "But when we get something, you'll be one of the first to know. Community involvement is a big priority with us, right, Frank?"

DeSales nodded without enthusiasm. The waitress giggled like a teenager and moved off proudly.

"Starfucker," Kavanaugh hissed, bobbing his three chins in her wake. He turned to DeSales, "Hey, Frank, how come you always get on the network affiliates and I never do any better than channel eleven or five?"

DeSales ignored the question. Bernie was on one of his anticipation-of-food highs. He considered suggesting that his chief aide lose some weight, polish his TV image. Instead he asked, "How's the old lady? Mrs. Kosciolek?"

"Crackers. One minute she's in Warsaw, the next San Jose. Anyplace but the here and now."

"You don't think she actually saw the guy?"

"You bet she did. But by the time we get him in a lineup, if we ever do, she could decide it was really Moshe Dayan was the perp. Eyepatch and all." He contemplated his vision. "Or Golda Meir. Maybe."

"You're telling me she has a Jewish problem?"

"No shit Dick Tracy."

The waitress appeared with two heaping plates. She leaned across Kavanaugh's girth to set them down and took her time about it. When she was gone again, Kavanaugh shoveled some cabbage into his mouth, adding: "The dopiest Legal Aid broad would make mincemeat out of her, Mrs. K., on the stand."

"The neighborhood types," DeSales nodded toward the waitress, "seem to take her at her word."

Kavanaugh shook salt onto the pork and buttered a slice of white bread. "There's a social club on up Java Street. They're nervous about Hispanics moving in. So they've come to the obvious conclusion that it's the Jews are driving the Latinos up from Williamsburg. On top of that, they figure it was the Polack Catholics and not the Jews who took the real heat in the war. They've got some debts to settle. Since most of them are out of work, they've got the time. They're threatening to march down to Williamsburg."

"Hope they don't make a wrong turn and end up on one of those dangerous blocks. The ones with the *minorities.*"

Kavanaugh laughed out loud. He had finished the mashed potatoes and was wiping up the leftover gravy with bread.

"Seriously," DeSales continued, lighting a match, putting it to his Benson and Hedges Regular, then watching the match burn down to his fingers before dropping it in the ashtray, "we'd better notify the crowd-control boys."

"I already did. After I left Mrs. K. And before I bought the pirogis. How were the parents?"

"In shock. Like you'd expect. The biggest crisis either of them's ever been through before was saving a whale . . . okay, maybe only a couple striped bass. They work for environmental agencies. Lawyers."

"Any ideas, enemies, ransom?"

"Nothing. Can't believe it was deliberate. No enemies. Don't know of people who'd commit a violent act in revenge anyway. Some of their best friends are Jews, but not religious, hardly Hasidic. The only people in the neighborhood they know are people like themselves . . ."

"Yuppies."

"Whatever."

"So somebody's after their money, but slips with the kid."

"All their assets are tied up in the house. And in a mortgage they just swung to build a place in the Berkshires. That's when the wife broke down. She started off about how they'd gone into serious hock to have a country place where Noah could climb trees in the summer. And swim, because the pool here is unusable. And the playground is unsafe . . . The husband kept clutching his wineglass. I thought it was going to shatter in his hand, his knuckles were so white.''

Kavanaugh drained the Diet Pepsi and wiped his face. "Somebody could have *thought* they had money. I'll bet our waitress does.''

DeSales shook his head in dismissal. "We're not going to solve it from this end. There was blood in the locker room where the cinderblock had been knocked in. That suggests rage, passion, whatever. He must have hurt the kid bad, if not killed him, moments after he picked him up. Second, the presence of the kids in the park at that particular time and place was chance also. It's not where, or when, they normally go. And I'm assuming the guy even got lucky finding all the holes in the fence and the rec building. Did Mrs. Kosciolek ever see the guy in black before? No. Has anyone else? No. I think he's a loony from some entirely different place. A stranger to Greenpoint. So, we'll only make progress two ways. We go back to the pool now and go over it one more time to see if he left anything behind we can tie to him; and we go to records and check the M.O. Usually it's somebody who's done the same thing before. Somebody in a halfway house from a state hospital, maybe.''

The two men looked at one another. Kavanaugh began to extricate himself from the seat, then his wallet from his pants.

"You're forgetting something, Frank. We've got a date at the morgue in half an hour; we've been over that rec center with a fine-tooth comb, and everything's been set in motion for the computer record search. There's no sense putting it off any longer. We gotta go look at the kid.''

At the cash register, Kavanaugh tucked in his shirt, then loosened his belt and pulled the shirt halfway out again. "Y'know, I think you're losing some of your appetite for your work, Frank. You always had the strongest stomach in the Task Force, which was as it should be, you being the boss. Me, ever since I had babies of my own, I haven't been able to look at a kid's corpse without wanting to puke my guts out.''

"Guess I'm lucky I don't have a wife and kids, huh, Bernie?" DeSales buttoned his blue blazer and straightened his neatly pressed flannels. His hand went to his silk tie as Kavanaugh pocketed the change. "You got your problems, I got mine, Bernie. I don't like religious nuts, and after the morgue I gotta go see this rabbi. While you and Peg are playing with the microwave in Bay Ridge. I talked to him on the phone and he sounds like he's gonna burn my ass. He's already got a conspiracy theory. It was the Nazis or the Arabs or some rival tribe of Hasids planted the body in his yeshivah. Or, worse yet, it was the Jews who dress and act like regular people. Getting straight answers is going to be like pulling teeth."

"That's nothing new. I always thought you held the world record for pulling teeth outa religious fanatics. I think your problem's something else. If I was a shrink, I'd say you look depressed."

"Maybe Williamsburg depresses me; maybe it's that I'm sick of Brooklyn. Maybe I keep thinking about that woman. The mother of Noah. Gillian Simmons. I feel sorry for her *and* her husband . . . his name's Jeremy . . . but these people. I mean, they've lost their only kid and they sit there talking to me about *real estate* for Christ's sake. Brownstone in Brooklyn. A-frame in the mountains. *That* shit."

"How's your old friend, Roz?" asked Kavanaugh, suddenly. "And the Internal Affairs guys?"

The reaction that passed briefly over DeSales's sharp features was part furtive, part caustic: "Roz? Oh, yeah, *Roz*. Haven't seen her in a long time. And the visits from Internal Affairs were strictly routine. I told you that when they came around."

"Sure," said Kavanaugh without feeling.

The two detectives—one tall, fat, florid, unkempt; the other of medium height, trim, swarthy, and nattily dressed—stepped out onto Manhattan Avenue, drawing stares. A husky woman with high cheekbones and fair hair paused in the window of the Wedding Store where she was adjusting veils on the faces of mannequins. Across the street, a man emerged from Polestar Liquors toting a bottle of potato vodka; he stopped and watched as Kavanaugh inserted the key in the door of the car. The hoarse-voiced old man hawking red poppies for the Veterans of Foreign Wars leaned back into a doorway.

Waiting for Kavanaugh to turn the key, DeSales looked for a long moment to the north where the avenue opened on the East River and the Upper East Side of Manhattan, where the peculiar right triangle of architectural arrogance that sat atop the Citicorp Building pulled the eye away from the banalities of Greenpoint.

"How many times, speaking of shrinks," Kavanaugh called across the roof of the Ford to DeSales, "have you told me that people exposed to sudden violence often try to . . . whadyacallit . . . *displace* their feelings onto something else, like motor-mouthing about houses in the country or the Polish blaming the Jews or the Jews blaming the Arabs?" He climbed into his seat and lifted the lock on DeSales's side.

DeSales slammed his door. "Drive," he commanded, then fell silent. There was no sense telling Bernie that all through his interrogation of the grieving parents he, too, had been thinking more about real estate than about Roz or department surveillance. The Syrian Jews had bought his building and were going co-op with it. DeSales couldn't even afford the insider's price for his apartment. He was convinced that the Syrians were trying to get rid of all but their own kind, other Jews included, and convert the building into another link, another mortar block, in the ethnic fortress they were erecting around that section of Ocean Parkway. The place he had called home for twenty-odd years would become a residential adjunct to the multimillion-dollar Sephardic Community Center down the street. Forty-five years old, a detective inspector, he couldn't even afford a one-room studio in the farther reaches of Brooklyn. Maybe he was losing it: not just the apartment, but the nut, the whole enchilada—he gave a parting glance to Polish Greenpoint as Kavanaugh pointed the car in the direction of yet another ghetto—no, the whole *holupki,* he thought to himself. Maybe now he'd finally really understood why there were rogue cops, cops on the take, cops who sucked the barrels of their service revolvers before saying bye-bye to the cruel world.

CHAPTER 3

THE CONVERTED RECREATIONAL vehicle made its way slowly down New Utrecht Avenue, squeezing past the graffiti-spattered pillars that support the groaning El, threading its way through the cars in various states of disrepair that stood as many as four deep outside the auto diagnostic centers. A few blocks after the intersection with Fort Hamilton Parkway, the white camper turned left and accelerated through a neighborhood of undistinguished brick semidetached houses. A number of these declared themselves, via signs in Hebrew and English, to be temples or religious schools. The streets were quiet, populated primarily by formally dressed young women pushing expensive baby carriages. Many of these women were already pregnant again, stomachs swelling under their tailored, long-skirted outfits. They paid scant heed to the van, in spite of the music—a cross between polka and college fight song, complete with background cheering—which blared from the loudspeakers flanking a rickety three-sided bamboo hut on the roof.

The Lubavitcher Mitzvah Tank made another left, onto a busy commercial thoroughfare, and pulled up in front of a restaurant:

THE KOSHER BLOSSOM—BOROUGH PARK'S INTERNATIONAL FAST FOOD NOSHERIA. The pavement was thronged with people. There were clusters of old folks in Depression-era secular dress, Holocaust survivors berating one another good-humoredly in a dozen languages. There were the bearded Hasidim, long-sideburned, in their wide-brimmed velvet black hats and black frock coats; most of these appeared in a hurry, and many were young and intense. There were more young mothers, more baby carriages.

A man in full Hasidic gear and carrying what appeared to be a bouquet of Indian corn and citrus fruits dismounted from the Mitzvah Tank. He leaned briefly against the WE WANT MOSIACH NOW sign painted on the side of the vehicle. He pulled at his beard, surveying the thriving kosher butcher shops and vendors of religious literature. He stepped forward to scrutinize a boarded-up former dry-goods establishment, and a tenement house converted into the Congregation Kahal Torah, which announced proudly, in English, from four prominent window displays: AIR-CONDITIONED. Then he took a few purposeful strides and entered The Kosher Blossom.

The layout of the restaurant was more or less identical to that of any fast-food chain in the Western world. There were fixed orange plastic tables and a long counter with two cash registers at the back of the room. Behind the register to the left was a Chinese man and behind him on the wall an orange billboard that offered Egg Foo Young, Fried Rice, and Moo Shoo Chicken. At the other register stood a glowering man with a beard, yarmulke, and large aquiline nose. Behind him, the wall menu included Chicken Soup, Pastrami, Tongue, and Brown's sodas.

It was only 11 A.M.; the restaurant had but two patrons, young men of college age wearing baseball caps, one Mets, one Yankees. The first was eating an egg roll, the other a chopped-liver knish. They were arguing passionately about computer software. The Lubavitcher stepped up to them and, not surprisingly, asked the required question prefatory to proselytizing for his sect: "Are you Jewish?"

The Yankee waved him away with the half-eaten knish. The other did not even look up. He said, "You gotta go with the IBM compatibles. Look, Leading Edge could be out of business in a year. It's a shit deal."

The knish eater responded, "My cousin in Jersey pirates everything; word processing, tax programs. Only a shnook wouldn't take it."

The Lubavitcher produced a snub-nosed pistol from his pocket and knocked the knish out of the young man's hand. Then he pressed the barrel into his ear. "I want both of you to crawl under your seats, put your noses on the floor, close your eyes, and pretend you're praying to Mecca."

"Yes, *sir*. Anything you say." They scrambled under the seats. The Mets cap fell off, revealing beneath it a yarmulke embroidered with a psychedelic design.

The gunman stepped to the counter. The smile remained frozen on the Chinaman's face. The Jew crossed and uncrossed his arms over the shiny apron. "Hit the deck," the Lubavitcher said to the grinning Oriental. And he did, emitting a sound not unlike laughter. "Now," he said to the other counterman, "it is Succot, and I think you owe a friendly donation to my *rebbe*. Put your hands on the counter. Good. Now your head. Right." He brushed the plain skullcap away, and struck the man sharply, with the pistol, on his crown. As the counterman began to sink, unconscious, behind the counter, the assailant dropped his lemons and Indian corn on the floor and caught the collar of the man's shirt. With one hand, he hauled the hefty restaurateur up until his torso stretched across the counter. He laid down the gun and produced a pair of scissors. Quickly and efficiently, he trimmed most of the man's beard, stuffing hair into his pockets. He cut the yarmulke to bits. He picked up the pistol again, assured himself that the baseball fans and the Chinaman had not moved. He replaced weapon and cutting tools in the pocket of his long black coat and walked briskly to the door. He stepped through the oblivious crowd on the pavement and climbed back into the passenger seat of the

RV. As it pulled away from the curb, the egg-roll eater appeared in the doorway of the nosheria.

"Motherfucking schmuck!" he yelled.

Later, one passerby asserted that the driver of the vehicle was a woman, but this was generally discounted around Borough Park. The witness was an Italian from 11th Avenue, walking to a pork store in Bensonhurst, and didn't know any better.

CHAPTER 4

MEGAN MOORE REMOVED the earphone, arranged her notes in front of her, dismissed the technician who had been adjusting a camera angle, nodded, and waved good-bye to the director who had been whispering frantically from a point about two inches from the back of her neck. Making sure her shoulder straps were right, she leaned forward and gave DeSales a reassuring pat on the hand, silently blowing him a kiss. He realized that her breasts, along with her face, had been rouged for the camera. Only the parts that showed, he assumed. She mouthed one word to him: "Later." There was something bold, rapacious, about her that had not been there in her radio days. This could turn out to be an interesting evening after all. When the show was over.

Megan, anchorperson for the nightly newsmagazine "New York Live," opened the show with a solemn pun:

"We may be *live,* but tonight's show is about *death.* Death compounded by other acts of violence, and by seriously escalating intolerance, even hatred, between and among some of the city's most prominent religious communities. Each of our guests is in his own way uniquely qualified to comment on the situation. Here at the top of the show, to review these unfortunate events with us, is Detective Inspector Francis DeSales, supercop," she glanced over with respectful affection, "head of the Brooklyn Violence Task Force and the individual primarily responsible for directing the investigation."

DeSales bowed his head briefly in acknowledgment, wanting to wince at the "supercop" label; he buttoned and unbuttoned the jacket of his gray Italian suit with the thumb and forefinger of his right hand. He was uncomfortable. Of course, he had been on TV frequently before, but never sitting at a conference table on a show like this, looking for all the world like some professor or government expert or politician happily prepared to bullshit his audience to death. *His* specialty for the tube was standing in front of an ambulance or next to a body bag on a bloodstained sidewalk, dispassionately intoning phrases like "no comment" or "the alleged perpetrator" into a sea of microphones waving before him.

Instead, now Megan Moore turned from her talking-head position facing directly into one camera and stretched herself languorously in the swivel chair, facing DeSales. She crossed her legs, so that the open toe of one of her pumps almost touched his knee. She had reinserted the earphone in the ear facing the camera, DeSales assumed, to accentuate for the viewer the sense that late-breaking stories were imminent and she was tuned in, alert, as usual. DeSales felt in his pocket for his box of Benson & Hedges, but then remembered he had been cautioned by the chief not to smoke. Bad for the image. The chief would owe him one—at least—for this, for agreeing to be standup guy for the whole department.

"First, let's go to the videotape," she said, and a large monitor, one of the two on the facing wall, came alive.

The tape had been nicely edited, a montage of scenes accompanied by Megan Moore's prerecorded narration, tracing the events of the past week: children playing in McCarren Park; Mrs. Kosciolek interviewed on her bench; a helicopter shot of the enormous empty blue-green swimming pool with the broken-down fountains at each end; the bed-frame factory; the yeshivah in Williamsburg; the distraught parents, sobbing, trailed by microphones; a whirlybird overview of the Brooklyn-Queens Expressway from Humboldt and McGuinness to Flushing Avenue; "Christkillers" scrawled on placards waved by toughs on Bedford where the police blockade had stopped them just short of the yeshivah; on the steps of the adjoining synagogue, hundreds of irate Hasidim shaking fists at the mob. Some of the Jews wore pale brown fur pillbox hats that resembled automatic shoe polishers turned on their side.

DeSales's smile was first tinged with solemnity. He remembered sadly the days when he and his buddies had trekked all the way from their Italian neighborhood in South Brooklyn to the famous McCarren Pool in North Brooklyn for the privilege of splashing about under the gushing fountains with thousands of other proletarian adolescents, all white Christians it now seemed. There were Italians in Greenpoint, of course, lots of them, but DeSales's group always aimed to meet some Polish girls, reputed to be tall, blond, and round-heeled.

Then he flashed an ironic squint, showing the crow's feet at the corners of his eyes: the camera had failed to record, besides the past glories of McCarren Park, the building around the corner from the temple that advertised itself, in bright neon, as THE BIRTHPLACE OF THE SQUARE KNISH. Sometimes he knew too much. That was why he was a detective. He was encouraged to take the offensive.

"I'm impressed," he said. "How much air time did that take, about two minutes? It's good for *your* purposes, but to me, professionally useless. The situation is so much more complicated. And it's the nature of TV news—or of film—to have to gloss over things." Like the home of the square knish, he thought. Like Sylvia Shears, who in 1954 was the most beautiful and French-kissable girl in McCarren Park.

Megan Moore was too quick. She grinned like a cat having discovered a lame mouse, and sat forward, clasping her knee with interlocked fingers.

"And that's *exactly* why we need you here, Inspector. We need *depth*. Are you implying that there is undisclosed evidence in the case?" She raised one eyebrow, a nice feminine version of William F. Buckley, Jr.

DeSales stumbled, then recovered. "No. I'm not implying anything. I said it quite directly. This is a complicated situation."

Moore shuffled her notes: "Then let's proceed. You find the evidence of Mrs. Kosciolek, and the man—Mr. Smirnov, who was walking near the rec center—unassailable?"

"No evidence is 'unassailable.' "

"Do you believe them?"

"Of course I believe them. They're sincere, upstanding citizens. But all they tell us is that they saw a man in black carrying the child through a hole in the fence toward the closed building. And that there was no indication that the child was struggling."

"We saw Mrs. Kosciolek on the video saying that the kidnapper was dressed like an Orthodox Jew."

"Like an Orthodox Jew doesn't mean he *was* one."

"Dershowitz Bed Frames, on Bayard Street adjacent to McCarren Park, is owned by Orthodox Jews. The body was found in a Hasidic academy in a box that originated at the Dershowitz warehouse. Isn't this a lot of coincidence?"

"Sure, but the bed frames had been back-ordered by the yeshivah for some time. They were for a group of newly arrived South African rabbinical students who, in the meantime, have been sleeping in sleeping bags on the floor of an attic at the school. It's just as likely that this has something to do with a South African protest—don't quote me on that: I can see it in a misleading headline already—or, more likely, the killer, whatever religion he happens to be, merely used what was available. The entire sad story could be coincidence. A sick man is watching children at play; he sees one of them sneak away from the group; impetuously he abducts him, for what motive we do not yet know, but we can guess, and when the child cries out or resists in some way, he strangles him in a fit of rage or fear or whatever turns him on."

"What about the blood in the locker room?"

"Less helpful than I had hoped. It's the same type as the boy's: O, the most common in the country. It's still being subjected to dating tests. Until we know *when* it was spilled, we know nothing. That locker room has been broken open for some time now, we've learned. Teenagers go there to use drugs; bums sleep in there. Lots of reason for blood being splattered around."

"How do you know this?"

DeSales winked. " 'Undisclosed sources close to the investigation.' Think I can get a job as a reporter?"

Megan Moore sat back again, tapping her temple with her pen. "Well, at least our viewers are getting to see why you're called the Saint."

"You mean because of my directness and honesty?"

"Forget it." She consulted her notes, took a breath, and looked up. The green eyes were as clear and piercing as ever, enhanced in fact by the touch of red she had added to her hair since switching to TV. It occurred to DeSales for the first time that she looked younger than she had five years before. She must have felt him studying her, for there was a hint of a blush beneath the makeup. She cleared her throat. "However circumstantial the evidence is in the murder of Noah Simmons, it seems to be clear that the unprovoked attack on a Hasidic businessman in Borough Park this morning certainly adds fuel to the fire of religious speculation and anti-Semitism."

"Right. My men are working on that case right now, except that there appears to be little to find out. The murder of the child is an open book for interpretations. Nobody saw the actual crime; we haven't established beyond a doubt where it took place; we don't know at what point the body was put in the box; we don't know if it was by chance or preconceived plan that it ended up where it did. And, of course, we don't even know if the selection of the victim was premeditated. In Borough Park, as I understand it, there were literally dozens of witnesses. Each has identified the vehicle—which, by the way, was abandoned in the parking lot of

Washington Cemetery directly adjacent to the F train stop at McDonald Avenue, less than ten blocks from the incident. Everyone also agrees that the man was exactly and precisely dressed as a Lubavitcher—that's another Hasidic sect from the one in Williamsburg—that he carried Succot plants, that he declared quite publicly to the victim, before knocking him unconscious and clipping his beard, that this was a kind of grudge retaliation from another group of Orthodox believers. But from what we've learned in our interrogations down there, it will take a theologian more than a cop to untangle things. The relations between the various Jewish groups seem far more complicated than the crime.''

Megan Moore swung in her seat back to face the camera. The camera dollied in for a closeup.

"Wonderful segue, Inspector. Thank you. Now let me introduce our other guests for tonight's edition of 'New York Live.' First, live on the video monitor from his congregation, Rabbi Shlomo Glickstein of the Congregation Lev Chaim in Williamsburg.'' The head of an old man with a hawk eye, a long white beard, button nose, and black hat sitting casually off his forehead appeared on the screen. "Next, here in the studio an official at the office of Housing and Urban Development, who also happens to be an ordained Reform rabbi, Dr. Nathan Foss.'' Foss entered and sat down quickly. He was very short, wore a chalk-striped blue suit, and smoked a pipe. His salt-and-pepper beard and mustache were neatly trimmed. His head was uncovered. "And finally, an expert from outside the world of Judaism, Professor Timothy Desmond of the Institute for Urban Studies. Professor Desmond is the author of a highly regarded recent book, *Ritual and Revenge: Criminality and the Cloak of Religion.* Professor Desmond?'' The familiar tall, tweedy figure ambled in and settled himself into a chair beside Foss. Above them, on one screen, Rabbi Glickstein appeared to be meditating; on the other, a hastily assembled film clip on Borough Park ran its short course, ending, like its predecessor, with angry Hasidim shaking fists.

DeSales felt a kind of vertiginous outrage. Megan had pulled a fast one on him, sneaking Desmond into the equation. Perhaps she thought the good professor's presence would provoke DeSales into the sort of combative indiscretion he knew she expected to achieve when the two rabbis went after one another. Desmond had once insinuated himself into DeSales's pursuit of a mass murderer named Tyrone Ward, whom Megan herself had dubbed the Grim Graveyard Reaper; and it was Desmond who had saved the lethal psychopath from drowning in Gowanus Bay, thus thwarting DeSales's effort to spare society the bother of having to try the man or suffer the possibility he might walk the streets again. Because of Desmond, Ward now languished in a mental institution: at the whim of some soft-headed shrink or soft-hearted judge, the Reaper might someday be loose in Brooklyn again. Very likely, as was the killer of Noah Simmons. Thanks to the overdeveloped sense of justice of people like Desmond.

But it was the video monitors that made him momentarily dizzy. They seemed to have taken on a countenance of their own, sightless and unforgiving inquisitors, invoking a sense of a plunge into the depths of hell.

The scene crystallized in one intense moment a cop's chronic dilemma: punishment or lenience, conservative or liberal, order or chaos. Life or Death. By the time DeSales shook his head clear, the debate was well begun.

DeSales noticed first that Foss had placed a pair of rimless half spectacles on the tip of his nose and was calmly taking in Glickstein's denunciations while lighting and relighting his pipe. Then Foss glanced sideways at the detective and lifted an eyebrow as if it were DeSales's turn to do something. Glickstein, in an Eastern European accent, was saying, "The New York City police might as well be the Gestapo for all the protection we get."

DeSales supposed he was being called on to defend himself. He said, with as much conviction as he could muster, "We're doing the best we can. None of your congregation has been hurt and we've minimized any material damage to your property or the neighborhood in general."

"There are still racists throwing stones, calling names, roaming and threatening. And on the basis of what? Testimony from two senile anti-Semites, one of whom had Stalinist connection. Pogroms will be next." The rabbi waved his finger. "And what of allegations you allow to be published? That the killer was one of us? That one of us has attacked a good religious man in Borough Park so as to cast shadow on Lubavitcher. Untrue. We are peaceful people. Unlike Lubavitcher we mind our own business. We are peaceful, we know God exists in everything. A man dressed as I am is religious man. Entire existence, twenty-four hours a day, is devoted to holiness of everything and everyone around us. We are mystics, we study our texts, the outside world is residence of holiness, and is of interest to us for only that reason."

"Mr. Foss?" said Megan Moore. "Any response?"

Foss shifted in his seat, fingered the spectacles, and tapped his pipe on the ashtray. "Were it so simple." He chuckled. He faced the camera, looking sincere. "First of all I'd like to make it clear that, whatever I say tonight, neither I nor anyone at HUD or in the city government condones or even remotely tolerates the outrageous displays we have seen in three of our oldest and most cherished ethnic neighborhoods in recent days. Gentile versus Jew, Jew versus Jew . . ."

Glickstein hissed, then broke out, "Jew against Jew! It's a conspiracy against true Jews. How you define Jew? You're no . . ."

"Please, Rabbi, let him finish."

"Jew against Jew, I was saying. There is a tradition in your sect, is there not, Rabbi Glickstein, of treating other Jews who tread on your turf, namely Lubavitchers, roughly: cutting beards, removing trousers, that sort of thing."

The old man appeared to tremble; he looked off to the side as if he were being cued. "One instance," he conceded. "Some overzealous young men . . . a Lubavitcher invaded our place of worship and was attempting to brainwash one of our people into defecting . . ."

"Defecting?" Foss asked. "Sounds like Russia. I thought *our* people came to this country because there was freedom to practice the religion of our choice."

Glickstein looked wounded, then summoned together his energy, puffing himself up: *"Our* people. Hm, we shall see. In any case, you distort the picture, *Commissioner."* He used the title with biting sarcasm. "How we deal with our *own* problems, on our *own* property, is quite a different matter from what is at hand. A child is dead, completely unrelated to us—and I do not necessarily include *you* among *us*—in any way. A man who appears to be a member of another congregation, Hasidic of course, but also unrelated to us, assaults another religious Jew who is not one of us *either.* And, this is all the way across Brooklyn. Greenpoint, I acknowledge, is nearby our Williamsburg community . . . There is no question but this is Hitlerism, an anti-Semitic slur . . ."

Foss interrupted, sounding pleased with himself: "You speak of *your* property, Rabbi, and address me as if you were divorced from the rest of the city, from the rest of Jewry. The reason I am here today is to testify that your *people,* as you call them, have indulged in many forms of illicit and semilegal activity to preserve and expand your real estate, also in order to promote your separateness. And," he leaned forward and pointed his pipe vigorously at the screen on the wall, "these activities plus your aggressive maintenance of a radical stance, in language, manners, dress, housing . . . this has prolonged, even extended in this country the very anti-Semitism of which you claim victimhood . . ."

Glickstein appeared almost apoplectic; then his voice exploded from the screen: " 'Radical'? 'Radical'! We are not the radicals: my beliefs, my Talmudic study, my observance of dietary laws and of Shabbot—these are not radical, but *traditional;* it is scum like you who have deserted the tradition to assimilate into a foreign culture." Glickstein looked about, as if searching for the appropriate villain, and pointed a finger at Desmond, who had not yet spoken: "You are no more Jew than *he* is."

"Your hostile stance on Israel would suggest the opposite." Foss banged his pipe.

"Israel! Whose Israel? Ours, or that of Babylon? There are lewd advertisements on the sacred walls of Jerusalem. This is the Promised Land? A land without a Messiah?"

"Gentlemen, please."

Megan was loving it, DeSales thought. For her this meant ratings; for him it meant crowd-control problems, vandalism, the works. He looked at Desmond, who seemed not to mind having been selected as role model for what a Jew should *not* be.

And their eyes met.

Desmond raised his eyebrows, a tentative greeting. DeSales remembered that he had not been such a bad guy after all. Smart, a hard worker, had a sense of humor. And no religion: that almost rated him three stars. And he had been having woman trouble, with his wife, when they had last met. That moved him up to four stars.

Foss now spoke with the measured complacency of a graduate of Yale Law School, which he was, about to make a decisive point in a brief: "If you are so traditional, Rabbi, so involved with the universality of God, why do you insist on setting yourself apart from the country of which you are a citizen? If someone stones me or calls me a 'Christ killer,' that is not a definition of me as a Jew, a particular kind of Jew, or something altogether different. It defines the stone thrower or the name caller as a sick person. If we truly believe in a universal creator or power in the universe, how can we maintain a separate social identity? If this power is in us all and all we touch, think of what this implies in the matter of women. . . . Your sense of them as unclean, needing ritual baths."

"Women!" Glickstein shook his head. "Your so-called liberation of women portends the destruction of the family—*your* families, not ours . . ."

Megan Moore glared at Glickstein, then interrupted: "Sorry, gentlemen. We must hear from Professor Desmond before we take a break. Then we can get back to your discussion. Professor

Desmond, what light can the student of crime and religion shed on this issue?''

Desmond pulled at an earlobe, faced Megan Moore. "There is of course no *one* issue here, and I don't pretend to share the inspector's expertise in detection, or the rabbis' passionate involvement in their religion. But I can tell you that what happened in Greenpoint and the social consequences of a Jew being identified as killer or criminal outsider is part of a long tradition, justified or not, in Western civilization. We can go back not only to the *Canterbury Tales,* but to Shakespeare and Dickens, to find the most visible works that deal with this theme. And here I refer only to *English* literature.''

Desmond gave DeSales a questioning glance. He was doing his best not to appear to be talking down to his audience.

"Could you please be more specific," the anchorwoman smiled understandingly, "in about twenty seconds?"

"Geoffrey Chaucer wrote 'The Prioress's Tale' in the late thirteen hundreds. It's about a Christian child abducted by Jews for the purpose of a ritual murder. The tale is set in an unspecified city in Asia, but is based on the true story of the killing of an English boy called Hugh of Lincoln in 1255, which was blamed on the Jews, and that particular racial indictment was based on an ancient libel, widespread throughout Europe, that Jews routinely sought the blood of gentile children. Then, of course, more recently, there's Fagin in *Oliver Twist,* which first appeared in 1837 and continues to be revived in one form or . . .''

"And would you argue that familiarity with these literary classics can help illuminate these recent acts of violence?''

Desmond put his elbows on the table and spread his palms. "You mean am I prescribing a course in literature as an antidote to crime?" His mouth was whimsical. "Hardly. I mean, real events tend to outstrip the most fertile imaginations of storytellers. The Jews were in fact banished from England in 1290—not long after the Hugh of Lincoln incident—and not allowed to return for over four hundred years. And Fagin was based on a real-life character named Ikey Solomons who most likely made Fagin pale by comparison as a villain . . ." He shrugged his shoulders. "Look, all I can say as we run out of time is that we need to comprehend the past to deal effectively with the present."

"We will return after these commercial messages, ladies and gentlemen."

DeSales found himself liking Desmond, in spite of what had happened five years before. Maybe, along with everything else, he—the Saint, supercop—was getting soft. On the past.

"Bernie, what's happening? I call into the office and the guy on the front desk says it's *imperative* I call you at this number. *Imperative.* And the guy has marbles in his mouth. Where we recruiting these days? The International Cotillion? The St. Regis Roof?" He paused. "And where are *you?*"

Kavanaugh ignored the question. "I *could* have pulled you off the air, but I didn't want to interrupt your little star turn. I knew you'd call in. Anyway, corpses can always wait. Even when the evidence boys don't want to."

DeSales stared at the receiver and thought about hanging it up, pretending he'd been disconnected, hadn't heard what Kavanaugh was saying. He held his breath as Megan, across the studio on the sound stage, said good-bye to the Reform rabbi from City Hall. Desmond was still sitting at the conference table talking to one of the producers. Then the detective looked up at the blank video monitors; he wouldn't have been surprised if Glickstein reappeared like some wrathful Jehovah and stepped out of the screen into the room.

"Another body? Jewish?"

"Circumcised."

"You got his pants off already?"

"He don't have any. Naked as a jaybird."

Megan Moore sat down with Desmond and started an animated conversation. DeSales looked at his watch.

"Give me some more facts, Bernie. I got a date."

There was the sound of Kavanaugh turning pages; then he began to read: "Black. Male. Five-six, mid-thirties . . ."

"Sounds like the profile for three-quarters of the suspicious deaths in the whole borough. You have me call in after hours for this? What's wrong with Shultz? He's in charge over there at night this week."

"Well, there's some interesting details. The fingertips have been surgically removed. All his teeth have been pulled. Could make I.D. a little tough."

DeSales remembered he had been craving nicotine. He lighted up and took a deep drag.

"It could, Bernie, but to tell you the truth I'm not that interested tonight. Can't I deal with this *mañana*?" He exhaled. Through the haze of smoke, he could see the expensive cut of Megan Moore's outfit, a baggy Japanese-French suit with padded shoulders and slit skirt. It was a sort of pale green that set off the hair, the eyes, and the low-cut white silk blouse with the rouged boobs swelling out of it. She looked *comfortable,* that's what had changed, like a Mercedes or a Rolls. Before, she had had lots of looks and breeding, but no sense of *comfort,* like one of those classic MGs with irresistible lines but always the looming likelihood of bad shocks and a leaky top. He imagined her now, rich from TV stardom, living in a penthouse on Central Park West. A sunken Jacuzzi, maybe. There had been the implied offer before the show, and the looks she kept giving him. He would take her up on anything she had to throw his way. "Besides," he went on, "I've already done my overtime for today, been put through the wringer for an hour with two fucking rabbis and our old buddy, Professor Timothy Desmond, the limousine liberal."

Kavanaugh was not impressed: "And Megan Moore. You forgot to mention her. It's her show, right? Does that mean you're maybe feeling a little touchy because you've finally decided to give her a break, awready, after all these years. *Mañana* you serve yourself up a little warm anchorperson. For breakfast. Between the sheets . . ." He began his heavy-breather imitation.

"Very funny. I asked where you were."

"I'm in the office of a Mr. Frick, administrative associate of the Botanic Gardens."

"Brooklyn?"

"Where else? And we got something just a little more complicated than your run-of-the-mill Black Male Victim report."

"Yeah?" DeSales began to take short, swift puffs on the cigarette.

"Definitely. There's these Jap Gardens. Inside the regular Botanic?"

"Yeah."

"With a fence around and a little lake in the middle?"

"Yeah." DeSales looked for a place to drop the smoldering ash.

And suddenly Megan Moore was standing there, holding out a glass tray. As he pressed the butt down, she stood on tiptoe and whispered, "I've got an original idea. *I'll* buy *you* a drink."

He covered the mouthpiece with his hand: "A drink. That's all?"

"Okay. Dinner too."

"And in these Jap gardens," Kavanaugh was saying, "there's a shrine. Shinto. That's some kinda Buddhist, right? Well, that's where the stiff is. Lying in the shrine."

"Shit," DeSales swore, "more fucking religion." Now he knew why Bernie had called. He would have to go back to work after all.

"But I refuse to submit myself to a mikvah bath," Megan winked. "It's not my *period*." She tossed her head at Desmond's back. "I find their practices dis*gust*ing, *and* chauvinistic."

"Also," Kavanaugh continued, coughing, "there's an abandoned wheelchair outside the shrine."

"An *abandoned* wheelchair?"

"Well, nobody's claiming it. And it was made in Japan."

Megan Moore appeared to have given up on Jewish women's

problems. "And I *would* like you to see my new apartment. You like Chinese? We could just send out."

"Japanese," said DeSales, thinking out loud. He saw that Desmond had reached the bank of elevators, briefcase in hand.

"Why not?" Megan shrugged. "Sushi, sashimi. They have takeout too." She beamed.

"The chief is afraid this could be very important, Frank, if you see what I mean."

"Meet you there," said DeSales.

"Washington Avenue gate. Right up from where Ebbets Field was." They hung up simultaneously.

Megan Moore made a face: "Whom are we meeting?"

"Sorry, babe. Gotta cancel for tonight."

"I don't believe it. Isn't this where I came in?"

The author of *Ritual and Revenge* was pressing the DOWN button.

"Hey. Desmond! Tim!" DeSales yelled.

Desmond turned.

"You know anything about Japanese stuff? Religion and crime, I mean. Shintoism?"

Desmond pondered the question. "Some," he said finally.

"I need a favor. You still living near Grand Army Plaza?"

"Yes."

"Give me . . . let's call it a consultation . . . near there. A few minutes. And I'll give you a ride home. I've got a car and driver waiting outside."

"You're on. Anything beats the D train."

"Hey, guys," Megan Moore pouted, "that's not *fair*."

CHAPTER 5

IN THE DIM, BARREN ROOM, there were only two sources of light. There was a television sitting on the floor at the foot of the mattress. There was the beam from the peephole fashioned in the sliding metal security door that shut off the disused storefront from the street. Naked, the man crawled over the woman lying face down next to him on the mattress. With knees bent like an ape, he made his way warily toward the window. The woman lifted her head an inch from the pillow and asked, sideways, "Wha's happening?"

The man was crouched over, peering through the hole at the street, at the same time fondling himself. He grunted, waved his hand in admonition of silence, then vigorously scratched his buttocks.

After Megan Moore's feature on the Brooklyn crimes, he had switched to another station. There was a commercial for Disney-World, then a heavyset black man with a lisp introduced a segment of *another* kind of "newsmagazine," this on Rock Hudson's tragic death from AIDS. A petite blonde with a beehive hairdo out of the fifties appeared in the studio. She was introduced as the wife of a prominent entertainer and one of the leading citizens of Beverly Hills, California.

"I went to see him in his last hours," she wept. "They tried to stop me, but I had fellow-believers among the staff."

"But how did you communicate? Wasn't he in a coma?"

"I spoke to him in tongues. I touched his hand. With mine." She held up her own dainty fingers, gaudy with rings, as one might hold up a limb that has been lost and miraculously recovered. "He opened his eyes!" Her voice had a Southern tinge and a gospel rhythm. "He sort of blinked at me," she mimicked the gesture with false eyelashes, "and there was a twinkle there." She pondered this. "But it was a *pious* twinkle, a *Christian* twinkle. It was as if in his pain he had repented his sinful past and broken through to the Lord." She looked up, dewy eyed. "He had the charisma; he would have made a *heck* of a preacher."

The naked man in the storefront stood upright. He was deeply tanned and heavily muscled. He walked back toward the bed. He twirled the dial on the TV, switching channels. Finally, he had to settle for Rock Hudson again.

"We should have brought the VCR," he said. "One of those new tapes, Al Goldstein gives it four peckers on his Peter Meter in *Penthouse.*" He thought for a minute, rubbing his chin. "I'd like to get a crack at that bastard. Alone. Sometime. He'd . . ."

"Who? Rock Hudson? You a secret fairy or something?"

He planted his feet at the woman's side of the bed and unleashed the back of his hand at her face. "Don't ever talk to me like that," he hissed as her head snapped back and she clutched her nose.

With blood gushing over her hands, she stumbled toward the tiny, soiled cubicle that served as a bathroom and emerged with a fistful of paper towels. She sat gingerly on the bed, back against the wall, and applied the compress to her nose. Her naked thighs were spread before the TV screen as if she were submitting to a pelvic exam or photography session. She, too, was brown as a nut from the sun. All over.

"You're evil," she sobbed. "Now I do believe you killed that kid. Now I *know!*"

The man ignored her. He had returned to the peephole. "You idiot. Not some faggot. I mean this guy DeSales. On the TV. Supercop, my ass. I'd show him. Hey, the Hasids just finished their meeting in that little air-conditioned tax shelter they got across the street. Are they pissed, or what? They must have seen the show." He began gyrating his hips with his eye still glued to the hole. "They're going *bullshit.* Completely turned around. Better than the boogies on Nostrand Avenue. They won't even notice we've been here until we're gone."

The woman removed the paper from her face. There were splotches and streaks of red on her cheeks and chin. She brought her knees together. Slowly. She trembled, but only slightly, a movement suggesting more ready anticipation than fear. "Maybe he's queer too, this DeSales. Maybe everybody's queer. Except you." She wiped her cheek again.

The man paced deliberately back from the window now, once again stroking his genitals. He climbed on the bed, straddling the woman's waist.

"Here's a dude that ain't," he breathed in a mock Negro voice.

She slid down from the wall, now horizontal beneath him. He knee-walked forward on the mattress until he was dangling himself over her mouth. "Now, you talk about *hung,* huh, sweetness?" He pressed his knees in on her ears as if to say, "Hurry up!"

She extended her tongue, then retracted it, a bit of a tease. "When's the delivery?" she asked quietly.

The man sighed. He looked around the room, littered with rubble and opened packing cases. He looked up at the broken plaster in the ceiling and caressed himself again, a long, slow, gentle pull.

"There are two," he said, sounding now quite businesslike and precise. "Seconal and Tuinal tomorrow. Percodan the next day, if we can keep the Hebes *hot.*" He chortled. "The asshole from Eli Lilly sounded suspicious, so I had to order a case of insulin and a lot of laxative antacid. For starters, I said. Told him we were still renovating our shelf space. Y'know any constipated diabetics?''

She showed her appreciation with a wide, open-mouthed smile, then brought her hand around behind his bulging thigh to wipe some more blood from her nostrils. "Rand," she whispered, raising her head to greet his entry with her lips, "will you give me a poke, the other kind, after?''

He rumbled with self-satisfaction. "I got the works. You just do as you're told." He pushed her shoulders back and began his slow bump and grind. He laughed again. "Fucking Eli Lilly. *Laxatives*! At least *they* didn't make me take any wheelchairs.''

CHAPTER 6

DESMOND AND DESALES FOLLOWED the Botanic Gardens official through the Magnolia Plaza and up a set of stone stairs into pitch darkness. For a moment the names Linnaeus and Darwin, engraved over the door to the giftshop, occupied Desmond's consciousness; then he began to get his night vision and could make out the balding, bearded figure ahead of him, gesticulating, as it were, to the trees that arched above them.

"*Quel dommage*," the administrator, whose name was Edmund Frick, exclaimed. "A *most* inappropriate day for such a thing to happen! It was glorious here: the Asiatic Sweetleaf and the Orange Trifoliate were *just* holding on while the Beautyberries were coming into season a touch early. It was *serendipity*. The Dwarf-Winged Euonymous was positively *scarlet*."

"I thought you had a flashlight," said DeSales, bringing up the rear.

"Heavens, I forgot." He snapped it on, played it on the drooping hemlocks, and then focused on the entrance to the Japanese Gardens, the floating teahouse framed behind the turnstile. They entered the Japanese area and turned right again, box hedges on each side of the path. The hemlocks brushed the head of Desmond, six inches taller than the other two men, and he stooped as he walked. The pond materialized through a gap in the hedge on the left and soon they were skirting the edge. The wind came up a bit, fluttering across the surface of the water. A fish jumped.

It was a scene that implied the awesome silence of deep woods, but instead Desmond could hear guard dogs growling behind the hedges and an ambulance screaming down Eastern Parkway, only a few hundred yards away. And Frick continued to conduct his guided tour, flashlight bobbing as his voice rose and fell in excited inflection.

"The water here is full of shorebirds at this time of year. Sandpipers and bitterns heading south for their winter holidays; the gulls, *of course*." He put his hands on his hips, a camp gesture of annoyance, then relaxed again, leaning against an enormous tree trunk. "They come for the berries, then have a little drinkie from the pond." He emitted a humorless staccato laugh, not unlike something one might hear in an exotic aviary. Then he raised the flashlight. "Why, there was a *humongous* blue heron in this very Bald Cypress just before noon."

DeSales said, "Let's keep moving, Mr. Frick. We've got work to do and I want to get it done before it rains."

When they had crossed the bridge from Manhattan a short time before, the sky had been starry, New Jersey bright beyond the harbor. Now it was gloomy, threatening.

Desmond reflected that, under the tree where the blue heron had rested that midday, he and his son, Nick, just turned four, had frolicked ankle-deep in cherry blossoms the previous May.

Now he was trying to beat a rainstorm to a corpse.

Frick strode forward. There was an intersection, the glint of pebbles, a waterfall to the right. They crossed a footbridge and began to press on uphill. There was a flash of lightning backlighting the stand of white pine, then the roll of thunder in the distance. A car alarm went off on Empire Boulevard. At the top of the hill, the headlights from the park ranger's Jeep lit up the shrine like a window exhibit. It was a tiny building, no more than four feet by four feet on the floor of its one story. The pagodalike roof sloped from a peak not much higher. It looked more like a church organ than a church.

Bernie Kavanaugh emerged from the Jeep as Desmond and DeSales approached. Frick hung back, chatting with the ranger. About the relative translucence of Mistletoe Honeysuckle fruit this year.

Kavanaugh said, "Jesus mighty, if it isn't Professor Desmond, the messiah of the Montauk Club! Last time he walks on water; what's his encore, the Loaves and the Fishes? Hey, I'm starved." Kavanaugh held his belly with both hands.

"Lay off him, Bernie. He could help with this one."

"You wanna help with this one, Desmond, do a Lazarus. There ain't no other way we're gonna figure this stiff out."

They passed the abandoned wheelchair and entered the temple area through a little gate with statues of wolves or wild dogs on each side. A sign declared that the shrine was dedicated to Inari, the Shinto god of the harvest and protector of plants. There was a tiny wooden porch, then a sort of cabinet door. This door had been kicked in, and now the lower half of the dead naked man protruded from the splintered opening. The soles of his feet were pink; his legs were heavily muscled; and there was a tattoo on the inside of his cocoa-colored thigh. His genitals—the penis, purple and ponderous, resting on the swollen scrotum in statuesque harmony—suggested they had been scrupulously arranged for a viewing.

Kavanaugh looked over his shoulder to make sure he was out of earshot of Frick and the ranger and pointed at the tattoo: "How do you like this, Frank. St. Patrick running the snakes out of Ireland. I've known some Black Irish, but not like this."

DeSales got down on his knees and crawled into the minimal space remaining in the broken door. With Frick's flashlight, he gave the rest of the corpse, and the inside of the shrine, a thorough once-over. After a while he backed out and handed the light to

Desmond. "Take a look," he said. Then he turned to Kavanaugh.
"I assume Friedman's been here already."

Kavanaugh imitated the medical examiner's nasal accent:
"Nothing can even be inferred until we have the body in the lab."

"What did he think of the surgical job on the fingertips?"

"Wanted the number of the guy who sharpened the scalpel.
Said they could use him at the morgue."

Desmond got down on his knees, trying not to tremble or
visibly hold his breath. He had no idea what he anticipated, but it
included some vague notion of intolerable putrefaction and poisonous fumes. The last thing he wanted to do was let on to the cops
that he was experiencing fear or loathing.

"Don't be bashful, Professor," cracked Kavanaugh. "He's
clean. Too clean." He looked back to DeSales. "Like embalmed."

DeSales nodded. Tentatively, Desmond poked his head in the
hole, clumsily bringing the flashlight from behind. He looked at
the man's carved-up fingers, which were interlaced on his chest.
The undertaker's, or window dresser's, signature again. He noted
that the chest was hairless. He looked at the face, fascinated, for a
long time. Kavanaugh was right. The man was clean. There was
almost no blood, except for the brown dried line where the throat
had been slit and the rough spots on the lips and gums where the
teeth had been pulled. The only odor was of aftershave. English
Leather. And of course the funky residue natural to the inside of a
closed wooden cabin: animal droppings, spiderwebs, mildew. He
prepared to back out, but then saw something where the far arm of
the corpse joined the shoulder. He pulled it out, taking it with him,
back into the fresh air. The sky was completely black now and
gusts of rain were beginning to blow from the west, but he felt in
emerging as if he had ingested some kind of amphetamine. The
world was immeasurably more alive than when he had gone in; his
mind seemed slick and sharp as a summer morning. The rain, as it
struck him, enhanced his sense of invigoration. Pine needles rested
in silence underfoot.

The two detectives huddled on the leeward side of the temple, jackets pulled up over their heads. There was another bolt of lightning and the thunder struck almost instantly. Frick, now inside the Jeep, called out that it wasn't safe for them among the tall trees.

"Well?" asked DeSales.

"When I saw the tattoo, I had an idea," said Desmond. "And this tends to confirm it." He held up the feather he had found in the armpit.

"What is it?" asked Kavanaugh.

"A feather," said Desmond, with a mocking smile.

"What kind of feather, wiseass?"

"I spent part of my childhood on a farm in Pennsylvania," said Desmond, "and there it would have been a chicken. To someone like Frick over there, maybe it's a Dwarf-Winged Euonymus."

"And what does that mean? If it's a chicken?" asked DeSales.

"With the tattoo, it suggests a Voodoo ritual. Or, more properly, Voudon."

"What the fuck does St. Patrick have to do with voodoo?"

"Look," said Desmond, "I'm getting wet, my family expected me home an hour ago, and you said you only wanted me for fifteen minutes. Besides, you have to wait for the post-mortem results—the autopsy—tomorrow anyway. Let's call it a night and I'll meet you tomorrow, okay? Then we can talk this out."

"Irish voodoo," spat Kavanaugh. DeSales's dark eyes burned into Desmond's.

"What kind of jerk-off is this, Desmond?"

Desmond wiped his spectacles with his tie and readjusted them on his nose. "Look, DeSales, I'm not pulling your chain. Before I go off on a tangent with this voodoo thing, I have to look something up in the library in the morning. Besides, there's also something weird, contradictory . . ." He cupped his chin.

"Yeah?"

"Well, did you notice that guy may have had brown skin, but now he's got a kind of purple tinge, and he looks Oriental? Japanese or Korean, I'd say."

"I noticed," said DeSales.

"Like a fucking eggplant," said Kavanaugh.

CHAPTER 7

IT TOOK ONLY A FEW minutes for the police car to drop Desmond at the house on Berkeley Place. The brownstone was flaking from the façade on the parlor floor. The light bulb over the tenant's doorway under the stoop had burned out. Desmond wrinkled his brow with annoyance, then turned the key and crossed the threshold, greeted by the wiggling, pawing golden retriever they had purchased as watchdog and companion just before Nick was born. Ralph, the dog, was nice enough in a general way, if you liked large goofy animals with bad breath, but totally inept in any practical sense. He devoted most of his waking hours to watching the Siamese cat sleep on the stove. He was waiting for the cat to make a move toward the litter box in the downstairs lavatory so he could chase her and indulge himself in some general harassment. He only attended to the front door when he recognized as a friend the person entering. A friend, to Ralph, was anyone who might conceivably offer him food.

The house was silent and all but the hall lights were out. Nick and Mona had gone to bed.

In the kitchen, Desmond gave the dog a biscuit, then another when he sat up and begged. Then he made sure that the espresso machine was turned off and that the icemaker, which had a habit of hurling cubes all about the freezer, was under control. He checked the locks on the door to the deck from the rear parlor, and on the windows that faced the street from the dining room. He inspected the garbage to ensure that nothing was in the plastic bag that would encourage midnight foraging by Ralph or the cat. He put soap in the dishwasher and turned it on full-cycle. He patted the cat, secure and half asleep in her niche over the rear pilot light; poured himself a glass of milk, and extinguished the lights. Having completed the nightly ritual, he trudged up the steep flight of industrial-carpeted stairs.

The top two floors of the triplex had been recently remodeled from the state in which they had existed as part of a decrepit rooming house for forty-odd years, before the Desmonds had bought the place—parlor and tenant's floors refurbished by a speculator—some seven years before. They had originally hoped to restore it to its Victorian grandeur, stripping paint from hidden treasures of fine wood, reopening fireplaces, and so forth, but any plan they came up with had seemed too expensive, or too tedious, or both. So they procrastinated until, spurred on by Mona's pregnancy, they had settled for the pragmatic modern solution. Desmond was satisfied. He lived within walls of plasterboard painted gleaming white; all the machinery worked; and the hand-me-down furniture was comfortable if undistinguished. He could ask no more.

The ultimate bonus, of course, was that Nick had arrived; the presence of a child . . . and such a child . . . had breathed life into the physical plant. What to Desmond had been once a pile of wood and brick and brownstone and pipes threatening to burst at any moment had taken on human—and humane—qualities. The house nurtured; it protected; it provided a hedge against age and depression; an investment, an inheritance to pass on.

The pathetic fallacy.

Desmond slipped into his son's room. The storm had passed

and the moon rested at a point in the sky over the harbor, not far from the Statue of Liberty, and cast a beam across the sleigh bed where Nick sprawled, sheets kicked off by his ever-busy feet. The boy's breathing was deep and regular, his pale delicate features ringed by a mass of golden curls. He wore He-Man pajamas and clutched under one arm the medium-size version of Swiftheart the Blue Rabbit. The miniature Care Bear, Tenderheart, had been cast off and dangled precariously at the edge of the bed. Desmond tucked the bear in his proper place on Nick's pillow, then pulled the sheets back up to his chin. As an afterthought, he added a light blanket, the air having cooled after the storm. He planted a kiss on the child's forehead, wondering where he had come from, what genetic trickery had created him. He resembled neither Desmond nor Mona nor anyone in either family; he was much better looking, better coordinated, more imaginative. In summertime in the country he even had golden freckles on his nose. Desmond had always wanted freckles. Desmond for that matter had also always wanted the fearless energy and taste for adventure that made Nick a popular favorite in his preschool class, particularly among the boys. When he wasn't getting into fights.

For the briefest moment, Desmond imagined the muscular corpse in the Shinto temple; wondered if in life that man had been timid or brave; felt again the gust of chill, baptismal, cleansing rain on the back of his neck. He hoped Nick would never have to see his father dead. As he had had to when he was a boy.

He shivered.

In the bathroom, the proud but unsettled father brushed his teeth and gargled and promised himself that he would begin using the Water Pik regularly as soon as he had more time. He stripped to his shorts, discarded the rest of his clothing in the wicker laundry basket, and stepped into the darkened bedroom. He decided not to turn on the light to read, so as to avoid waking Mona. But he saw her movement under the covers and knew instinctively that she was not asleep.

"You're late," she murmured.

He crawled under the covers. "Did you see the show? After it was over, that detective, DeSales, asked me to consult about a corpse they just found in the Botanicals."

"Yuck." She rolled against him. She was naked, her skin warm and reassuring. She touched his chest with her fingers and walked them down to his navel. Slowly. "First you're on TV talking about killers, then you're looking at corpses instead of coming home to your waiting family. I'm going to write my own book: *I Married a Necrophiliac for the FBI.* They'll serialize it in the *National Enquirer.*" She moved her hand lower, inserting it in the waistband of his shorts.

"This one was incredible. A black-Asian guy with no fingertips and a voodoo icon tattooed on his thigh."

"A real necro," she said. "Man gets erection talking about death. Wife has difficulty pulling pants down over rising obstruction."

Desmond lifted his hips to facilitate the undressing. They lay facing one another, touched lips, and without further ado she raised a leg over his and he was inside her. They moved together in a gentle rhythm, as to an old song they knew by heart. The bed was the swell of a tranquil sea. She stretched her torso and he bent his neck, taking her left nipple in his mouth.

"Wow," she said. "Nobody ever told me about the side benefits of breast feeding." After a while, she moaned, riding him now, faster and faster. She put her tongue in his ear as he began to quiver. Their tremor was one. Then they lay still, balanced, a study in equipoise.

"Let me tell you about the corpse again. Maybe we'll be up all night," Desmond whispered.

She laughed. "Wishful thinking, old man. Remember that D. H. Lawrence story about the sexy resurrection of Christ in the pagan temple?"

"The Man Who Died?"

"Right."

"Tell me about it. I only remember it in a general way, not the details. Nick was asking questions about what religion we were today. His little friend Harvey told him he went to temple and now Nickie thinks Harvey goes somewhere in the *desert* to worship. Anyway, I was thinking we ought to tell him we were a little bit of *everything*. Instead of a *lot* of nothing. Religiously, I mean. And we could sort of tell him stories like the Lawrence one . . . without the sex . . . so he gets some sense of what it's all about. Only without the doctrine.''

"In Lawrence the sex *is* the doctrine.''

"You sound like a professor. Just give me the facts.''

"The story had Christ wandering forty days and nights in the desert after his crucifixion and meeting an Egyptian priestess of Isis on the beach or something and they go to the temple and make it on the altar. I think.''

Suddenly, a car alarm went off outside the window.

"Oh, shit,'' said Mona. "Another one. Can't we have one night of peace?''

"City life,'' Desmond said, pulling away from her and stepping quickly to the shutters. He peered down into the street.

"So much for postcoital affection. And my little lesson in literature,'' sighed Mona. Then, propping herself on an elbow, she asked with resignation, "What is it now?''

"Just the Griswolds again. They've had that new Saab for three weeks and every time they lock it the alarm goes off.''

"Shoot him.''

"Ian Griswold?''

"No, the Saab.''

"Him?''

"I always think of fast cars . . . with 'Turbo' written on them and stuff like that . . . as *male*. Phallic and all that.''

"Sex is all you think about these days. *I Married a Nympho from Madison Avenue* will be *my* next book.''

"You used to accuse me of the opposite. Too cold, too hot. Men are never satisfied.''

Desmond did not respond. He had spotted a familiar figure

making his way down from Eighth Avenue. One of the houses on the block still had a gaslight in front and the man paused before it, casting a spectral shadow into the street. As usual, he appeared to be talking to himself. He carried a shopping bag.

"Sweetie," said Mona.

"Yeah?"

"You're tuning out."

"I was just watching that guy with the beard and black coat who hangs around the park. He's checking out Mrs. Romulo's gaslight."

"How exciting. Get back here."

As the man in black continued on his way to Seventh Avenue, Desmond got back in bed. Mona rolled on her stomach, and, taking the clue, he began to massage her. He said: "The older Nick gets, the more I get sort of right wing. I see hobos in the park, I want to get the rangers to remove them. I hear black teenagers making noise, I want to call nine one one."

"Well, I don't think you have to worry about our friend in the black coat."

"Why?"

"Remember that time before we were married we went to visit your parents and they wouldn't let us sleep together, so we left early and checked into that motel in Pennsylvania Dutch country?"

Desmond had found the spot under her shoulder blade where she liked him to apply pressure. "Sort of."

"And the bed squeaked and the bathrooms were in the hall and they had dispensing machines for Kotex in the ladies' and for french ticklers and rainbow rubbers in the men's?"

"A classic selective nympho memory. So what? We were talking about Nick's safety and the guy in the park and to tell you the truth I've been thinking about this Greenpoint thing."

She rolled onto her back and scissored him with her legs. "That's exactly what *I've* been thinking about, dummy. Park Slope is *not* Greenpoint. Park Slope is *trendy*. I read it in *New York* magazine. And our local vagrant is *not* dangerous. I looked him over pretty closely yesterday while he was sitting outside the Third Street playground and I was watching Nick and Harvey swinging on the tires on chains, and I found myself thinking about that night in Pennsylvania, and I realized the guy has this kind of holy look about him and then it hit me: he's whatyacallem? Dutch, *Amish*. They're the most peaceful, obedient, nonviolent people in the world. Remember that movie, *Witness*. It won an Academy Award for Best Screenplay. Look, I figure he hangs around our playground because it's the *safest* place in Brooklyn. He's escaping *murderous* reality. Hey, I say 'murderous' and I detect another resurrection taking place. You *are* trying to set the sex record for middle-aged scholars.''

''Looks that way, but before I test the limits of human endurance, who's picking up Nick at school tomorrow?''

''You are. But you'd better take him up to the Ninth Street playground. Third Street will be under water after that cloudburst. At least the sand will be too wet.''

''And, please, *you* remind me that I have to get three competitive bids for stonemasons to do the façade and I have to change the bulb under the stoop. Before I go to the library and then meet the cops and then pick up our son and take him all the way to Ninth Street. That, of course, is if *I*, as parent in charge, decide the sand is too wet.''

''Poor sweetie. Always overworked.''

''As we used to say in Pennsylvania, 'Overworked and under . . .' ''

She put her finger to his lips. ''Not anymore.''

He kissed her eyelids, then, when she reopened her eyes, looked into them. They were large, dewy. Somehow, they made him think of Nick's freckles. Her grin was slightly, fetchingly, off center; she was gap toothed.

''You're a *wonderful* caretaker,'' she said, ''and father.''

''But a necrophiliac.''

''A handsome, virile necrophiliac.''

Their lips met again, then opened. Their tongues found one

another. Her legs tightened briefly, then relaxed. Her heels rested lightly on the backs of his calves.

"Why do they call this the *missionary* position?" she asked.

"The ways of God are not for man to question," he murmured, most solemnly, then began to hum "Onward, Christian Soldiers."

Desmond had a dream. He was in the pub that had become his local during the sabbatical year in London when he had written *Ritual and Revenge,* when Nick was just two. The Queen's Larch was inhabited by upper-class bohemians and Irish nationalists, but in the dream the clientele was entirely black, garbed in colorful Caribbean costumes. The barman was alternately an Orthodox Jew and an Amish elder, each bearing a striking resemblance to Bob Dylan. Then he became Francis DeSales. The Saint. The Saint sold not drinks but snakes to his customers. The poisonous serpents were most expensive. Desmond found he could not afford one of these, so he settled for the least pricey: a baby boa constrictor. It would be a nice pet for his son.

"It'll grow," said DeSales, winking.

"Country'll grow," rasped the voice of Bob Dylan from the yawning jaws of the snake.

When Desmond awoke with a start, he tried and tried to remember the early Dylan song from which the line had come. But he could not. "Masters of War"? "Maggie's Farm"? "The Times They Are A-Changin' "? No. It was upsetting, and he slept fitfully the rest of the night, but could not bring himself to get out of the warm bed—separate himself from the glow of Mona's flesh—and look it up.

Instead, when awake, he lay rigid, alert for any sound of distress from Nick's room.

CHAPTER 8

"YOU SEE ABOUT THIS Cuban on the Staten Island ferry?" asked Kavanaugh. "He goes bananas during rush hour, pulls out a sword—a fucking rapier for Christ's sake—and slashes ten people?"

DeSales finished his bagel-with-schmear, drained his coffee, and tossed the *News* in the wastebasket. "I saw it," he said. "C'mon, the guys are waiting for the meeting to start." DeSales opened the door and stepped into the plushly carpeted hallway of the new Task Force headquarters.

Kavanaugh took his time, bringing up the rear. "And you get why he said he did it? *God* told him he had to. He hears voices; he's got a direct line to the Almighty."

DeSales spoke over his shoulder: "Like you said to the waitress in Greenpoint who asked you about the Black Hebrews in Queens, Bernie: *not our jurisdiction.*"

"The harbor? Or the Almighty?"

"Neither. This is Brooklyn. Kings County. The ferry left Manhattan, New York County, headed for Richmond County. The water out there by the Statue of Liberty might belong to the feds, for all I know, but I don't care. Let them fight over it.''

"Seems like we've been running into the Almighty all over the place lately, though.''

"Like I said, I'm going to continue to assume that this is Brooklyn, Kings County, that it's a real place and not the goddamn happy hunting grounds. Not our jurisdiction.'' DeSales began to turn the knob of the conference-room door. *"Juris*diction, *juris*prudence,'' he said half to himself. "That's why I've called this meeting. I'm making a judgment about jurisdictional priorities, and I've got to cover my ass, get the force behind me, before I sever the cases. Because I prefer not to mess around with spiritual matters. So some reporter or politician doesn't try to second-guess me if I fuck up.''

He paused, hand still on knob, and waited for Kavanaugh to catch up. Once again he experienced the sensation of losing it—his nerve, whatever.

He had hesitated to act, no longer sure of his instinct, and now here he was seeking advice and consent because he was worried about the press and the bureaucracy.

Kavanaugh seemed unaffected by his malaise. His step picked up as he neared the door. "Did you see the picture, Frank? The sword the Cuban bought on Forty-second Street looks like the same one Teddy Roosevelt used leading the charge up San Juan Hill.'' Laughing, Bernie Kavanaugh poked DeSales in the ribs with his finger, propelling him through the door.

The two detectives filed into the room. DeSales nodded to his staff and took a seat at the head of the table, Kavanaugh at his side.

Jurisdiction. Judaic. Jews. He had come here to talk first about Jews. He opened a folder that Kavanaugh had slipped in front of him and said gruffly, without looking up, "Colon?''

"Sí, Señor.''

Hector Colon was wearing snakeskin cowboy boots, Levi's, and a silver satin Porsche racing-team jacket. He made eye contact with DeSales while slipping back into his wallet the pictures he had been proudly showing Shultz of his sister's new baby boy.

"Pay attention, Colon. I got the Greenpoint-Williamsburg dossier in front of me. You can tell because it has the green cover, right? And it's nine A.M. Thursday and we're in Room D, right? And for the past ten days you've been tracking one case only, right?"

"Absolute."

"So what am I asking you for?"

"The name of my hairstylist, maybe?" Colon's head was a mass of tightly lacquered curls. He ran his hand through it. "You gettin' a little thin on top, Frank." Some of the other men snickered. Shultz and Kavanaugh guffawed. DeSales remained expressionless. Colon waited for the commotion to die down, then tipped his chin forward. He pursed his lips, then passed his manicured fingers over his face in an attempt to rearrange his handsome features into a semblance of solemnity. Finally, he said, "I gotta make jokes, Frank. Nothing is happening, absolutely nothing. Last few days I been with my *compañeros* up and down Broadway. By South Eighth and like that all the way to Myrtle. I don't get shit. I act the pimp, the dealer, the fence. *Nada.*"

"You only talk to Latinos, Hector? You discriminating?"

"Like I tell you last time: for a week I wear a dark suit, I talk correct English, and I got my master's degree in communications stamped to my forehead." He turned to the room in general: "Who knows? Maybe I get offered a job in broadcasting where I make some *money*?" There was another outbreak of hilarity around the table. "I talk to more Polacks and Jews than I ever want to talk to again. The Poles are edgy, like maybe I got a shiv strapped to my ankle, but they open up because they're pissed. In general. The mailman on the Simmonses' block in Greenpoint, who lives there and has been on the beat for thirty years, sums it up nicely. He don't like three things. First, he don't like Jews. Second, he don't like spics. Like me." He pointed his thumb at his chest. "Third and most important, he don't like these new nondenominational people in the neighborhood like the Simmonses and the PlaySpace Co-op crowd. Know why?"

"He's jealous of their money?" ventured Kavanaugh.

Colon shook his head, grinning broadly.

"How about he don't agree with modern child-rearing practices?" Shultz said, pensive.

"Nope. Not even close."

"C'mon, Hector, we have a lot to do this morning."

"Okay," said Colon, "give up? He don't like their mail."

"Their *mail*?"

"They get too much. Books, magazines, credit-card mailings, museum brochures, college catalogues. The neighborhood people get a letter from the old country, and the Con Ed and telephone every month. That's all. It's breaking the mailman's back. The weight. He's taking early retirement because of them."

"And the Jews?"

"They look at *me* like I got a dead rat in my pocket. But they don't actually dislike me. Or the Poles. Or the yuppies. They don't even know I'm there. As soon as the body was taken out of the yeshivah and the Greenpoint bullies were sent home, they went right back in their own little world. Inside the string."

"String?"

"String, fishing line, whatever. Called an *eruv,* I think. See, these Orthodox Jews, and particularly the Satmar Hasids in Williamsburg, got more rules and regulations than the Department of Sanitation. As a consequence, human nature being what it is, they're always preoccupied with getting around these rules and regulations. For example, besides having their own bus service so the men don't have to ride with women and not allowing anybody to watch TV, they're forbidden to carry anything off their own property on the Sabbath. So some smart guy gets the idea, you put some fishing line, more-or-less invisible, up on the utility poles so it surrounds the whole neighborhood, that makes the neighborhood enclosed so it's all one property. Technically speaking. Then these guys can carry their prayer books and whatever. Even on Yom Kippur. But only inside the string.''

"You're getting a real cross-cultural education, Hector.''

"Like, I need it. All I know is these characters got their heads in the clouds all the time with Gd.''

"What?''

"Gee, dash, dee. G-d. I pronounce it Gd. They believe if you actually write it out, *G-o-d*, God, you make God pissed off or maybe he, like, disappears. Anyway it's always Gd.''

DeSales asked no more questions. He held his chin in his hand. He looked contemplative. He blinked. He played with an unlit cigarette. Finally, he spoke: "Let's get back to the real world. A guy gets attacked in Borough Park and the Hasids there start screaming at one another about Mitzvah Tanks and Israel, not Gd.''

Colon shook his head. "Borough Park I don't know about, but it doesn't make any sense that one of these people would hurt a gentile kid, let alone kill one, even to put their enemies in a bad light.''

"And the ritual-killing angle?''

"Forget it. There's no such thing, nor was there ever. An old wives' tale. Frank, we gotta look somewhere else. We're wasting our time, my time, in Williamsburg.''

Kavanaugh knocked his knuckles on the table. "Just like we been saying all along.''

"Thanks for the reaffirmation, Bernie. And thanks for your hard work, Hector. I had to put you through the paces, kid, make sure we were doing the right thing taking you off down there.'' DeSales exhaled, baring his teeth for the sardonic clincher. "Now instead of wasting manpower on, what is it up there, Hector, the population?''

"Sixty-odd thousand if you count everybody together. From the Hasids' point of view there's about half that. Themselves.''

"Instead of wasting a fellow like Hector on a mere sixty

thousand people, now the Task Force can just watch and wait and let Hector loose on the other three and a half million prospective killers and victims.''

Kavanaugh raised himself slightly from his seat, unsticking the seat of his pants. For a change, he looked solemn. "You think he's gonna do it again, don't you, Frank, hit some kid?''

"Right, but there's not much we can do about it. We're only equipped to *react*. We can't police the entire borough now,'' said DeSales, his blue eyes not wavering as they passed from Kavanaugh to Colon to Shultz. "What about your end, Dutch?''

Shultz did not answer immediately. Instead he worked his lips in and out. His eyes looked transfixed. With his crewcut, he appeared to be some sort of Nazi buffoon. Indeed he often expressed a longing to do an audition for *Stalag 17*. Although he had elicited many a leading clue or confession in his day by appearing to criminals as a kind of benighted idiot, he had also driven any number of his superiors crazy. DeSales was the only man who had been able to tolerate him on his staff for more than a few months.

Finally Shultz spoke. His speech pattern was similar to that of an adolescent imitating a play-by-play sports broadcaster. "Double *nada, nyet,* nix. I know Bernie's working the computerized stuff, and there's the partial print we sent into the I.D. network, but I don't see anything out there either. I've called all the precincts, gone over six months' worth of blotters. We've had lots of child abuse, sure. But the everyday kind. An unwed mother with a new boyfriend. The mother goes to work or to pick up the welfare check and the boyfriend gets a headache from listening to the kid cry and sticks her or him in the oven or out the window.'' He stopped for a breath, then dribbled on. "There's a lot of perverts out there too, sometimes the parents themselves. But everybody knows who they are. There are no mystery men in black coats and beards. The danger is mostly at home.''

"Mental institutions?'' asked DeSales.

"Followed up all recent releases. All accounted for.''

Kavanaugh jibed, "Including the guy on the ferry yesterday."

"Nobody told me I was after a swashbuckler," retorted Shultz. "Wasn't lookin' for Captain Blood."

"There are new sex offenders turning up every day," DeSales went on. "A guy goes along until he's in his thirties even, then something goes pop in his head or between his legs and . . ."

"Sure, Frank," Shultz got as serious as he ever did. "But we can't anticipate something like that. Besides, the Simmons kid wasn't technically a *sex* case. Nobody stuck anything up his ass or did unspeakable things to his pee-pee. Or even stole his underwear. Like you said on TV last night, it's too random. Even if the sexual motivation was there, it was never acted out. The kid takes a blow to the head, then soon afterward he's strangled . . ."

"Okay," DeSales took off his coat and hung it over the back of his chair. He remained standing. "I also asked you yesterday to run down to Borough Park. Anything on the Jews beyond what Hector says?"

"Plenty, but nothing at the same time. The Satmars of Williamsburg are at serious odds not only with the secular types and the Israeli politicians, but with other Hasids from other neighborhoods. They jostle one another now and then. Over Israel. Over the Lubavitchers' evangelistic buttonholing. Only a few years ago, also in Borough Park, a former Satmar rabbi who had jumped to the Lubavitchers was taken into a van, beat up, and de-pantsed; beard also shorn. But there never was a trial, never a positive I.D."

"You think this business yesterday is part of the same feud?"

"If it was the Lubavitchers doing this, why would they wait three years for revenge? And they're not violent in any case. And who's going to abandon his own Mitzvah Tank a few blocks away?"

"Thanks, Dutch. By the way, I was informed this morning that the Lubavitcher Center on Eastern Parkway has just reported the vehicle stolen."

Shultz nodded. "Another country heard from. Crown Heights."

Watkins, the black man with the shaved head and long aquiline nose who had his chair tilted against the far wall, interrupted: "Go back to what Shultz said before, Frank. About the hypothetical boyfriend of the welfare mother. You don't have any kids of your own. I have a few and I love 'em, but I've had my days and nights without sleep where one of them wouldn't stop crying and I could see myself . . . almost, anyway . . . smothering him or her with a pillow. You take anybody who's the least bit off center, out of work, substance abuse, whatever. Give him a frightened child who can't listen to 'reason,' " he made inverted commas with his long fingers, "and the situation is potentially explosive whatever the original motivation." He looked around the table. "Or *no* motivation. Anybody with a kid has been there. We've *all* been there. Maybe we never even raised a hand or voice in anger, but we know how close it is. Inside."

"So?"

"So, I think—even if watching three and a half million people is a hopeless task—we better take a shot at it. Get manpower to the playgrounds, the parks. Child abuse is a human epidemic. It's not Jewish or gentile, white or black. We can't turn our backs because we'd rather deal with other things."

The room was silent. The men assembled looked at the table or the ceiling or into their laps as if they had been instructed to observe a moment of meditative prayer. And were uncomfortable with it.

DeSales leaned against the wall, crossed his ankles, and frowned. This was what he had hoped to avoid. He pointed a finger at Watkins: "Otis, sometimes I feel like a deprived person, as if not having a family makes me a sociopath."

"I didn't say *that*, Frank."

"Okay. So will you trust me already? I'm reallocating assignments, sure. I'm changing our focus out of what I take to be practical necessity. Think of it as not abandoning the Simmons kid's murder, but as maximizing our resources, and still keeping a finger in the right pies.''

"C'mon, Big O," said Colon to Watkins, "we need some action, a change of scene. We're not producing where we are."

"Put it another way," said DeSales. "I'm trying to sever what Bernie likes to call 'The Almighty' from the case."

Watkins shrugged his shoulders. An impish grin twisted the corners of his mouth. "Oh, I get it, Frank, sorry. You just playing God again, right? Be my guest."

DeSales smiled in return. "If God is the guy who wants to just do one thing at a time, then I'm it, Detective Watkins."

DeSales took a new, unmarked file from the pile in front of Kavanaugh. He took a step behind his chair, moving toward the window that was not there. Windowless conference rooms were for privacy and concentration. It was another one of countless details of the design that he had ignored when the headquarters were being built. Now he was sorry. He found himself going to the window in his own office more and more, whenever there was an excuse. Sometimes he thought that maybe he was actually looking for something. But what, he didn't know. Maybe, like all these other characters, he was searching for meaning, a miracle, a visitation. He wasn't playing God. He was a potential visionary. A broad in a blue-and-white gown with a hood would float over the Manhattan Bridge toward him and they would name her "Our Lady of Flatbush Avenue Extended." Make a movie about him: *Song of St. Francis, Supercop.*

"Watkins," he asked, "you first in the reassignments. Do you know anything about voodoo?"

Watkins tilted the chair back away from the wall, shook out his lanky frame, and sat up straight. He seemed to have forgotten for the moment the wounded children of the world, regained his wacky sense of humor. "I object, Inspector. I was raised in one of the oldest *Anglican*—not Episcopalian, *Anglican*—churches in the city. My father served as deacon there for years. And *you* ask *me* about this jungle-bunny stuff. What do I look like, Screamin' Jay Hawkins? *'I put a spell on you!'* '' He stood up, made a Watusi move toward the head of the table, clawing the air with his fingers, face distorted.

"I forgot you were the champion of affirmative inaction," said DeSales, "but if I said 'pretty please,' would you ask around where you might go if you wanted to put an ear to the ground on that world?"

"Put an ear to the ground, hear the wild pounding of the drums, see the naked, buxom, brown-skinned beauties writhing in the light of the torches?"

DeSales indeed saw Roz for a moment—her sensual savagery at once alluring and painful—but didn't blink: "You got it."

"No problem, boss," said Watkins, sitting down heavily. "Nostrand Avenue, Rogers, from Empire to Church for starters."

"And didn't you put on your résumé that you knew some French?"

" 'Knew' is past tense."

"I've got a guy coming in later who may be able to open up this Botanic Gardens mess. Says there's probably voodoo mixed up in it. Will you stay around today and help Bernie with the computer work? In case I need you to be my man on the street in Little Haiti?"

"Sure. I just don't want my French held against me."

DeSales shuffled his files, looking absentminded. Then he said, "Oh, yeah. Since, in effect, we just terminated Colon's and Shultz's specific roles in the Simmons murder, we have to find something for them to do."

There was a low groan around the room.

"As you know, the D.A. has a permanent lien on us for expendable men on a temporary basis. Her office is particularly disturbed about the spread of cheap prescription pills and new designer drugs on the streets of Crown Heights. Colon, I'm reassigning you to Narcotics."

Colon shrugged: *"Por qué no?* Like I always say: I came

over here for the action. Forget the gray-bearded rabbis.''

"It also just happens the Orthodox Jewish community has started to pressure the mayor's office about the spread of smut and prostitution from Sunset Park and Flatbush into Borough Park. Trying to out-moralize the Williamsburg gang, I guess. So Shultz, I'm going to allow you to indulge your vices, temporarily, in Vice.''

Shultz beamed and the other howled.

Colon strode over to the blackboard against the far wall and began a crude chalk drawing. A map. "You're a real sneak, Frank,'' he said admiringly. "I'm gonna snitch. Look,'' he pointed with the chalk to the contours of the map. While I'm chasing uppers and downers and XTC all over West Indian Crown Heights, I'll be conveniently adjacent to the largest Lubavitcher community in the world.''

Shultz jabbed a finger in the air. "And while I'm protecting Borough Park from the pleasures of the flesh, I can also keep an eye on what's happening with the people whose most recent martyr lost his beard.''

Colon came back: "Need I add that Crown Heights also adjoins the Botanic Gardens and I heard a rumor that the stiff in there may have been an O.D. from an unidentifiable drug. Or that Shultz will be assaulting immorality well within shouting distance of Watkins on Nostrand, which in turn happens to be an avenue that runs a West Indian course right through Crown Heights beyond Empire. We're still going to be indulging Inspector DeSales's penchant for the spiritual side of things.'' He drew an arc connecting the locations on the map. "So forget this 'no reference to the Almighty' shit. We're into it up to our necks.''

DeSales shrugged. "We squeeze the pimple, the pus comes out.''

CHAPTER 9

THE MORNING SUN strobed through the ever-diminishing cover of oak and maple leaves. The man in the black raincoat sat wearily on one of the stone benches that separates the playground at the 3rd Street entrance to Prospect Park from the Litchfield Villa. He put his gym bag down beside him and, seeing that no one was nearby, removed the dark felt hat with the low round crown and widish brim. The filter of yellow-and-red light caught his sandy hair and brought out the strawberry blond in it. His unkempt beard, darker than the hair on his head and showing traces of premature gray, merely emphasized the contrasting pallor of his cheeks and high shine of his swollen nose. His eyes, except for an occasional flicker of interest, were barely animate, lizardlike.

But when he spoke aloud, his voice had a pleasant lilt and the timbre of velvet: "The Lord sayeth to me to come out and be separate, and I have done so."

Then he realized that he was indeed more separate than he intended, for there were no children in the playground, no laughter, none of the prickling cries of combat. Barren.

So he looked skyward and the light reminded him of home,

transported him readily from the empty city park. The hum of traffic from the Park Drive put him in the back seat of his dad's old Chevy hurtling down Route 22, splicing Pennsylvania north from south; past the barns with the hex signs; past Roadside America, the nation's Premiere Miniature Village; past the dirty-book store behind the Midway Diner; past the black fecund earth, the endless rows of green cornstalks in midsummer that sadly turned to husks as the orange light of October—this very light—approached. He missed the birch beer on tap, the pork barbecue on a bun, Twinsicles.

"Now I am Truly Plain," he said aloud, replacing his hat on his head, wondering again where the little boys were, the blond little boys like home, the playground an oasis in this dark city, city of coloreds and Jews and Spaniards and Greeks and Italians and Russians and Arabs. You could walk across Brooklyn for days, like a man lost in the desert, without encountering a fair-haired, blue-eyed Aryan child. Finding this park had been a stroke of luck.

But a mixed blessing: the fence was secure and the children had babysitters, fat black ones—from some South Sea island, he supposed—who sat on the benches like alligators, sleepy-eyed but ready to snap; besides, the hollow had steep, sloping sides that threatened containment, like some of the rooms he had been locked up in. This was before he had seen the Movie, and realized he had been living next to truth through his childhood, shielded from it by a wicked father and a profane, deceitful society. Then he had decided to be Plain. And Separate. He called himself the Stranger. He recited:

> *Look out for the stranger*
> *Because he's not in danger.*

Dad of course had not started locking him up right away. In fact he had figured out that if Dad went out to the barn, you were free to do pretty much what was available for a good long time because he stayed long hours there in the barn. So one morning just like this, with the leaves falling and the sun low on the horizon, and dew on the splintered cornstalks, he decided he could afford to take a trip to the lot next to the cornfield off the dirt road that ran back off 22 from Ono; the town that had the O Yes Diner. That was nice: the name was clever and the hamburgs were well-done, even crisp around the edges as they should be; and there were little miniature jukeboxes in each booth where they played, endlessly, Gene Vincent's "Be-Bop-A-Lula." And there was a guessing game where you put in a penny and the answer was Yes or No. It was nice but not as nice as the lot down the road where couples parked at night and threw the rubbers out the window after they were finished, sometimes the boxes too. So he was pretty young when he began his collection: Excellos, Trojans, Sheiks. The morning his father had gone out to the barn, he got the Heinz girl from the trailer next door and that idiot brother of hers with the hair as wispy as corn silk and big buck teeth, and they went out to the lot and took the Heinz boy's pants down and got him hard. He didn't know if it was he or the sister that did it, but it was probably the girl because they used to say she could give thirty-five or sixty-eight varieties or however many it was on the billboard with the official pickle. The Heinz Pickle. Anyways, he got one of the old Trojans out of the dirt and was trying to pull it on this idiot Heinz boy so they could take him over to the farm on the other side of the corn and have him fuck a sheep or cow or whatever was available . . .

He spoke with resonance this time the line from the movie, shaking his fist in the air. "I've got nothing to do with your laws. Come out from them and be separate."

. . . And then his father appeared, came running through the fallen stalks like the wrath of God waving the razor strop, and he got the idiot first across the bare heinie and the girl in the chops and then took his time stropping him, his own son, and punching him into the dirt until he was unconscious. He was locked in the cellar for a long time after that, and he sometimes thought he heard his mother crying through the door.

Dazed with the memory, the man in black hoisted his bag and

stumbled down the macadam path through the gates of the empty playground. It dawned on him now why the children were missing: the enclosed lowland space had flooded during the night and was not yet drained. Water seeped into his socks. He would have to take himself to the open, sunny meadow to dry out. Later there would be kids; or, of course, he could go down to the other playground where the class of people was not so nice.

Irish. You can't trust a mackeral-snapper. His grandfather said that.

And then Ricky Nelson's voice was overlapping Gene Vincent's on the track in his head. Ricky Nelson, the travelin' man who had made a lot of stops . . . but Ricky Nelson was dead. Standing ankle-deep in water in an all-sand playground adjacent to the world's largest community of preserved Victorian housing, the man with the hat chanted:

Dead in his plane
Smoking cocaine.

Ozzie and Harriet had raised their boy well; they would be sad.

He saw that one of the guards was watching him from the pathway behind the Litchfield Villa. He had better be moving on. With his clothes and his name, they always thought he was a Jew and it was getting pretty hard to take. That was why he had become the Stranger. There was nowhere in New York City where anyone knew the difference, the devout from the pagan, the pure from the contaminated.

Still, he did not move. His feet were soaked, the cuffs of his trousers clung to his ankles. He scuffed his toe against the wet sand. He never knew why his dad would take the strop against him when he did. The Heinz girl and boy were wicked schemers; they always tricked him into doing what he didn't want to do. They were tainted and his dad didn't know it.

He saw his father's horse-face, the close-cropped dark blond hair with the ducktail in back, cut square across the neck, longer there than on top. He felt the gaze of the crossed eyes, remembered the way he wore his T-shirts, white and clean, with his pack of Camels folded up over the shoulder into the sleeve. There was a tattoo of a fire-breathing dragon on his bicep. There was a time before his little sister was sent off, before he had moved to Gramps's house, before the shunning and the foster homes, when Dad had taken the two kids, him and his sister, all the way to the Carlisle Fair. After the demolition derby, Dad bought them some cotton candy, gave them some money for the rides while he went into a big tent with a barker and a lady in a kind of bathing suit outside. Well, they rode the tilt-a-whirl a few times. They fished up the wooden ducks with the numbers on the bottom and lost. They wandered back over to the midway and went in to see the half-man, half-woman. Then they pitched pennies until they were broke.

So they went looking for Dad.

The man taking tickets at the flap in the tent was engrossed in the show and they sneaked past him. They crept up behind the backs of the burly, noisy men until they could see the stage. There was the lady up there, stark naked. Her tits stood out like torpedoes and she was doing a kind of dance.

"Be-Bop-A-Lula" played on the loudspeaker, then "Shake, Rattle, and Roll."

The woman kept shaking her tits while she squatted at the edge of the stage and the tall, dark-blond man in the front row who was his father handed some paper money up which she stuck inside her, something he had never seen done before or since; then he thrust his head forward and started eating hair pie right then and there in front of half the farmers in Cumberland, Perry, and Dauphin counties and everybody cheered and his sister started to cry. There was their father with his face buried between the dancer's legs and his D.A. all mussed up, and then a fellow with a John Deere hat on waved some more money and the woman sort of side-straddled leaving Dad wiping his lips so she could give another taste. They got out fast before they got caught.

On the way home, the old Chevy with the cigarette burns in

the upholstery ran out of gas on the Harrisburg Pike. They had no money left and Dad whipped them both for spending all of theirs pitching pennies. Sometimes he still wondered why his father thought rootin' and snootin', as he called it, was a better way to spend your money than pitching pennies.

CHAPTER 10

DE SALES WAS FIDDLING with the electronic map of Brooklyn that occupied an entire wall in his office in the new headquarters. Timothy Desmond crossed his legs, leaned back in the swivel chair, and remembered that in the ramshackle old place there had been turn-of-the-century light fixtures, and DeSales sometimes referred to another map he had stuck into the crumbling plaster with thumbtacks. The detective's desk stood in the middle of an open space next to a holding pen, and the profane cries and maniacal laughter of the prisoners being booked provided an appropriate subtext to the parade of distraught parents, sleazy ambulance chasers, and general chaos that pervaded the room. Now there were private offices and carpeting underfoot that looked like it belonged in a white-shoe country club in Florida. Bernie Kavanaugh sat in an alcove to the left before a bank of new computers.

"You've upgraded your real estate," said Desmond when the swarthy detective did not bother to acknowledge his presence.

DeSales did not look back. He pointed at a flashing red light at the far right of the map. "That's telling me that there's an emergency situation out in East New York. Of course, there's always an emergency situation in East New York. But it allows Bernie to type up a code on that machine there, and . . ."

Kavanaugh took him up in midsentence. "We find out that one Ismail Godbole, an Indian immigrant with history of mental illness, stabbed to death his five children while they slept this morning, then threw his wife out the tenth-floor window. Unemployed, thirty-five years old, city housing project." Kavanaugh paused as the machine took a break, then resumed: "Attempted suicide by jumping out same window. Unsuccessful. Landed on a terrace on eighth floor. Intensive care at Kings County Hospital."

"So now," DeSales turned to face his guest, "I know twice as fast what I never wanted to know in the first place. What do we do with poor Godbole except officially book him, do the paperwork, and hope he's more successful getting rid of himself the next time he's despondent?" He sat down at his desk. "Did you know that ninety percent of what we do has no mystery, no detection whatever to it? We know in seconds, thanks to modern technology, whodunit, how, and—in a general way—why. We clean up the mess and carry the red tape part of the way. That's it. We're paper—or, more exactly, keyboard," he nodded at Kavanaugh, "pushers more than we are investigators." He turned on his charming smile. "But you're over here to help us actually play detective for a while. So welcome. Let's get to work."

Desmond gave him a look of shared irony. "I thought you were looking gloomy. Now I see why. And even the color scheme doesn't work?"

DeSales almost blushed, and then laughed out loud. "The mayor found this Iranian in an Italian Restaurant on the Upper East Side. Name of Omar. A Persian ass-kisser with crocodile moccasins and no socks. He said we need carpeting of Aegean Blue to introduce a sense of gentle harmony into our troubled and violence-strewn existence."

"Has it?"

"Has it, Bernie?"

"Has what?"

"The goddamn Aegean Blue."

Kavanaugh tittered. "You bet." A yellow light went on on the map. Kavanaugh typed, then read aloud the incoming message: "A ballet dancer's been raped and stabbed on Eastern Parkway, across from the Museum and Botanicals. This is just the kind of thing the Chamber of Commerce loves. She's conscious, but calm and only superficially wounded. Ambulance taking her to Methodist for observation . . ."

DeSales became animated. "Perp?"

"Next-door neighbor."

DeSales's mouth began to turn down at the corners. His hand hit a buzzer. A tall, slender black man peeked in the door. "Watkins," he said, "check out this Eastern Parkway rape-stabbing before you set yourself up at Nostrand. See if it could be connected to the Shinto temple. Then go on to Nostrand. I may look for you around the corner of Empire later on." He turned back to Desmond and raised an eyebrow. "We were discussing Aegean Blue, as I remember?"

"Forget it," Desmond said, as Watkins backed silently out the door. "I'm here because of last night. To play detective."

DeSales rearranged some paper, found a pen and notebook and promptly dumped them back on the pile. He lighted a cigarette and put his feet up on the desk. He flipped the match into a wastebasket. "Last night we were discussing a corpse, voodoo, and uncertainty. The uncertainty was yours. We knew nothing. So we had nothing to be uncertain about."

Desmond was aware as he began that Kavanaugh had switched on a tape recorder. The notepad was a throwback, a mere atavism. It should have been left in the old office. "There were obvious signs of a Voudon rite . . . okay, to simplify I'll say voodoo . . . at the Gardens last night. In the first place, I had exotic religion on my mind, because of the TV show and the circumstance in which you asked me. Then, the man was black. Or at first appeared to be . . . let's say *Negro*. . . . There was the chicken feather . . . and the absence of large quantities of blood suggested to me—although I include no medical knowledge in my portfolio—that maybe the man had been cut up *after* he was dead. My mind clicked: voodoo.''

DeSales looked toward the recorder: "For the machine we need some 'why' in here."

" 'Why'? Because black in Brooklyn often means Haitian these days; because the Haitians' fear of zombis sometimes leads them to 'kill' a corpse a second time by mutilation to make sure it's really dead and won't rise from the grave. Because it's common voodoo practice to pass the body of a live animal, often a chicken, over a sick or dying person. Then to bite off or rip off the head of the bird . . ."

"Did anybody look for the rest of that chicken, Bernie?"

"Not so far."

DeSales brought his feet to the floor abruptly, butted the cigarette, slammed open a drawer, and fished around until he found a stick of chewing gum. He stripped it, put the gum in his mouth, rose, and stood next to the window, contemplating the flourishing car wash across Flatbush Extended and the perennial traffic jam at the entrance to the Brooklyn-Queens Expressway on Tillary. He folded his arms, still intent on the street scene. "What about the tattoo?"

Desmond drew a breath and decided to pretend he was giving a lecture. He didn't like DeSales's high level of agitation. A few years before, Desmond had secretly envied the man's cool, unflappable, even amoral, detachment from his physical surroundings. "The representation of Christian icons, particularly Roman Catholic ones, is a characteristic of Voudonist practice. In reflects the deep-running social tensions that permeate Haitian society, its potential for savagery and violence. Haiti, or Dominica, was an incredibly rich island when it was discovered by the Spanish. After the French succeeded in wresting the part now known as Haiti from the Spanish, they set about importing African slaves to provide free labor which would in turn provide wealth for the mother country from the sugar and coffee plantations. The slaves were of course not Christians, and the French required not only that they break their backs, but that they convert.''

"From what, exactly?''

"That's not easy to be precise about, their original beliefs. The slaves were of a number of different tribes: Ibo and Dahomians particularly, as I remember.'' He scratched his head and made a gesture toward the briefcase he had rested against his chair on the floor, then pulled back. "That's right, it was the Yoruba who went to Cuba and started a similar cult to Voudon called Santeria. In Brazil there's Macumba . . .''

"Okay,'' said DeSales, impatient, "get us to the tattoo.''

"Right. Forgive me. When you study a lot, it's not easy to keep the focus.''

"You've got my sympathies.'' DeSales waved toward the map, as if the very size of the borough implied the absence of focus. Knowing *it* was knowing too much. Just like reading too many books.

Desmond continued: "The African spirit religions were assimilated rather than suppressed. The result is Voudon. The French told them if they didn't want to be killed or beaten they had to worship Christ as the Son of God and venerate the saints. The Africans wanted to continue to find *their* expressions of God in their *loa,* the spirits found in all natural living things. One of the favorite *loa* is the snake, which also in special circumstances doubles as the Great Serpent who is directly responsible for the Creation, for procreation in general, for the taking of blood as a sacrament, and for the whole tricky business of spirit possession. So,'' he held out his arms, half-smiling, "a representation of a saint, like old Patrick, with a snake under his foot, was conveniently adapted by the Africans because they could put it up in their quarters, pretending to venerate the saint but in reality worshiping the snake!''

"I love it,'' DeSales said, shaking his hand in the Italian gesture of much exasperation.

"You talk about zombis," said Kavanaugh. "I hear zombis, I start thinking about witch doctors sticking pins in dolls, casting spells, black magic, that shit. Are we supposed to be believing in this stuff? Do the Haitians out there in Flatbush believe it?"

"It's a tricky question," said Desmond, "trickier than you might expect. You can find legitimate voodoo priests around who've gone more-or-less public here in the States. They give lectures at the Museum of Natural History and college campuses, for example. The party line I've heard is that they want to be recognized as a legitimate religion, as peaceable and spiritual as Islam or Christianity. That Hollywood and sensationalist writers have created the image of the pagan bogeyman doing black magic. Then in the next breath we see slides or film of the *houngan,* or priest, exorcising curses and evil spirits from people who appear to be truly possessed."

DeSales had perked up again. "But that's a contradiction. They either believe in it or they don't."

"To us it certainly appears a contradiction, but there are plenty of Catholics who believe in exorcism. In any case, the *houngan* has an answer to your challenge. You'll love this one too: he, the Voudonist, practices *white magic.* The zombis and possessed people are created by *black* magic, by a sort of witch doctor called a *bokor.*"

"So they believe in black magic, but they don't practice it, so they're clean. It's just racist America that makes them out to be pagan savages. Terrific."

"More than that: they say the voodoo priest's very function, his reason for being, is to combat the evil of the *bokor.* White magic versus the black."

"That's some kind of back-ass logic."

Desmond raised a hand. "Hold on. That was my first reaction, but if you think of it, we were all raised to see God largely as filling the function of battling the devil. What's the difference?"

"At Our Lady of Peace, they told us God came first and that

Satan was a bad boy, a rebel condemned to eternal fire, and he exists because God wants to test us, give us some rope to hang ourselves, so to speak.''

"Which Adam and Eve promptly did," Kavanaugh interjected.

"And in voodoo, God is unreachable so the Great Serpent came first. I find the serpent a more interesting metaphor, to tell you the truth.''

DeSales chewed his gum and watched for a while men with squeegees intimidating motorists on Tillary to pay them to take a swipe at their windshields. Finally he said, "Let's get back to the case at hand. You telling us we got a corpse whose death is the result of some spell, some black magic?''

"Not at all. Do you have the autopsy yet?''

DeSales looked at his watch: "Within the hour.''

"That'll tell you more than I can. But what I'm telling you is not just theology. It's part and parcel of an everyday reality that is sometimes quite violent.''

"How so?''

"The voodoo societies have always fulfilled a rebellious, marauder's function in Haiti. One of Papa Doc Duvalier's greatest political triumphs was that he brought the Voudon priests directly on his side, which gave him some control of them.''

"And?''

"And he did this by persuading the chieftains of the voodoo societies in previously ungovernable regions to become the heads of the Ton Ton Macoute.''

Kavanaugh sat up. "The big black guys with the shades and submachine guns? The secret police?''

"Right.''

"And how does this bring us back to murder in Brooklyn?''

"Since the Duvaliers have been run out, the Catholics and Protestants are getting their licks in. Here and at home. Remember the demonstrations on Liberation Day at Grand Army Plaza? When you read in the paper that the people of Haiti are tarring and feathering the Ton Ton Macoute since the revolution . . .''

"They're at the same time . . .''

"Right. At the same time they're killing the voodoo priests. And something parallel is probably happening in New York.''

"White-magic or black-magic department?''

Desmond shrugged his shoulders. "The impression I get is that a lot of these guys were playing both sides of the street. 'Serving with both hands,' they call it. Take the case of zombis. I read of one instance in which the writer conjectures that the *houngan,* the white- magic guy, actually put out a contract to a black-magic guy to poison a fellow so he appeared dead, so as ultimately to enhance his own reputation by using a pre-prepared antidote and bringing the guy back from the dead.''

"This is beginning to sound familiar,'' said DeSales.

"Like the Hasids. Everything an expression of 'Gd.' ''

"Huh?'' asked Desmond." 'Gd'? ''

"A cop joke,'' said DeSales. "And like City Hall. Doubletalk to cover up doubledealing.''

"One of my central themes in *Ritual and Revenge,*'' said Desmond. "Extreme religions, positions among which I will readily concede City Hall a place,'' he winked at DeSales, "represent embattled social minorities determined at all costs not to be swallowed up, assimilated, by the oppressive majority. This leads to violence.'' The half-articulated image of the man in black stumbling down Berkeley Place at midnight flitted across his mind. Like the Amish, he thought, but he chose not to give voice to the idea. He had, based on his previous experience, a resistance to getting his own life twisted up with the concerns of the police. Besides, as Mona had said, the guy was safe. And the Amish had chosen not rebellion nor an aggressive flaunting of their differences as their style: instead they retreated and turned the other cheek. In a way Desmond did as well.

He joined the detectives in self-congratulatory laughter.

·   ·   ·

"So what made you hesitate last night?" asked DeSales. "Put things off until you looked something up today?"

"It was the Japanese business. In combination with voodoo. The placement of the body seemed to me suspicious in the first place. Then when I saw that the guy had Oriental features, something went off in the back of my mind, something I just couldn't put my finger on." Desmond had been leaning forward; now he sat up straight and pushed his glasses back from the tip of his nose.

"And you have now?"

Slowly, Desmond shook his head. He leaned forward again, brushed the hair back from his forehead. Then he sat up straight once more, repeating the movement with the glasses. "Nope," he said. "I'm still stumped. I went over to the Grand Army Plaza library after I took my son to nursery school this morning, but I couldn't find the reference I was looking for."

"Maybe you had a general sense?"

"Oh, sure. It had something to do with eating, food ingestion."

"Poison?"

"That would be part of it: I keep seeing words flashing like distant road signs: *zombi, poison, Japan.* Then there's a sense of an eating place involved. I looked through all of the obvious references in the library, but I couldn't find anything on Japan, so maybe I'm dreaming."

"The Shinto Japs don't do tattoos, saints, snakes, chickens?"

"Not that I know of. And especially not anything related to motifs involving mayhem or revenge or problems with assimilation . . ."

"Poison," DeSales repeated, dropping the gum in the wastebasket and smoking again. "Bernie, get Friedman on the line. We need at least a tentative post-mortem right now."

"Check." Kavanaugh dialed the phone. DeSales and Desmond looked at one another across the desk. Desmond thought of the Amish vagrant again and again decided not to mention him. He would be taking Nick to the playground soon and he would consult with the other parents and caretakers about their observations before reporting the guy. He didn't want to be seen as hysterical or alarmist. He realized that this instinct was much more pressing than the more abstract resistance to involvement in a crime. He watched the ash on DeSales's cigarette grow longer, and he tried to think of a way to ask about the manifest air of sadness that enveloped the detective. But then he looked into the steely blue eyes and thought the better of that, too, because there remained artifacts of that macho confidence that had once intimidated him so.

I am still afraid of the bastard, he thought, of his stereotypical manhood. I cannot allow Nick to grow up like I did, passive, lacking the courage to attack before being attacked, to seize what he wants without needing someone to hand it to him on a silver platter. My son needs a touch of DeSales in him. More macho than he gets at home.

"Pick it up," said Kavanaugh. DeSales ground out the ash.

"Yeah?" he said, phone pressed tight against his ear. The high-pitched nasal response on the other end of the line was muffled. It went on for at least five minutes. Desmond looked at Kavanaugh but the man had returned to the computer. He noticed that the Irishman was jug-eared and bit his fingernails. He looked at the map on the wall. Lights flashed all over the borough, except in the brownstone strip from his own place in Park Slope to Brooklyn Heights and the river; also seemingly protected by the invisible shield was the sprawl of Borough Park south of Greenwood Cemetery. The two communities were connected, in fact, by a narrow corridor between the park and the cemetery. This was Windsor Terrace, Desmond realized, an Irish enclave that seemed not to have changed in fifty years, while all about it the borough had gone up and down, in and out, receiving immigrants and expelling them, whitening and blackening. Desmond was wondering if there was some significance in this rock of undistinguished ethnic consistency lying between the two areas, one the most assimilated and the other the most adamantly parochial; but then

DeSales was grunting into the mouthpiece, hanging up, and glaring across the desk at him.

"Preliminary report; *very* preliminary, Friedman says, but when he says anything at all, it's pretty complete. The guy's system was laced with drugs: uppers and downers and a dash of marijuana and coke. But none of this killed him."

"What did?"

"He doesn't know. There are substances he can't identify and some weird organ damage. He's waiting for a toxicologist who specializes in tropical plants, from Columbia-Presbyterian."

"I wish even more now that I could remember."

"If the toxicologist has any trouble we may have to hypnotize you to bring it back."

"Okay, get out the iron maiden and give him the old third degree, huh, Frank."

"Right, Bernie, we could try something like that. But I'd rather start with truth serum. Then the Jewish water torture."

Desmond made a face. "I have to go," he said, looking at his watch. "Is there anything else?"

"There was some blood around the body that wasn't the victim's." He nodded. "Chicken blood. And there was some powder, also not yet chemically identified, on the boards underneath the body. Looks like it may have been deposited in the shape of a cross. There are also some interesting physical details we missed in the dark."

"Yeah?"

"Scratches all over his ass and another piece of minor surgery to go along with the missing fingerprints. There's been a piece of skin removed from his arm." He made a circle with his thumb and index finger. "The size of a silver dollar, Friedman says. Any of this ring a bell?"

"Reminds me that Friedman is rumored to spend his holidays in Vegas and Atlantic City playing the slots."

"Desmond?"

"Something that's not pleasant to contemplate."

"Not much *is*, in this business."

"In the early days of Haiti, when the Voudon secret societies were being formed?"

"Yeah."

"Bounty hunters were often sent out by the authorities to bring back runaway slaves and other rebels. There was also another class of free-lance bounty hunter. Anyway, the slaves were branded and rather than go to the trouble of bringing back the entire body of the recaptured slave, the hunter would simply remove the skin with his brand on and bring it back so he could cash in."

"Just like . . ." Kavanaugh began.

"Just like ripping off a cereal boxtop, or a coupon out of the paper," said Desmond. "They do it with paperback books that the store returns to the publisher too. Just rip off the cover and send it back. Trash the book itself."

"You're getting the idea, Professor," Kavanaugh rejoined.

DeSales got up and paced the wall with the map, hiking up his trousers on his slender hips. With his finger he traced the route that Colon had drawn crudely on the blackboard earlier in the day. "You stay here and keep after that machine, Bernie. I'm going back to the scene-of-crime and giving it one more look. Then I'm going to take a walk." He looked at the map again. "A long walk."

"Looking for voodooists or Jews?"

"You name it. What the streets have to offer."

"Don't forget your beeper, then."

DeSales was strapping on his holster, inspecting the chambers on his .38.

"Or your piece."

"Or my piece," said the detective inspector.

CHAPTER 11

THE MAN CALLED RAND FURLONG closed the steel door behind him and secured the lock. He trotted across the hardwood floor of the loft to the corner with the mini-gym and dropped onto his back on the plastic mat. After lying still, chest heaving, for thirty seconds, he turned onto his stomach, raised himself with hands and arms, poised in the air until his butt was in line with his spine, and began to do pushups. Rapidly. After fifty, he dropped again and rolled back over.

"Who's minding the store?" he asked, between intakes of breath.

The woman was reading a magazine, *HerOwn,* on the spare futuristic couch. She looked up, then back down at the page. "Don't worry," she said, without much movement of the lips. "They don't start coming until noon. And I'll hear the buzzer." She wiped her nose, still swollen from the blow it had absorbed the night before. She kept her eyes glued to the page.

"What's so interesting?"

She held up the cover to him. "Something about multiple orgasms."

"What about multiple orgasms?"

"Women who survive near-fatal accidents are twice as likely to have them—multiples, that is."

"Twice as likely as *whom?* Those who *don't* survive?" He let out a deep belly laugh, clasped his knees with his hands and drew them into his chest. He rocked back and forth, still manifestly pleased with his own sense of humor, then crawled to his feet.

"How'd it go?" she asked. "I still can't believe you dragged me outa that dump in Borough Park in the middle of the night after we went to all that trouble to be there when the truck arrived."

He had backed over to the gleaming-new galley kitchen on the opposite exposed brick wall. Now he stripped off his headband and was wringing it out into the sink. He appeared to be thinking about her question. When he spoke, his normally deep, resonant voice was defensive, an octave higher. "It came to me in the night, the vibes. Why the fuck should we hang around there overnight when the only people liable to even peep in the place were the cops! And this guy who's going to make the delivery, I never dealt with him before. He's J.P.'s man. What if he's done a double-cross?" He tossed the headband into the laundry closet and stripped the orange-Day-Glo jogging shirt from his gleaming torso. "I did the right thing, believe me."

"Well, I lost my beauty sleep." She yawned. "And the delivery?"

"Not a hitch. Our little kosher pharmacy-to-be is locked up tighter than a drum; inside is not only the cases of downers and the laxatives, but the supplier threw in a load of Darvon on top to make up for Lilly being so pricky about the laxatives. *Then,*" he adjusted his genitals under the tight satin shorts; it was clear he wore no supporter. "Then, I did two laps around the cemetery. Second time around the 'Ricans from Fourth Avenue were waiting by the BMT yard. They'll take all the Seconal and Tuinal off my hands tomorrow. The market's still a little soft on the narcotic analgesics, so I'll hold on to the Darvon a while. We still got room here."

"And the Percodan and Dexies?"

"I got a contract with the big Jamaican motherfucker. He comes by today with fifty percent up front. I run back over to Thirteenth Avenue, just like today, in the morning with the van, and wait for the other supplier. I take delivery, sign the invoice with J.P.'s name and wait for the 'Ricans and the Jamaican to pick up. When they do, I put the painkillers in the van, leave the laxatives and insulin behind, and close up shop. The landlord's got three months' rent in advance. He won't even fucking *look* at the place until Christmas, when the next rent is due. The lease is in the name of one Jean-Paul Pic, who old Teitelbaum thinks is me, a white Frenchman, and not our dearly beloved, departed, dusky colonial friend."

"You're so smart. You think of everything." But she seemed less than pleased. She knit her brow and pressed the pages of the magazine back roughly.

Rand dropped his shorts and began a vigorous toweling down. "Smart is right. You know any other dealer has a Harvard MBA?"

"I don't know nobody has a Harvard MBA." She touched the sore area on her nose tentatively. "Rand, are you gonna try to keep up Jean-Paul's line of special products?"

He stiffened, hands at his sides gripping the towel against the small of his back. "Why not? I got the ingredients." He nodded toward a bank of locked metal cabinets. "I'm building a lab." He indicated the marble-topped table and siphons and pipes being assembled in front of the cabinets. He started rotating his hips again. A male stripper without G-string. "I got the talent," he concluded.

The woman dropped the magazine and stood up, facing him. She wore a diaphanous beach shift, a white bikini underneath it. The tan stood out in stark contrast. "I'm sorry, baby, but that I don't think is so smart."

Rand was outraged. "Why?"

"Look what happened to J.P. fucking around with that stuff."

"J.P. was Faustian. He had to take a fall. I know my limits. I'm educated as a practical businessman."

"Does Harvard Business School teach you somebody should be cut up after he's already dead?"

"Your nose is real pretty from last night. Wanna try for a mouth fulla loosies this morning?"

She took a step forward, then hesitated. "You think it's not normal for somebody like me to not get spooked by this shit? I'm *scared*, Rand. If you just deal straight pills and don't cross the wrong dude, you got a good, safe, profitable profession. You get into the weird stuff, next step we're mutilating people. God, I feel *dirty;* I got blood on my hands." She held them out. Her long fingernails were painted a spectral white, once again setting off the sun-darkened flesh.

Rand turned to the refrigerator, dropping the towel. He pulled the handle and grabbed out a bottle of carrot juice. He shook his head, disbelievingly. *"Mutilating,"* his voice rose in pitch again. "What a word. You been reading too much trashy shit, seen too many chain-saw videos. J.P. was responsible for his own demise, nobody can deny that. And what I had to do I had to do. Pure business. Cover your tracks and beat ass. Set up a smokescreen. Cloud the mind of the fucking supercops." He gulped his juice.

The buzzer rang. The expression that crossed Rand's visage, the wide-set gray eyes, straight nose, flaring nostrils, and pencil-thin lips, suggested that things were again in place, that a stage direction had been neatly followed. "You got a customer," he said. "Get to work and leave *my* business to *me.*"

She threw her head back, a silent act of defiance, ran her hands through the thick bleached hair, and went to the stairs.

The buzzer sounded again.

"There's another one. Move your ass."

She descended quickly to the ground floor, heels clattering on the old metal staircase. Rand heard her open the door to the shop and say, in that hookerish voice she thought made her sound businesslike, "And what can I do for *you,* sir?"

Wired, a bit paranoid after the intensity of the morning's transactions, not to mention Merry's assaultive interrogation,

Furlong slid back the panel in the floor that concealed the one-way mirror looking into the store. There were two men standing in line at the counter. They were about average skin-flick jerkoffs. Beefy, middle-aged, working-class types. The first he recognized as a regular customer, a retired court stenographer from Windsor Terrace. He walked all the way down to the South Slope regularly because the parish priest on Prospect Park West wouldn't allow the distribution of adult magazines or videos in the neighborhood. Besides, thought Furlong, as he watched the old drunk's hands quivering, this guy would probably be afraid to rent the stuff in his own area even if he could: somebody might find out. Rand remembered his own childhood in Greenpoint, when you had to go twenty blocks to buy a pack of rubbers or a *Playboy* because the druggist, old man Fibak, would tell your parents or, worse, the nuns.

What blew him away was the second man. At first, the anachronistic crewcut, ill-fitting suit, and long nose had rung only a minor bell in his memory. But something rankled and he hesitated before closing the panel. Then it hit him: the guy was a cop! And not just any cop, but one of DeSales's men. Furlong had seen him nosing around the kosher Chinese joint in Borough Park after the Hasid got his beard trimmed. On the edge of panic, he closed the panel gently and went back to the mat, clutching his knees again and rocking. How had they found him so soon? Should he grab as much of the dope as he could carry and run for it? The dope! This introduced a calming thought: this guy wasn't a narc; he was in Violence. They weren't after the dope. But, worse, that meant they had connected him to Jean-Paul. Fucking J.P., even dead, was like a bad penny.

He started to do one of his breathing exercises, but his head wouldn't clear.

Shultz stood behind the old Irishman, contemplating the walls of the store that featured posters advertising skin flicks mixed with travel agent's promotions for tropical islands. Doing his bit on loan to Vice, he had been working his way from Sunset Park through the south fringe of Park Slope and on to Borough Park, stamping out smut. He had seen some slimy operations, but this place was so brazen it was outrageous. At first the name, "Video-Rays" had suggested to him a tape place owned by a guy named Ray. But here it turned out to be a tape rental place specializing in X-rated flicks combined with a *tanning* parlor, presided over by an almost naked broad who had recently been knocked around a bit. If anything ever smelled of pussy-for-sale this was it.

The man in front of him asked, "You got *Bavarian Cream*?" He wore thick glasses on the tip of his blue-veined nose and smelled of stale beer.

The girl in the see-through gown scanned the shelves. "Nope. That one's almost always out."

"Jesus, Mary, and Joseph." The guy leaned over, peering at the catalogue of adult entertainment. "Maybe you got *Roman Orgies III*?"

The girl didn't even bother to look, just shook her head. "That's out too."

"*Inside Eva Brawn?* Sounds German. I like the foreign stuff. It's classier."

"Mr. Joyce, I know you told me once you were disgusted by the Gay Rights Bill. And *Inside Eva Brawn* is transvestite S and M stuff. I don't think it's for you." Mr. Joyce's face took on an expression of profound distaste. "I give up, honey, what do *you* recommend?" He raised his watery eyes from the sheets of paper. The girl turned them around so she could consult. Shultz had to restrain himself from putting in his own two cents' worth. He was something of an expert on porn himself, not from the viewpoint of the law-enforcement officer but from that of the consumer. He was a single man now because his wife of twenty-five years had thrown him out after stumbling on his private collection, particularly a videotape of Detective Shultz himself performing an act of criminal sodomy with a Chinese prostitute at the Patrolmen's Benevolent Association convention in Vegas some years before.

Indeed his collection of books, magazines, and tapes had achieved widespread notoriety in northern Westchester, when, the day after he moved out of the house in Mahopac, his wife had invited the Lutheran minister and all the neighbors and conducted a public burning of the offensive material in the fieldstone barbecue pit Shultz had built with his bare hands in the backyard. Anyway, he knew his way around.

"Here's one," said the girl behind the counter, leaning over so you could see her nipples where the shift and bikini top hung loose. "Very popular. *Bad Girls in the Badlands*."

"What country is that?"

"It's got, like, a Wild West theme."

Mr. Joyce looked skeptical. "It got girl-girl?"

"You bet."

"Black on white?"

"You kidding? There's a triple gangbang featuring runaway slaves. One of the slaves is played by Whopper Goldberg. What a piece of equipment!"

The customer appeared pleased with this information. Then he recovered his air of caution: "But no faggots?" His eyes narrowed.

The girl turned up her hands. She smiled blithely. She did a King Tut movement with her neck. "Not exactly, but gimme a break, Mr. Joyce. This is based on *true* history. What do you think those cowpokes had to do with themselves after chuckwagon out there on the lone prairie?"

"Okay," Joyce gave in, "I'll take it."

As the man walked out the door with the tape safely camouflaged in a plastic shopping bag, she looked at Shultz, raised an eyebrow, and said, "I *work* for my money."

"You sure do," Shultz agreed heartily, thinking that this was a come-on if he'd ever heard one, but wary that he must play her along, catch her in the act of open solicitation without himself risking being accused of entrapment. He decided to stick to videos for a while, let her lure him into the "tanning" parlor in her own good time. He leaned on the counter and gave her his most

ingratiating smile. "I'm looking for something a little different,"
he said, running his hand through his brush cut to give himself an
aura of boyish naïveté.

"Yeah?" She appeared interested. "Like what?"

"Kiddyflicks. Somebody told me there's a new batch out of
Amsterdam."

"Hey, you hear more than I do." She turned and contemplated
the shelves. "The best I can do for you is *Pubescent Pink*. They got
a girl in there's legal, eighteen say, but she got no boobs and they
shave the crotch so she looks maybe twelve."

Shultz put his chin in his hands and thought about this for a
moment. "Nope," he shook his head. "I only like the *real* thing."
He waggled an eyebrow. "Got any *snuff* movies?"

She made a face. "Disgusting. I wouldn't touch one with a
ten-foot pole. And *expensive*." Then a cloud of suspicion crossed
her face. "Hey, who are you anyhow?"

Shultz took this easily. He produced a plastic card identifying
him as Fred Otto, a member of the longshoremen's union. "Look,
I'm one of the old-time stevedores. Down at Bush Terminal. Now
that Jersey's got all the container business, we got a contract but no
ships to unload. So me and the other guys gotta show up every
morning and punch in. Then we got all day to do what we want. On
Fridays though we still get a nice fat paycheck. So I got *all day* to
enjoy. Listen," he confided, shrugging with a certain diffidence,
"some guys go to the gym, some guys drink, some guys even just
go home for the day. Me, I'm creative and I'm looking for a new
hobby. See, I even wear a suit to work in case I get invited
someplace fancy."

She looked at him with renewed interest. She flicked her long
tongue as if in sudden comprehension, then ran it slowly over her
upper lip. She stood back from the counter and looked Shultz over
for a while.

"I think I got just the thing," she said. "Follow me."

She led Shultz to a door in the wall with the tropical island
scenes. He found himself in a long corridor with white louvered

doors opening off it. She opened a door on the right. "This is the dressing room. Take off all your clothes. There's a stack of white towels there. Let me know when you're ready. We go to a room over there," she pointed across the corridor with her thumb, "so out of modesty you oughta wear one towel and carry another." She winked. "You know, to wipe off."

Shultz grinned broadly. "Terrific. Hey, they call me 'Dutch.' What's your name, sweetie?"

"Merry. Merry Pace."

"That's a real nice name."

"Just push the button on the wall when you're ready, Dutch."

Merry Pace hurried upstairs, where she found Rand in a yoga meditation posture, with one of J.P.'s special bottles in front of him.

"We got a cop downstairs," she said.

"I know. He's one of DeSales's men. I've done a couple mantras but I can't settle down. It looks like it's me against him, DeSales. I gotta get him before he gets me."

"Shit, Rand, you're blowing it all out of proportion. This guy is from Vice. He thinks this is a whorehouse."

"Clever, a clever front. He gives us the once over and we think we're clean. Then: bam!" He made a fist and drilled it into the palm of his other hand. "I don't know how he could have caught on so quick. He should be chasing niggers all over East Flatbush."

"You're crazy. If they wanted you for J.P., or for the pills, they'd come get you. This guy, believe me, is a misguided soul from Vice." A bell tinkled. "There he is, all eager for some action."

Rand looked up, eyes brightening. "What're you gonna give him then?"

"The works," said Merry Pace.

Rand remembered why he kept her around: she could evoke the Power of Positive Thinking.

. . .

The blonde opened Shultz's door, looked at his grizzled hairy chest and fish-belly-pale corpulence with unconcealed pleasure. She beckoned with her finger and Shultz, holding up the towel around his waist, walked barefoot through the thick carpeting, which he realized was the same color as that at the new headquarters, Aegean Blue, into the other room. Here there was a machine the likes of which he had never seen before. It resembled a large professional clothes-presser, maybe seven feet long by three feet wide, with the inside of the top and bottom halves glass or a clear plastic. At the hinge there was a control panel, tape deck, earphones, and eye shades. It looked like something they might put you into permanent orbit in.

"Lie down on the glass," said Merry seductively, "put on the earphones, and relax. I've adjusted the timer so you don't get overdosed with sun; it's just the right amount for a first-time tanner. I'll turn on the machine. You stay prone. Take off your towel. I'm sure you want this to be an all-over experience. Tee-hee. And, oh yeah, I've selected a tape for you already: Madonna, 'Like a Virgin.' "

Shultz opened his mouth to protest, but she was gone already and the top of the machine had begun to lower itself onto him, humming ominously. He supposed he could have escaped if he had rolled off the pallet right away, but he was still waiting to make a collar, and who knew if she'd be back in five minutes offering him half-and-half for an extra hundred? So it was too late when he felt the sweat oozing out of him and he was overcome by claustrophobia. The press was grinding to a halt an inch or so short of the tip of his nose and he had to suck in his belly to keep it from touching him there. He sucked a little harder and was barely able to whisk away the towel from his crotch with his all-but-imprisoned hand, flicking it to the floor. He held his breath and said a rapidly improvised prayer, then began to breathe easier. He had to keep quiet; he had to not have a heart attack. It was six of one, half dozen of the other, whether he raised hell and the cop on the beat had to come to the aid of a trapped naked detective or whether they had to call the morgue to take him away. It wouldn't look good.

So he gave in, rode with it. With two fingers on his left hand he turned on the cassette player. The singer's watery voice came through at once loud but undistinguishable, enveloped as Shultz was, in junky studio noise and a creeping seductive warmth. Then, in the face of potential indignity, embarrassment, folly, for putting himself in the position of a giant hot dog in a bun, Shultz did what he had become infamous for doing over his long career—in barroom booths, toilet stalls, at his desk, on stakeouts. He fell asleep.

Merry Pace went back upstairs to see if Rand had calmed down, to tell him that she had finessed the cop. Rand had showered quickly and was now sitting at the laboratory table in a Lacoste shirt, chinos, and thong sandals. He was intent on opening the red and blue Tuinal capsules and arranging their contents in neat piles adjacent to doses of ocher powder spooned from J.P.'s old rum bottle, and of mounds of multicolored sprinkles from three-hundred-milligram Thorazine spans.

"I wanted to pick you up," she said. "Not send you on a power trip. You're fucking around with that stuff after all."

Rand looked up quickly. "Hey, we still have to get them before they get us. *They* is this asshole, DeSales. I'm four steps ahead of him now, you're right, but I want to make it five. Five big ones. Our marketing strategies and defensive-offensive positioning has been sound. At this point in time. But I better get to work."

Shultz, more or less fully dressed, staggered out of the dressing room and into the shop.

Merry looked up cheerfully from the video catalogue. "Say, Dutch, you look great already. What time do you want to come in tomorrow? I think you'd better take the ten-ticket book. In two weeks you'll be looking like you've lived on the beach in the Caribbean for years. No more stevedore's pallor."

Shultz shook his head, peeling off some bills. "That enough? I'm not sure I'll make it tomorrow, to tell you the truth." He looked into her eyes and for a moment he thought he was gazing into yellow solar rays again. They *were* yellow. "I'm not sure this is exactly what I was looking for, Merry."

"Oh, well," she shrugged, "everybody's gotta do his own thing. This just happens to be mine. All that Vitamin D. Never have to take a pill, it's beautiful."

Shultz waved limply as he stepped into the street. He walked north for a block on the same side of the street, then realized he was disoriented, that Molloy's Bar was across the street and back up toward Video-Rays. He waited for the light and crossed. He felt hot still, and removed his jacket. Slowly, peeking in shop windows, he made his way crablike back south. A bus pulled up, and he used it for cover as he slipped into Molloy's and sat at the corner of the bar, peering across at Video-Rays from behind a coatrack. He drank a beer, then a shot of Paddy and another beer. He saw Merry Pace take care of a number of customers, mostly middle-aged men renting tapes. One wrinkled old lady presented a book of tickets and was shown into the tanning parlor. Then Merry answered the phone, laid it down gingerly on the counter. She stood in the entranceway, gazing up and down the street. Apparently satisfied that whatever she was looking for was not in evidence, she nodded her head briskly and went back to the phone. Her lips moved, only a word or two, and she hung up, returning her attentions to the catalogue.

Five minutes later, a limo pulled up and out of it stepped a man well known to Brooklyn detectives as Big Bird. Big Bird strolled casually up to the Video-Rays window; Merry gave him a reassuring nod, and he went into the shop. He passed the counter without looking at Merry and opened a door on the other side of the shop from the tanning area. It was the door from which Merry had emerged when Shultz had first arrived in the wake of the man with the blue-veined nose.

How interesting, thought Shultz and, feeling a great thirst, ordered himself another Irish and beer. It was unlikely that Big Bird had come all the way across town to rent a cassette and even less likely that he had come for a tan, since Big Bird was from Jamaica, West Indies, and was black as the ace of spades.

CHAPTER 12

THE FLEET OF MITZVAH TANKS—Chevrolet Leisurecraft they were, in fact—breezed down Eastern Parkway, heading to points throughout the city where they would spread enlightenment among the worldly and misguided of the Chosen People. Francis DeSales, stepping out of the subway exit in front of the Brooklyn Museum, took note of the young scholars bent over books at their pop-out tables in the rear of the vehicles and tried his best to picture the event at which these solemn and unhealthy-looking characters had been induced to record the frenzied chanting that blared from the speakers atop every van. He found himself laughing out loud at the image of Shlomo Glickstein's Lubavitcher alter ego leading a horde of his pallid, bearded followers, men only, all naked and goat-footed, into an orgy of dancing and homoerotic abandon.

DeSales felt good for a change. His feet were on the ground, specifically the pavements of Brooklyn again. He had been spending too much time being driven in official cars from meeting to meeting, worrying about politics and public relations and snoopers from Internal Affairs. He needed action.

In the wake of the Hasidic convoy, three ebony-skinned bicyclists wearing *Haiti Liberté* T-shirts pedaled by, each in turn flashing V-signs to pedestrians. An appropriate foreshadowing.

Frick met DeSales in the administrative office of the gardens. At his desk, wearing a Dacron suit, the shiny-pated man seemed to take on more ballast. The night before he had appeared as so much fluff, ready to be blown away by a big wind. Without ado, he led the detective back past the turnstile entrance to the Japanese section, in the direction of the Cherry Esplanade. He showed him the service gate in the stockade fencing where the lock had been forced and the wheelchair rolled in the day before. It had been done sometime before 4 P.M., when the guards made a sweep to make sure the gardens were empty. Weight, presumably dead weight, had caused the wheels of the chair to leave an impression in the soft earth.

"That's why the guard at the turnstile didn't remember anything unusual," said Frick.

It was a short way to the shrine, and Frick pointed out the obscure corner where the chicken carcass and its severed head had been discovered. DeSales nodded. "About what we expected. It fits in with the voodoo scheme I mentioned."

Frick unbuttoned his suit coat and put the tip of his forefinger on the tip of his chin, a Shakespearean pose. "There's something I don't understand, Inspector, and I've barely slept worrying about this. It's why someone would go to such elaborate measures to put a corpse on display, and then take such *drastic* measures to conceal its identity."

"Did you come up with an answer?" asked DeSales.

"*Well!*" Frick's eyes grew round as saucers. "If *I* had done it—God forbid!—I think I'd have been trying . . . Well, this is just too literal-minded I'm sure. I would have been trying to use all this black- magic stuff as a decoy, while at the same time concealing the man's identity. Let me say that again. I would have a need to do three things. First, dispose of the body. Second, conceal the identity. Third, send the police on a wild goose chase, a diversionary tactic it would be, so I could get away with something else. What that something else would be, of course, I haven't the foggiest.''

"Not literal-minded at all." DeSales was in a hurry, and he politely steered them back to the gate. "Absolutely penetrating. You would make a first-rate detective.''

Frick let out a sound of self-deprecation, but obviously he was pleased. DeSales, his feet on the ground, itching for movement, felt kindly. "Ask yourself another one," he said. "Why choose the fingertip-removal route?''

Frick struck his thinking pose again. "The person obviously had *fingerprints*. That sounds silly. I mean he had *known* fingerprints.''

"Right again," said DeSales. "And a person with *known* fingerprints is either the holder of some sort of classified job, or . . .''

"Or," said Frick, obviously more familiar with criminal matters than he had at first been willing to let on, "or he's got a yellow sheet. Maybe even done *time*.''

"Exactly," agreed DeSales, as they turned the corner and headed back to the Magnolia Plaza, where he would step through the neat, aromatic gift shop and right out again to Washington Avenue. Into the mean streets of Crown Heights. Through the Looking Glass. Frick tarried a moment, inspecting a plant, and DeSales noticed for the first time the Herb Garden. He stepped onto the raised terrace and inspected the name tags. "Golden carpet?''

"A laxative," Frick tittered.

"Persian cow parsnip?" DeSales was thinking of Omar the Decorator.

Frick rubbed his hands together as if he hadn't felt so positively functional in a long time: "A condiment. For pickles.''

"Black snakeroot?" DeSales squatted, looking up at Frick and squinting interrogatively. "Poison?''

"Hardly. It's medicinal.''

"So's a lot of poison. What's it used for?''

"Oh, dear. Sorry, Inspector. I just don't know."

"Find out and you'll get a crimestoppers' badge."

Frick laughed. "How *marvelous.*"

DeSales began to move briskly in the direction of the exit. Frick hurried to catch up. Near the official entrance to the Japanese Garden, they were momentarily arrested by the spectacle of a wedding party having formal pictures taken at the shore of the pond. They were Russians, in their early twenties. The groom and ushers wore white shoes, gray cutaways, white shirts, and pink bow ties. The bride's party wore strapless taffeta gowns that matched the bow ties. The photographer barked orders in Yiddish. The men all flicked their cigarettes toward the pond; the women looked nervous.

"Smile," the photographer pleaded in Russian, then English.

Now composed, the group smiled as one. With their Oriental cheekbones and narrow eyes and heavy pale chins, they appeared to be all of one large porcine family.

A group of visiting Hispanic schoolchildren stood by and alternately cheered and howled.

Frick took DeSales's arm to lead him around the blockage. "Can you believe it? They applied for a permit and everything. Came all the way from Brighton Beach?"

"I can," said DeSales. He shook Frick's hand. "Now don't forget finding out about that snakeroot, and . . ."

"Yes?"

"If you find a piece of flesh about the size of a silver dollar," DeSales joined thumb and forefinger in a ring, "let me know. It should have a brand or some kind of identifying mark on it."

"You bet," said Edmund Frick.

Well, thought DeSales, if there are any more murders in the Botanicals, we've now got friendly connections.

In the streets of Crown Heights, adjacent to the Botanic Gardens, faces were all black or brown, except for the proprietors of Chinese restaurants and pizza parlors. As DeSales headed east, he saw old folks sitting inanimate, caged, behind the bars of ground-floor tenement windows; naked infants hung over the sills on the upper levels. Farther on, between two tiny ramshackle wood-frame houses, someone had literally wedged a beaten-up Dodge Dart. Across the street, an enterprising gentleman had hooked up his soldering iron to a street lamp and was endeavoring to reattach a muffler to the chassis of a gypsy cab.

Soon he found himself in Hasidic country. The houses were at first undistinguished, semidetached residences. Within a block, these became free-standing stone mansions of the eccentric designs of the 1920s and 1930s. Pretty girls in neat frocks chatted idly on spacious balconies. Mothers, and grandmothers, wearing babushkas, pushed strollers. Gardeners prepared for spring. There were BMWs in the driveways.

The war was over.

On one corner there was a well-preserved Anglican church with substantial, beautifully kept grounds. An annex housed a school, and the schoolyard was full of well-dressed, well-disciplined students. They were all black. Somehow, this forced DeSales down for a moment, aware of his mortality. In his lifetime, after the respectable WASPs, who had founded the church, Crown Heights had been home to tough Irish and Italian immigrants, then assimilated Jews, then the Hasids, now the blacks. The sense was of time observed through a quadruple exposure. Here, for a few blocks, at any rate, the housing had been maintained as it was when first built, but the faces had changed so often—in one generation, really—and so radically that he would not be surprised to return in another decade and find Martians occupying the big houses and refugees from Hong Kong carrying the banner of the Church of England abroad. If he were to live so long.

There was something doubly deadening in the thought. Briefly, in his youth, DeSales and his mother had rented an apartment on Dean Street, only a few blocks on the other side of

Eastern Parkway. But, except for the pizza parlors, there hadn't been an Italian within miles for years. Francis DeSales, through his mother, was a member of an extinct race. In more ways than one.

He remembered that he had been on an up because he was back on the street, doing his business. Looking for trouble, in other words. And the only trouble he would find here was trouble in mind. He headed back where he had come from, where violence was everyday, humdrum, where he was to meet Hector Colon.

At Bedford Avenue, DeSales glanced downhill at the sand-colored pile of apartments that had once been Ebbets Field, crossed the street, and leaned against the corner of the 42nd Supply and Transport Armory. Colon sauntered out from the entranceway, from the shadow of the sign that said BASE OF THE RAINBOW. Colon leaned against the wall a dozen feet from DeSales, hands in pockets, and watched the traffic on Bedford intently.

DeSales concentrated on a poster on a telephone pole for a Calypso-extravaganza. Sponsored by Guinness Stout. What had Bernie said about the corpse in the temple? Black Irish.

"I've hit something already, Frank."

"The pot of gold?" DeSales looked from the poster back up at the rainbow sign again.

"As good as. I was just getting into it around here, some dudes were telling me there was a new kind of drug on the street, something expensive and fearsome to mess with, when Watkins shows up."

"He's supposed to be down on the other side of Empire."

"Check, but he called the office and Bernie told him you were heading over this way first. So he ran up to tell me you'd better hustle on down there double time."

"And why is that?"

"He'd been hearing about these pills, too. About strange rites involved. Then he tapped right into the source."

"The dealer? Is he connected to the guy in the Japanese Gardens?"

"Not the dealer, he says, a *victim* of the dealer who can lead us to him. I presume it's connected to the stuff. Watkins says, 'Tell Frank I got me a real zombi, and he'd better get down here before he fades away.' "

CHAPTER 13

NICK DESMOND, THIRTY-NINE inches tall and all of thirty-nine pounds, was defending the wooden platform from a massed armada of Imperial Forces and assorted outlaws working for Jabba the Hut. These two contingents were personified in the figures of the little red-headed girl from the Montessori School and the boy named Jason, other details unknown, who often filled the role of adversary in the young Desmond's scenarios. Nick menaced each in turn with the flourish of the long plastic glow-in-the-dark sword he clutched in his right fist, laser gun in the left. He was Luke Skywalker, pronounced "Wook."

He called out, in his warbling voice, "You be the brown man, Daddy, and you throw me the light saber just before I'm going to fall into the pit." He pointed four feet below to the sands of the 3rd Street playground, which while still damp had drained rather nicely in the sunshine. To Timothy Desmond, this was a deliverance. For a parent, going all the way down to 9th Street with one four-year-old, a GI Joe bike, a shovel and bucket, and a sand-moving truck, was no picnic. Not to mention, speaking of picnics, the little red backpack with the natural-food fruit bars and boxes of juice, which Mona insisted be carried on all expeditions out of the house.

This latter was a particularly unwanted annoyance to Desmond, who felt it was more practical to buy a hot dog and Coke from a vendor and be done with it, if anyone got hungry. But Mona worried about the nutritional problems associated with sugar, caffeine, and preservatives. A healthy picnic had to always be on hand.

Desmond in fact was more than annoyed, he was losing his temper. Neither wife nor son had managed in the course of the day to comply much with his wishes. "Nick," he said, standing sufficiently near the platform to prevent the children from falling and breaking any limbs, "I've asked you three times to share that sword. Or the gun. You can't have both if you want Jason to play with you."

"Daddy, it's not a sword, it's a *wight saber.*"

"What pit?" asked the little girl.

Nick lunged at her with the light saber, narrowly missing her ear. "Dummy," he said, pointing again at the sand. "The Sarlat Pit! Haven't you seen *Return of the Jedi?*"

"I saw *Strawberry Shortcake.*"

Jason took advantage of Nick's distraction and moved in from the left flank, grasping at the laser pistol. Nick pushed him away. The boy stumbled on the boards, then fell in a heap onto the sand, just out of Desmond's reach, below where the Tarzan rope hung. Jason screamed. The little red-headed girl hightailed it for the pyramidlike slide structure where four other girls had formed a circle and were peacefully building a sand castle. Jason's baby-sitter, a plump black woman with straightened hair in a net, detached herself from the group of other West Indian women who had been chattering away in a high keening dialect at the edge of the sand, and waddled over to Jason. She picked him up. She said, wagging a finger, "I tell you, stay away from that platform, boy."

"He pushed me," Jason cried, pointing up at Nick. Nick shook his blond curls and looked triumphant. Desmond grabbed his son's arm. Mortified, he commanded, "Apologize, Nick."

"No way, José. He tried to steal my *waser.*"

Desmond pulled Nick down from the platform and held him in midair. "You didn't *listen.* I told you if you didn't share, it would come to this."

Jason wailed again: "I want my own wight saber!"

The babysitter scolded: "You momma don't want no war toys. They make you vile-ent!"

Desmond settled Nick on the ground. He had almost bitten through his lower lip. He tried to regain his patience, turn things around, salvage the moment constructively, use one of the techniques that he and Mona had worked long and hard on. He knelt down, so he was almost at the level of the two boys. "Look, guys," he said, in what he hoped were soothing tones, "if you can't play together, I'm going to have to take Nick home and there will be no light saber, no laser gun, at all, for *anyone.* So let's apol-
. . . no, let's work on playing together, on sharing. Say how you *feel.* Don't act it out. There's no game at all if you can't cooperate. You're cutting off your noses to spite your . . ." Desmond hesitated, wondering if the metaphor would be understood. Jason took advantage of the moment to dive for Nick's legs. Nick neatly outmaneuvered him and was preparing to deliver a crushing blow with the sword to the back of the boy's head when his father, six-foot-three and almost two hundred pounds, lost all interest in talking things out or learning cooperation and swooped the boy up angrily, roughly, and carried him kicking and screaming to the GI Joe bike. He planted him firmly onto the seat, saying: "Start pedaling, kid. You're going home to your room." But Nick scrambled to get away, lost his balance, and fell onto the macadam, scraping his arm. Desmond felt the eyes of the playground on his back as Nick now let out a scream. The West Indians were probably clucking their tongues, Desmond being a prime example of one of these people who spares the rod and spoils the child and then things go too far; the mothers of the castle-builders saw him as a brute who imposed violent implements on the child and now was reaping what he had sown. He fought the urge to

throttle Nick; instead he picked him up, checked the bruise, and, as fast as he could, carried his son out of the park, weeping, on one arm, while he managed the bike and toys and backpack somehow with the other.

He was feeling terrible, like a child abuser, a murderer, worrying that this would be the way Nick would remember him when he grew up. Then Jason yelled, happily, "See you tomorrow, Nick." And Nick raised his head smiling through the tears, and in a flash was squirming out of his father's embrace and onto the tricycle, pedaling away. "Look, Daddy," he yelled—with extraordinary good humor, considering what had just happened—"there's Zorro!"

And Desmond looked up from readjusting the load he was carrying and saw the Amish derelict sitting on the bench. Out of the mouths of babes, he thought, for close up the man's outfit, the hat particularly, resembled more the Disney Mexican missionary-style than either Amish or Hasidic. Now he heard Nick, bent over the front of his plastic cycle, pick up the loudspeaker attachment from the handlebars and, imitating a dozen cartoons and police movies, impersonate a policeman on his bullhorn: "It's Zorro, Zorro. Mayday. Mayday!" And Desmond saw the man rise threateningly in Nick's direction, right there under the peaceful orange oak and maple leaves, and he rushed to protect his only child. But the man, sensing him, turned away.

Desmond reached the boy, hand on his back, and pushed him up the hill, looking over his shoulder just in case. "That's not nice," he whispered to Nick.

For the first time, he found himself looking straight into the eye of the man in the black hat, and he saw the look of not a desolate soul, a peace-loving outcast, but a cornered rat, a killer.

Desmond pushed harder, running now himself, until he and Nick were in the open safety of the streets, the hot-dog man, Prospect Park West. He had been frightened there for a moment. The hair had tingled on the back of his neck. And, he realized ruefully, his fear had not been entirely for Nick.

. . .

On Empire Boulevard, DeSales was able to find a convenient spot to demarcate Jewish and black cultures. On one corner, a shuttle bus pulled up and a dozen Lubavitcher men disembarked, pushing and shoving. On the next, there was a car repair shop, a solitary concrete block in a dirt wasteland surrounded by wreckage. There was no sign of life, no activity, no pounding of fenders. But someone had painted on the outside walls—in red, white, and blue—the entire Twenty-third Psalm using the balloonlike calligraphy of Zap comics. It was one wrap-around run-on sentence reading from front to side to back to side to front of the cinderblock cube: "The Lord is my Shepherd I shall not want I walketh with him in green pastures . . ." DeSales turned onto Nostrand with great anticipation. It was a feeling aroused in him only when he felt strongly the juxtaposition of Death and Life, intensely spontaneous life. He touched his shoulder holster briefly.

The Caribbean fairly exploded upon him, a kaleidoscope of color and rhythmic sensation. There was a familiar green Blimpie Base altered by a red-and-black sign offering Jamaican beef patties; the smell of cooking fish and spice: take-out caloo, conch, chive-peppers; a half dozen storefront churches; groups of men, drinking beer and smoking *ganja* as they shuffled about near the blaring speakers set out in front of stereo shops; women marketing, sailing regally in bright fabric turbans through the throng. Roz would do herself proud here. DeSales watched his back as he entered the crowd. As he drew nearer the source, the words and music from the speakers resolved themselves into the eloquent clarity of the anthem, the redemption song, the incantation.

> *When I analyze this age*
> *To me it makes a lot of sense*
> *How the Dreadlock Rasta*
> *Was the Buffalo Soldier . . .*

With street noises and a haunting percussion backup, the lyrical question was at once gentle and full of menace. DeSales had to shake his head to keep out a sharp eye. Then Watkins's elongated profile became visible among one of the groups of men across the street. DeSales cracked his knuckles, moving from one side to the other until he had a full view of what was going on.

Watkins, in dress slacks and a short-sleeved white shirt, was having an intense discussion with a young fellow, not much more than a boy, wearing army fatigues. The boy's dusty hair had been woven into individual braids, an incipient Rastafarian hairstyle. There was a hint of ocher to the hair, which brought out the red from the brown in his skin. At the tip of the chin was a wispy goatee, and he wore a hat that would not have looked out of place on one of Santa Claus's helpers. When Watkins, leaning over to be heard in the cacophony, stopped speaking and drew himself up to his full height, the young man opened his mouth. He appeared agitated. Expostulation turned to shouting. Watkins made a sort of conciliatory gesture, hands spread wide, then appeared to lose patience. The music was relentless:

> *Stolen from Africa*
> *Brought to America*
> *Fighting on arrival*
> *Fighting for survival . . .*

Watkins jabbed a finger into the boy's chest; some of the men stepped back; DeSales heard the recurring phrase from the reggae song, ''The war for America/The war for America,'' echoing in his brain as he watched, helpless, the boy pull a pointed instrument from his belt and plunge it into Watkins's chest. The cop fell slowly to the pavement. The boy looked about and then melted into the crowd. The drinking men first made a larger circle around the body, reallocated their bottles and burning cigarettes, and then drifted off to re-form in new units at a respectable distance. DeSales had by this time pulled out his revolver and was desperately making his way through screeching brakes and blowing horns across Nostrand Avenue, but he felt as if he were moving in slow motion, under water. When he reached Watkins, hearing the approach of sirens in the distance, he could do nothing but cradle his lieutenant's head on his knee and hope he would live, at least to tell what he had found out.

"Frank," Watkins said, a sound of bubbling in his windpipe, "you got here a minute too late."

DeSales had to steel himself to not try to remove the stilletto from Watkins's torso. "I came as soon as I could, my man. I saw what happened. Who was it?"

Watkins moved his head slowly back and forth. "No matter. A nonperson. Mind blown."

"That was the zombi you told Colon about?"

Watkins gasped, then nodded. DeSales noticed for the first time that the whites of Watkins's big eyes had smudges of brown in them, like so many clouds.

"He looked like a Rasta . . ."

Watkins spat. "Mind blown. Don't belong . . . Trinidad . . . Obideah . . . Haile . . ."

DeSales's knee was shaking, so he sat down on the sidewalk and adjusted Watkins's head and upper body so it had a more comfortable and stable cushion in his lap. "Take it easy, Otis. There's a squad car here now, and the ambulance is a block away."

"Finish, Frank."

DeSales couldn't remember how many kids Watkins had. He wondered if they knew how much he thought about them. He wondered if Watkins thought he was dying, dropping the *ed* in *finished*, returning to his black English roots, or if he wanted him to complete his interrogation. Either way, he'd better find out what he could.

"Who's made him into a zombi?"

"Pretty pills . . . hears voices."

"How'd you find him?"

"The Botanique. Voodoo store. Next block."

As Watkins attempted to raise the same long, bony finger—the one with which he had given the zombi a paternal, admonitory poke—to point toward the voodoo store, the ambulance squad arrived, lifting him away from DeSales and onto a stretcher, and the uniformed cops began rousting everyone on the block. DeSales couldn't tell if what he had felt at the moment his man was taken away from him was the convulsion of death or merely the engaging of gears of the forces of law enforcement.

Buffalo Soldier
Dreadlock Rasta . . .

As an afterthought, DeSales told the ambulance man, "He's an Anglican. There's a church up on Union. Get him a minister, priest, whatever they call them."

The Botanique de St. Jean Baptiste had, in its brightly decorated window, a sign that said SE HABLA ESPAÑOL and an impressively eclectic array of statuary. As DeSales entered the shop, he took in at a glance a Madonna, an army of saints, a Siberian tiger, and an Indian chief. A little old lady with Negroid features and skin that was more gray than brown or black stood behind the counter, with two books open before her: a Catholic missal and a red pamphlet. Upside down, DeSales made out the title: *Obideah*. The word that Watkins had muttered. Behind her were a jumble of shelves, devoted to candles, incense, aerosol sprays, and jars of powder.

"Yass," she looked up at him, indifferent, as if white men wearing Armani suits and Bally loafers spattered with blood stopped in at least hourly.

DeSales looked about, curious. He located in a dim corner a three-foot-high statue of a fat black man wearing a loincloth and gold necklace and sitting, with his legs crossed under him. Next to him stood a life-size Christ on distinctly twentieth-century crutches.

DeSales walked back and put a finger on the shoulder of the black Buddha. "I'm interested in this," he said. "What does it represent?"

"Yoruba," she said, bored. "African God. Cubans like him." Her accent was at once distinctly Caribbean and Brooklynese.

DeSales looked around again. At the back of the store, there was a curtain. The woman saw him looking in that direction, registered a moment's alarm, then looked down at the floor.

"Voodoo?" he asked.

She looked at him scornfully. "Santeria."

"What's the difference?"

She shrugged her shoulders. To try to explain to someone so uninformed would be worthless.

DeSales thought he detected movement behind the curtain. He decided to hold on for another minute or so. He put his finger on the pamphlet in front of her. "And this is voodoo?"

The same shrug. "Obideah. Black magic. Trinidad. Is different."

Her cheek twitched. There was the light tinkle of a bell from behind the curtain. The woman held up a finger and paddled to the rear of the floor. DeSales decided that whoever was back there was not leaving. He considered the consequences of pulling out his .38 and conducting an unwarranted raid. And thought better of it. Instead, aware of the covert whispering coming from behind the curtain, he moved soundlessly to the part of the store nearest the back room and picked up an aerosol can marked "Love Spray." The directions, in English, French, and Spanish, instructed him to spray his bedroom nightly, preferably making the sign of the cross while doing so, and that "passionate embraces" would not be far off. The illustration on the can depicted a male and female, white, naked, in a decidedly passionate embrace. He was reaching for the "Lucky Number" spray when the woman came back out.

"What you want here? Really?" she asked.

DeSales flashed his badge. "My partner, tall skinny black guy with big ears? He tells me you know something about somebody who's making zombis.''

She walked back to the counter, apparently wiping away a tear. She lighted a candle and took a pinch of powder from one of the jars. She shook her head no and made a cross on the countertop with the powder.

"My partner says you could tell me about a boy who's become a zombi and how he got that way.''

Her eyes flashed a brief defiance; then she cast them down. "All zombis made the same way. A *bokor* does black magic.''

"And where is this *bokor*?''

The bell tinkled again. She went to the curtain, stuck in her head, then leaned out again. She beckoned to DeSales with her finger. DeSales took out his pistol and held it next to his ear, pointing to the ceiling. He walked toward the woman and the back room.

"Who's in there, lady? No zombis, no *bokors*?''

Her smile was vicious. It said, "See for yourself.'' She drew back the curtain. DeSales darted to the side of the door frame and allowed his weapon to precede him into the room, but instead of some witch doctor or the young man in the fatigues and wispy goatee, he found a legless man, coal black skin, lying on a cot. Next to the cot was a shiny new wheelchair.

The old man drew himself up against the wall. He coughed hoarsely. "White man always needs a gun. White man's guns took my legs.''

"In the war,'' the woman said. "The Second World War.''

"For America,'' the man coughed again. "So why you had to come here? There was a black man this morning. He understood.''

"He's dead,'' said DeSales.

"A cop,'' spat the man. "For America.''

"Killed by the kid he said was a zombi. With a knife. A long knife.''

The woman gasped. The man reached for the stump of his right leg, as if he were suffering from shooting pains.

"So," said DeSales, still keeping the pistol extended. "I may be a white man and you may have lost your legs in a white man's war, but you can see I have to know who this zombi boy is."

The old woman sank into the wheelchair. The man rolled over onto his face. The woman said, "He's our grandson. We raised him up."

"And where did you get the wheelchair?"

"From our grandson. It was a birthday present for my husband."

"When?"

"About a month ago. September fifteenth. About the same time he start actin' crazy."

"You know where he is now?"

"No."

"Where he might be going?"

"Where the poison is. Where the *bokor* is. The boy is pos*sess*!"

"And his full name?"

"We come from Trinidad to Harlem just before the Second War. Murray is our name. English. Grandson is Winston. But he call himself something else now."

"What?"

"Haile Selassie. No, Rasta man don't like it one bit. But they leave him alone. He been pos*sess* since the summer; they don't mess with the pos*sess*."

As DeSales stepped back out onto Nostrand, he scrutinized the window more closely. Mickey Mouse grinned next to Christ crucified. Pinocchio and Yoruba stood side to side.

On Cortelyou Road, in the no-man's-land between Flatbush and Borough Park, Francis DeSales lost heart. He had started his walk energized by a sense of purpose, of significant action. The Botanic Gardens, then the Hasidic and West Indian ghettos, had reinforced this in a general way, in their own appearance of organized intent. The stabbing of Watkins had quite specifically lent force and meaning to the cop's trade, not to mention tragedy. But the banality of Cortelyou—from Coney Island Avenue to McDonald, say—had brought back in spades his earlier feeling that he worked in a borough that in itself constituted a universe of aimless nullity. This was the Brooklyn he had come to know too well.

The buildings had neither the potential for grandeur nor squalor, solid four-story apartment houses of pale stone. Each block seemed to have the same pizza parlor, dog groomer, dry cleaner, unisex hair stylist, fly-blown deli, and Arab newsstand. The people he encountered also suggested a germ of disorder in the commonplace. There were black construction workers and the odd black idler, looking as if he had been dropped from the sky. Koreans scurried about on the pavements, carrying leafy produce from one box to another. The whites were either elderly, shaky and unstable, confused by the passage of time; or impossibly young, teenage boys of the Heavy Metal, sleeveless-T-shirt variety, all pale bicep and blank stare. A group of these latter, with their girlfriends, huddled on a side street near the rumble of the F train, drinking from paper cups and circling a box radio like bums warming at a fire on a winter's day. The music was aggressive, dissonant. DeSales watched these kids for a minute, searching for some jog of memory that might connect him to them, for he, too, had once been a working-class Italian-Canuck Brooklyn adolescent without direction, who took his pleasures on the street. But there was nothing there. Things had either changed more radically than he had dreamed possible, or he had grown old, lost the cultural memory that had once given him a uniquely perverse taste for the ironies of the void, the void that was Brooklyn.

In any case, why had he been headed for Borough Park anyway? For a guy getting his beard cut off. Hardly top priority. Especially in the bloody void.

The reggae beat that had reverberated along Nostrand Avenue as Watkins had toppled slowly to the pavement now resounded again in DeSales's mind. The percussion of dry bones on jungle drumskins, the cracking of whips. Dreadlock Rasta Buffalo Soldier Fighting fighting fighting for survival.

He turned back to Ocean Parkway, the broad and prosperous thoroughfare of red-brick high rises that he had chosen to inhabit, where the impersonal, vulgar imagination that had created Las Vegas or Miami Beach held sway. Where, therefore, nothing counted, nothing obtained. Where the Mafia held wedding receptions. Where the Syrians were trying to get his apartment.

Someone had slipped a note under the door of DeSales's sparsely furnished, L-shaped studio. A man with a Middle-Eastern name proposed to bankroll the present tenant with a down payment on the apartment if the building went co-op, if said present tenant would sign a contract agreeing to then sell the apartment to a person represented by the undersigned at a profit of fifty pecent to said present tenant. DeSales dropped it in the general direction of an overstuffed wastebasket.

He took off his jacket and threw it on the bed. He sat in the swivel chair next to the table he used to pay his bills. He swung his feet up onto the desk, lighted a cigarette, and dialed the phone. Bernie Kavanaugh wheezed his name and grade into the other end of the line.

"How's Watkins?" DeSales asked without salutation.

"Looks bad, Frank. Critical. They've got him in intensive care."

"How about the perp, the kid?"

"Hasn't turned up yet. But Colon found a small-time dealer who gave us an address where these new pills were coming from. It's on Rogers, not far from where Watkins got it."

"You get a warrant?"

"Not yet. I wasn't about to bother Judge Giotto after hours without your go-ahead."

DeSales put his cigarette on the edge of the blond wood of the desk, next to a series of burn marks, and began to thumb through his Rolodex. Then he stopped. "It's always better not to cross that fat bitch," he said. "How urgent is this? Have we looked the place over?"

"Appears to be an abandoned storefront. But nobody can see inside because of the steel sliding gates. It's only a two-story building and the second floor looks empty too."

"You got it staked out?"

"Of course, but the only guys available were Caruso and Jackson."

DeSales grimaced into the receiver. He picked up the smoke, took another drag, and asked, "How about the landlord?"

"I'm tracing that on the computer now, but you know it's ten-to-one it's owned by some shadow corporation which it'll take months to get real names for."

"Hold on a minute, Bernie." DeSales stepped into the bathroom, dropped the cigarette into the toilet, listened to it hiss. He flushed the toilet and went back to the phone. "I want a warrant first thing in the morning. Let's not owe her judgeship one right now. I'm just worrying about the stakeout. Maybe you can get Shultz to do some overtime, go over and keep an eye on those two idiots."

"Shultz is not only off duty today, but he's not coming in tomorrow. Sick leave."

"Sick leave for what?"

"Sunburn."

"Sunburn!"

"It's a long story, Frank. He was doing a survey for Vice and he stumbled onto what he thinks is a major drug deal, so it's been reshuffled over to Narcotics . . ."

"Jesus motherfucking Christ. *I'll* have to go over and supervise. Remember when Caruso and Jackson shot that poor asshole in Red Hook when they . . ."

"Sorry, Frank. I'll take care of it. I'll find somebody. You got something else to do. The Professor? Desmond. He's been calling every fifteen minutes."

DeSales perked up. "He's remembered the poison and the Jap connection?"

"Maybe even better. He thinks he's spotted the perp in the Noah Simmons killing. A nut dressed in a black hat, black clothes, who hangs around playgrounds."

DeSales was skeptical. "Only the tenth sighting today. Any more details?"

"Nope. Desmond insists on talking to the boss, not the hired help. You're supposed to call him as soon as you can. Here's the number."

After Kavanaugh rang off, DeSales remembered he had missed lunch. He went to the refrigerator, found a couple of wilted slices of Genoa salami and poured himself the dregs of a half gallon of orange juice. When he finished the snack, he called Desmond's number but got a recording, a woman's voice apologizing for "Tim, Nick, and Mona not being available just now." Desmond's wife sounded breathy, interesting. DeSales, however, neglected to heed her instructions to leave a message so the Desmonds, individual or en masse, could "get right back" to him. He hung up at the sound of the tone.

He paced the apartment, trying to get a fix on the pattern that seemed to be emerging. He rearranged the covers on the bed without exactly making it. He found a garbage bag and emptied the wastebasket. He was contemplating doing the dishes, when it came to him that he had made his career as a detective by backing off from things when there was danger of overload. At a time like this, until just a few months ago, he would have given Roz a ring and dropped work until the fresh light of a new dawn, let it all hang out. So he began to feel empty, sorry for himself again, as he returned to the dirty sink. At the very moment he reached for the first dish, the phone rang. In the days when he had been blessed with luck, it would have been Roz, operating through that special telepathy. Now it was probably Desmond, and at this particular moment DeSales had little stomach for locating and nailing a pervert in a black hat, murderer of Noah Simmons or not.

Reluctantly, he picked up the receiver. No, it was a woman, an angry woman. Megan Moore's voice still showed she had professional training, but it had dropped that little overlay of objectivity required by her job. "Goddamn it, DeSales, you've done it *again!*"

"What say?"

"I come within a mile of you for the first time in years; you turn on the old charm, make me feel positively girlish, and then stand me up before we even go out. And now, you bastard, I've got another creep after me. And it's all *your* fault."

"Hold on, Ms. Moore, you're in the public eye. For people like you, heavy breathers come with the territory."

"*Bull*shit. This is no heavy breather, not even a stumblebum like the last one. This guy's a real smoothie. Tells me in so many ten-syllable words in great clinical detail that he intends to rip my ovaries out because he's seen me with you on TV and figures we're having a thing together somehow—God knows how anyone could think *that*—and is going to punish me to get revenge on *you.*"

DeSales couldn't help smiling to himself. Her intensity was arousing; he had never seen, or heard, her so worked up before. How was he to take her predicament too seriously when Brooklyn overload was suffocating him? Besides, this one he could handle. Brooklyn overload. He remembered his fantasies of the night before, before he had been called to the Botanic Gardens, of R & R in a big-city penthouse. Still smiling, he said in his most empathic tone, "Slow down, Megan. This kind of trouble is my business, remember. And I make house calls, hear? I'll be right over."

CHAPTER 14

THE MAN IN BLACK ran across the long meadow, toting the gym bag across his stooped shoulders, dodging the West Indian soccer players. A Frisbee landed at his feet; he stumbled, then lashed out ineffectually at the fair-haired teenager who came to retrieve it. The teenager was a strapping white boy in one of those shirts with an alligator on it. He could have been one of the old tormentors from the football varsity at Tomahawk Township High.

The boy looked at the man incredulously. "Asshole bum," he spat and snapped the plastic saucer at the older man, knocking off his hat.

The man grabbed the hat and scurried, seething with fear and anger, over the hill and across the road into the safety of the Vale of Cashmere, where only the druggies and lonely wanderers held sway. Where he found the secret ditch behind the elm tree that reminded him of home. Where he often slept, and soundly, on warm nights.

He dropped into the depression, out of sight of police, angry parents, football players, niggers, all the enemies who had pursued him without pity through these years—an angry endless mob, he saw them as now—from the black soil of Pennsylvania Dutch country to the Black Belt of Prospect Park, Brooklyn, U.S.A. He lay still for a long time, cringing now and then at the anticipated siren or even the baying of his father's beagles, but nothing came. Eyes closed, under pursuit, he bestowed upon himself power and swiftness. He was a truck hurtling down old 22, parallel to the new interstate, but the interstate wasn't there yet. The high-tension wires against the crow-spotted blue sky offered guidance, at least to the point where the Blue Mountain—really the color of smoke—rose from the plain. There were the neat ranch-style houses with garages and basketball hoops in the macadam driveways, and these provided a dull security. These were new, but not so new as the interstate, and he sensed them popping up like mushrooms as the odometer in the spacious cab of his rig ran up the miles. Positioned with monotonous regularity among these homes, rising out of the fields, sprouting lawns and raised blacktop parking lots, were the churches, plain red-brick cube after plain red brick cube. He saw the parking lots filling up with four-door sedans, saw the preachers greeting the parishioners in the ornamentless entranceways, and he knew it was a Sunday. Farmers' churches had paved driveways and parking lots so they needn't worship in gumboots on the Lord's Day. The anonymous passing truck rumbled on, heading for a new world in Maryland or West Virginia or Ohio, and there was the sandy-haired boy with the acne and rounded shoulders and gangly joints and dense gray eyes, mowing the lawn at his grandparents' house. Which of course was not split-level at all, but an old white frame with powder post beetles in the porch and a swing and the shunned boy—shunned from the church, the parking lots—mowing, or baling hay, or working on the soapbox-derby car they never let him enter in a race, watching the truck race by, begging it to take him away. But the truck always passed and the boy, bare-chested in summer, went on working alone, always outdoors.

The boy was himself.

Himself. Zorro. He who had striven mightily to be left alone. He heard the voices of the imagined pursuers translated into the child's falsetto, a thousand voices gleefully taunting, calling him yet another name: Zorrozorrzorro. . . .

From his bag, having opened his eyes to the incessant ringing in his ears, he removed a tattered piece of paper and read aloud: "Saul Jacob Swartz." He smiled, as if some dearly held orthodoxy had been confirmed in the face of subversion. He did not speak the other part: "4-F"; instead, clutching the card, he lay down again, closed his eyes, and had another vision. He saw the boy who did the chores on Sunday mornings pulling his father's head from between the pasty thighs of the woman he was eating out on the stage in the tent at the Carlisle Fair. He saw the father's frightened, wide-eyed look as the boy pummeled him to the ground. He felt himself step forward, taking the place of his father. Now he was confused; he knew not whether to bite or lick. The smell was overpowering; his ears were clamped by the white thighs and the ringing began again. He tried to close his eyes but, like some Bible story he had been told, he was compelled to peek. Like some old-time photographer under a hood, he squinted at life through a viewfinder and the viewfinder was the canal penetrating the private parts of the stripper. As through a veil of tears he saw the day of his own baptism, when he was thirteen, down country at the Zion Grove, near Indiantown Gap. After the government had moved all the soldiers to South Carolina or Georgia or Texas so the ones who made it, who got in, could come home and show off with their southern drawls. At the Grove, boys and girls of the congregation waded into the stream wearing baggy swimsuits. The preacher was waiting, holding the Bible against his chest. Waterbugs skittered across the surface of the slow-moving waters. The adults sat on picnic benches near the bank, beaming with solemn pride. When the minister called out, "Jacob Swartz," he saw himself step forward, but something strange had happened. Someone had pulled the drawstring of his trunks from behind and they slipped down around his knees. He heard a gasp, then a crescendo of snickering. He looked down and saw his pecker for some reason bobbing erect. His pecker was something he had always kept to himself. He never showered after gym class; never skinnydipped at the old quarry. It was funny-looking, had a kind of knob at the end, and was purple—blue-black almost—in marked contrast to the pallor of the rest of his skin. And down there he had no hair.

Melvin Spangler called out, "Look, Swartz don't have no hair on his balls, and he got a blackjack. A blackjack!" And the other boys took up the cry until the minister stifled them and his grandfather had plowed into the water after him with the switch, beat at it like it was a horsefly in the house, until it lay back, bruised and lifeless, against his thigh.

But before he actually felt the rain of blows, he had stepped away from the woman's pussy and given someone else a chance to get at it in there, and he heard the cries of protest from the naked boy as he was dragged from the stream. He heard these cries with satisfaction, from a distance, with a sense of something like justice, something like physical bliss.

Something like when he saw the startled look on his father's face as he threw him to the ground. Even if that had never really happened.

"Retribution is an end in itself sayeth the Lord," Jacob Swartz said aloud in the ditch in the Vale of Cashmere.

Zorro. The child at the playground had crossed the line, as did so many of them. They needed to experience the ritual sacrifice, the baptism of blood. To protect themselves from themselves. It was a stern kindness to provide escape from the terrible eventuality of growing up to torment or be tormented by others.

Swartz, relieved of fear and anger both, rose and stepped coolly into the Vale and washed his face at the fountain. He began to put his hat back on but realized that he could no longer afford to be Amish, the Stranger. Plain. *They* would not stand for it, would not allow him to be in peace. Plain. Still gripping the draft card in one hand, he determined to find himself a new I.D. Behind a tree, he removed the black outfit, rolled the hat up in it, and exchanged it in the bag for a set of threadbare army fatigues. He strolled, ever-cautious, down the deserted forest path to the zoo. He dumped

the black clothes in a garbage can, then leaned on the fence in front
of the polar bears. On the rocks littered with garbage, the mangy,
tired animals stared back at him. At him and the brown and black
and yellow faces of the teenagers who loitered alongside him at the
fence.

One day there would be apocalypse, plague, atonement. The
dead would walk on the bones of the living, for none of them
belonged where they were.

Neither the bears, the kids, nor Jacob Swartz.

Not in Brooklyn.

He liked to look at the tigers, but the stench of the big cat
house deterred him, recalling what he imagined to be the reek of
the stripteaser's crotch. Instead he went in the men's room and
stationed himself at the urinal, back to the door, so no one could
spy on him. After he hurriedly zipped up, he found a cracked
mirror and he studied his face for a long time. The eyes were still
a cloudy gray but the rest of him had changed from the boy so long
ago. There were only traces of the zit scars, and his hair was more
brown than blond, thinning as well, and his face had bloated. As
if the beatings had come back from over the years to haunt him.
And he would have to get rid of the beard. He knew a mission
where they allowed you to shave and wash up, and he knew a shack
where he might camp out on the West Side Highway, where they
didn't use it anymore, where he might stay for a while.

Outside the men's room, there was a flyer attached to the wall
that caught his eye. *A Panorama of Autumn Events*:

STRANGE HAPPENINGS IN A SECLUDED LOCATION

For many Brooklynites—and for Brooklyn children
especially—Autumn wouldn't be complete without the
popular park festival in the Nethermead. Besides free
balloons, refreshments, and carnival games, the Urban

Park Rangers will be present to escort daring children,
their parents, and friends, through the Haunted Ravine,
where such unearthly creatures as the Headless Horseman and Dracula will be lurking to greet them. You're
cordially invited to dress in your frighteningly finest
for what will be a safe yet harrowing experience. . . .

Swartz ripped the paper off the wall and shoved it in his bag. He
liked the idea of wearing his "frighteningly finest." Blackjack, the
Kike, Zorro. I.D. Halloween. He would have a new I.D. and
Brooklyn would be safe again. Sooner than he had expected. There
were so many good boys and bad boys who could be saved by
death from something much more terrible.

CHAPTER 15

OUTSIDE THE TALL casement windows, a leaf fell from a plane tree, tracing its fluttery descent against the patchwork trunk, and another Wall Street lawyer made his weary way home from a twelve- hour day at the office. Tim Desmond pushed aside the stack of essays he had been grading and leaned back smiling, basking in the glow of the educational process and the way it expressed itself in the diversity of Brooklyn. He had just read a cogent, impassioned argument against male oppression of females in New York Hispanic culture; before that, a recent Russian emigré had clumsily but effectively contrasted Dickens's London with Dostoevsky's St. Petersburg; before that, he had found little to fault in a painstakingly rewritten examination of race relations in Georgetown, Guyana, the product of a half–East Indian, half–Negro native of that city. And now, in his own hundred-year-old house (in spite of—perhaps enhanced by—the anomalous modern light fixture where there once had been a crystal chandelier, then, more recently, a gaping hole), he found comparable intricacy in the delicate filigree workmanship of the ceiling frieze, a complementary substance in the deep dark texture of the cherrywood mantle on the fireplace. And over it all there was the lingering warmth of having sat for the evening with Nick, as the little boy had traced the letters C-O-W in his new book with considerable pride, then colored the animal orange and green.

The professor returned to his task. He pulled the new bunch of papers from his bag, replacing them with the others. He had, characteristically, saved the worst for last. The earlier papers had come from an advanced urban-studies section; the ones he now confronted were from a remedial group. He did not put these off because he had disdain for this multihued assemblage of the educationally deprived, nor was he a defeatist about their prospects for success. He was a realist, and he foresaw for each of the students, and for himself, many hours of struggle before they would break out of their verbal and emotional ghettos and enter . . . what?

Brooklyn, the melting pot, the great world of Culture?

He picked up the paper on top, written by a pretty little doe-eyed girl from Colombia. She said that she missed her hometown on the sea coast because of "its beautiful beaches and warm climax." He dropped the looseleaf sheet and picked up the next: the black ex-Marine from Mississippi recalled fondly his grandmother's "black-eyed peas and colored greens." On to the next. The eighteen-year-old fourth-generation Brooklynite, product of the City educational system, child of the daughter of a Jewish machinist and the laborer son of an Irish civil servant—former hippies both—chose to evoke New York City in all its splendor, with its "Rockefeller Center and other such prehistoric monuments as the George Washington Bridge and the Statue of Liberty." He gave up on the next, an incoherent abstraction about the insubstantiality of the world and the eternal reward of Jesus. In his long experience he had found that Jesus and rational, grammatical, prose exposition tended not to mix. Jesus went hand-in-hand with run-on sentences and subject-verb disagreement.

Enough! He dropped the papers back on the table, scowled, then forced himself into a chuckle. If he didn't have a sense of humor, he would never get the job done. Just the same, these had better be saved for the cold light of day.

"What's so funny?"

Mona, having finally managed to read Nick to sleep, stood in the doorway, arms folded.

Desmond looked up, still grinning. "Some incredible howlers in my remedial class. Did you know that Rockefeller Center was a prehistoric monument, that you should sunbathe in South America to experience a warm *climax*?"

Mona was not amused. "Your superego is really on the alert today. Nick tells me you got so disapproving of him at the park you threw him to the ground. What was *that* all about?"

Desmond shook his head. "I didn't *throw* him to the ground; I . . . he got out of control and I had to carry him out of the park to stop him fighting. I sat him on the bike and . . . he fell off."

"And *then* you decide the Amish guy is dangerous. Maybe you're looking for villains."

"Nick started calling the guy names. The kid was out of control. And then I saw the guy was in a rage, a raving maniac."

Mona poured herself some orange juice, drank it, washed out the glass, and put her hands on her hips. "The kid is *not* out of control. He's in a normal developmental stage. He's learning to separate himself from others, which will eventually allow him to have empathy with the other person's point of view. He needs support, not to be dragged out of the playground kicking and screaming. That's no solution." For emphasis, a kind of punctuation, she slammed open the dishwasher and inserted the glass. She gathered up the *Times*, arranged it neatly on the counter, then reconsidered and dropped it in the garbage. Without asking her husband if he had finished it. It was going to be one of those.

Desmond jammed his papers into the bag. "You weren't there," he said. "What the fuck do you know? 'Superego,' 'developmental stage,' 'empathy,' 'support.' Buzz words. You're not dealing with *reality*. Nick was told to share and not to fight with the other kids and he didn't *listen*. That's the reality of the thing."

He rose and squeezed past her into the kitchen, opened the refrigerator, and poured himself a glass of jug white. Not looking at her, he continued: "Besides, where do you get so goddamn professional, talking like a shrink and not a human being?" He moved to the living room and sank into his chair. He sipped from the brimming goblet.

Mona followed, facing him, one hand on the wall near the thermostat, pointing a finger with the other. "After *too* many years of therapy and thousands and thousands of dollars, and dozens of childcare books, which *you* never had time to read, I have a perfect right to have some ideas about bringing up a child. And what's this 'reality' crap. *Whose* reality? Nick has feelings and they are *his* reality. If they're scrambled, if he's getting mixed messages, what service are we performing for him as parents?"

"I did *not* throw him to the ground. I was *not* violent with him. I responded in the most practical way. Given the real-life situation." He drank some more and looked up at her, eyes burning behind the rimless spectacles.

"But he *felt* thrown to the ground because he was responding to your rage." She softened her tone, dropped her hands to her sides. "Look: we're trying to teach him there are alternatives to aggressive acting out. If *we* do it, and sweetie, you know *I* do it too—we're presenting negative role models." She stepped forward and touched Desmond's shoulder, then brushed a lock of hair away from his brow. "Look, Tim. I'm not saying you're *bad*. I'm just saying we have our own problems because *our* parents couldn't deal with life. That helplessness was transmitted to us. That's why we're neurotic. So, when I feel frustration with him, and something snaps, I know I'm acting out the child with my mother again. *Sweetie,* you know if you lose it with a four-year-old that you must see something you despise in *yourself* in his behavior. The anger, the reluctance to share or listen. . . ."

Desmond reached for a magazine, feeling the old irresistible urge to hide, but Mona sat in his lap and put her arms around his neck. The warmth eased him, released him from the rigid resistance he had been compelled to set up. He responded to her embrace with a squeeze and a peck on the cheek. After a while, he said, "I'm sorry. It's the violence. I see it in him, and feel it in myself, and then walking into the crazy guy and having Nick taunt him instead of walking away . . . I don't know. I don't understand it. This aimless anger, violence, it's like a chain of creation, which links us all together."

She kissed his nose and began to get up, pinching his cheek. "What's this *we* shit, white man?"

"It was Zorro, not the Lone Ranger."

"Yeah, but I thought I felt your silver bullet under my buns when I was on your lap, or was it my imagination? You coming to bed?"

He shrugged. "Give me a rain check. I want to wait for DeSales to call. And finish my wine."

"Okay." She headed for the stairwell. "I can take rejection this once. But Tim, while you're sitting there . . ."

"Yeah?"

"Maybe we should rethink taking Nick to this Halloween thing in the park. Calmly. Just like we work out how to channel his anger. Look, he's going through a phase where he's projecting all those inner fears of his own angry omnipotence onto the outside world, populating it with monsters and all. Nightmares. When I was putting him to sleep tonight, he insisted that there are sharks in the pools in the big meadow over there and he doesn't want to go to that part of the park anymore."

Desmond bobbed his head, impatient again. "But we *know* there are no sharks in the park. And we can't shelter him in the name of psychology *forever*. C'mon, Mona. It's all in his mind. When he sees the real thing, he'll know it's just costumes and he'll have a ball."

"It's all in his mind." She put her hand on the polished mahogany banister. "Sometimes I wonder what I married. Your *brains* are all in your mind. As I said, I want us to reconsider this, talk it over. If that child feels forced and frightened, we'll set back his development indefinitely, not to mention losing his trust.''

She ran up the stairs. Desmond resisted a last parting shot. He had already had enough: sharks in the park, prehistoric skyscrapers, Jesus freaks. There was a heavy question about reality here, at home and at work, so he skirted it by pouring some more wine and opening the magazine. It was a slick glossy number devoted to the pleasures of the table. He had purchased it because he was interested in the results of a vertical tasting of twenty years of Chateau La Mission Haut Brion, in applying them to the modest collection of second growths that he kept in a dark closet in the basement. But, sitting down, he found himself confronted by a piece written by a prominent New York restaurateur: ''My Most Adventurous Meals.'' The man described a game dinner consumed while surrounded by a ravenous pack of hyenas on safari in Kenya; he recalled nostalgically an elegant luncheon at the Savoy in London during the Blitz, blacked out, bombs raining down around them as he groped for slippery sweetbreads with his fingers; he recounted with sardonic humor a visit to an underground restaurant in Tokyo that catered to a clientele with a perverse taste for the toxic innards of exotic fish.

It was then that Desmond remembered what he had been trying to tell DeSales about the dead man in the Botanic Gardens.

CHAPTER 16

MEGAN MOORE CHECKED him through the peephole and then again through the crack allowed by the chain before she finally opened the door. She stepped back skittishly, and he pulled the door closed behind him and turned the lock and reinserted the chain. She was barefoot, wearing tight jeans. She had let her hair down. Without makeup she was paler than he had expected and for the first time she resembled not so much one of the exotic race of WASPs, but the women in his mother's family, Neapolitans with thick, luxurious dark hair and creamy skin. She also reminded him of his mother in another way—his mother as he vaguely remembered her looking at about Megan's age when he was about twelve and she had first had the episodes—in that she had that hurt, angry look. As if someone were sadistically twisting a muscle behind her eyes.

"You're really scared," he said.

"What do you expect?" She sat down on a high stool at the bar in the far alcove, not welcoming him to join her, and began to handle a long, narrow black-and-gold Dunhill lighter. She thumbed the wheel, a flame shot out in a narrow stream, and she extinguished it almost immediately. "The last time I was threatened, your men fucked up and I spent the night tied up in the trunk of my car by a lunatic, not knowing if I'd ever see daylight again."

DeSales blocked out the memory of his mother and resumed his conciliatory air. "My men may have lost you, but you *did* help the lunatic by going out on your own when you were instructed to stay at home behind closed doors. We can't take responsibility for *that*." He raised his eyebrows and grinned.

She flicked the lighter again, allowing it to burn.

"You're wasting fluid," DeSales said, advancing toward her. She turned from him like a petulant child, allowing the flame to continue to flicker. He stopped short.

She said, almost to herself, "I was being used. I was a decoy, a sitting duck. Do you know what it's like to sit alone waiting for a homicidal maniac to beat down your door?"

"You *volunteered* to be used." His grin was fading. "You got the story you wanted out of it in the end. You made your *career* out of that case. That night in the trunk of the car made you a celebrity. You don't get something for nothing . . ." DeSales left the thought unfinished. His reasoning attitude was becoming close to a paternal one, an angry paternal one, which was unlikely to get him anywhere.

She had ignored him in any case. "And when I was finally rescued, you came to the hospital and schmoozed me into signing out before it was safe, just so you could make *your* case."

DeSales didn't remember it exactly that way; *she* had insisted on signing herself out. But he knew better than to get into a hassle about details now. That wasn't what she was asking for.

She went on: "And when you got your man, I was expendable. You dropped me like a hot potato. So," she waved at the beamed ceiling, "why should I believe you'll have *my* needs in mind now?"

DeSales loosened his tie and draped his jacket on the end of the bar. "What can I say, Megan? I'm *here*. I didn't assign anyone else. I didn't set you up as a decoy. I came myself. And I'm sorry you feel the way you do about the last time." He moved nearer, reassuring.

She slipped off the stool and went behind the bar, evading his approach. "I suppose you'd like a drink. Now that you're here." She made it sound like an accusation.

"*You* called *me* up. I'll take a scotch. Two cubes."

Hands shaking, she poured a precise measure and stirred the drink. She put it on the bar and then found a bottle of Perrier for herself in the mini-refrigerator. She pried off the top with an opener, looked at the bottle for a moment, then poured another ounce-and-a- half of scotch instead.

"So what did he say?" Their eyes met for the first time, as they sipped their drinks.

She jerked her head toward the other end of the living room, where there was a bank of recording equipment. "I've got it on tape. Personally, I don't ever want to hear it again."

He swirled the cubes in his drink. "So I can take it to the office and have a voice man go over it then. After I listen, of course."

"You're leaving." She said this with resignation, not surprise.

"I had another plan," he said.

"What?" She sipped, made a face, coughed lightly. There was a faint hint of tears in the green eyes now. A kind of dark cloud had replaced the angry brightness.

"Come around from behind the bar and I'll show you."

She looked bewildered, then made her way cautiously to where he stood on the Oriental throw rug on the hardwood floor.

"Put down your drink," he said. She rested it on the bar and nervously fingered the top button of her Brooks Brothers shirt. He reached out and took her hand. "I said I wasn't sending any substitutes this time. You're under protective custody and I'm handling the job myself." Gently he pulled her to him, felt her breasts squeeze against his rib cage. She looked up, ambivalent, ready to laugh or cry. "You know what that means?"

Now girlish, winsome, she continued to gaze up, warming at the embrace, and shook her head.

"It means I don't let you out of my sight, except to go to the bathroom."

"Where do you sleep?"

"Where I can keep an eye on you."

"And *other* things? *On* me, I mean." Her lips turned up in a plaintive smile.

"Not the custodian's choice."

She raised herself on her toes and quite explicitly ground her pelvis against his; then they kissed. They kissed for a long time. At first, he kept his thin lips gently closed, as an act of restraint rather than denial, but soon her tongue found a way and they were embracing open-mouthed, on their knees, then lying on the throw rug.

"Not here," she said. "The creep said he was watching the building. I'm no longer afraid of him, I *hope,* but the thought of him watching," she indicated the picture window, the myriad darkened commercial towers around them, "doesn't exactly turn me on."

He picked her up and carried her into the bedroom, lighted only by the spill of fluorescent bulb from the adjoining bath. He hesitated between the bath and the king-size bed: "You got a Jacuzzi?" he asked.

She shook her head, mouth open, grinning upward. She put on a New York accent: "For a little protective custody, you want already Plato's Retreat?"

"Just an idea," he muttered, almost embarrassed. He considered dropping her on the bed, but instead let her down slowly, so they stood facing each other. He put his fingers through the mass of hennaed chestnut hair, bringing it over her face, then allowing it to drop. They began to kiss again, bodies apart while he unbuttoned her shirt. Her breasts were as large as he had dreamed,

the nipples tantalizingly small and perky. He covered and uncovered them with her hair as she set about undressing him. When only
underpants remained, he began to move his mouth on her, brushing
his lips on her ear and throat, tonguing the swaying curve of one
breast, then the other. He knelt before her, nose at her navel. Then
he pulled her jeans and bikini bottoms to her ankles. He sat back
on his heels and watched with pleasure as she stepped out of them.
Her pubic hair was thicker even, a mass of dark curls, than the hair
on her head. And her belly and thighs were soft without flab and
white as ivory. He buried his face there for a moment, making no
overt move yet with his mouth.

He heard her intake of breath, felt her abdomen contract.

She held his head, tousled his hair. "Wait," she said. "I want
to start this relationship out on equal footing."

Gently, she guided him to his feet and was quickly kneeling
before him, lowering the tapered shorts over his taut thighs, the
knee with the ugly scar, the hairy calves. Then, teasingly, she
kneaded his buttocks while nuzzling, clockwise, his pelvic bones,
lower abdomen, and upper thighs. Now she sat back on *her*
heels.

"There," she said; and gripping his sex with her hand, led
him to the bed.

"This is equal footing?" he asked.

"Well, not exactly." She spread herself before him, the flesh
luminous, ghostly, in the refracted light. He knelt beside her, and
the weight on the bed tumbled her toward him. As she straightened
out, they began to embrace and the phone rang. Each went stiff.
For a moment. She whispered, "Wait it out. If it's him, we'll get
him on the answering machine. Fuck him. I mean I want to fuck
you. I mean I'm very confused."

The phone stopped ringing.

Rand Furlong came back from the phone booth, agitated. He
pulled with both hands at the tails of his white sport coat, then
fingered the gold Maltese cross that dangled in the open neck of his

Hawaiian shirt. He leaned on the gleaming chrome bar and drank through the straw of his blue margarita. His cuff slid down his arm, revealing a lot of wristwatch. Black and shiny.

"So?" asked Merry Pace, leaning back against the bar on her stool, holding her mimosa glass by the stem. She also wore white: a canvas jump suit. "You seem upset. I thought he bit."

"He did, he did. He got over here like a dog in heat. But now the lights are out and they've got the answering machine turned on."

"You think they sneaked out?"

"Impossible. There's only the one exit. I bribed the doorman before you got here. And I haven't taken my eye off the door."

"So, what's wrong then? You jealous he might be getting in a little sack time? A dog in heat's a dog in heat." She looked around the noisy, cavernous room with the white walls and hanging plants and paddle-bladed ceiling fans and at least a hundred young people at the elevated bar, raised like an altar above the crowded tables. "Relax, you finally brought me to a nice place. Maybe we can have dinner. I looked at the menu. They got Tex-Mex, Cajun, and Ethiopian. Three menus in one, actually. One hundred items. How can ya go wrong?"

Rand now had his elbows on the bar, staring intently at himself in the mirror. He wrinkled his nose. He tousled his already tousled curls: "Shut up. I'm thinking."

Merry beckoned to the barman with her empty glass. As he mixed another drink, she asked, "How long this place been here?" while batting her long eyelashes.

Like Rand, the man had impressive sets of Universal Gym arms and pectorals. Only more so. He wore a Keith Haring T-shirt that said CRACK IS WACK. He muttered, "I dunno. A week, two weeks. I'm new here myself. Just started the other night."

"I seen you talkin' to all the girls at the bar. You know your way around for somebody new."

He shrugged, then leaned forward on the bar with his hands clasped in such a way as to make his forearms look even bigger than they were. He took the swizzle stick out of Merry's drink and played with it a while before sucking it clean. Closeup, his features were vintage Hollywood South Seas. He could have been a stand-in for Sabu or a spear-chucker in a Jon Hall movie. He pointed the stirrer at the air in front of her eyes. "I get around, I worked in SoHo, Tribeca, NoHo, then somebody sees the drift is Uptown: Union Square."

"They got a name for this part of town yet?"

"HoHo, I call it."

This pleased Merry. She raised both eyebrows. "So you're where it's all happening, huh?"

"Check it out. It's bigger, the ceilings are higher, so it's noisier . . ." There was the sound of breaking plates and clattering silverware, followed by high-pitched laughter. He tilted his head toward the scene in the middle of the dining area, where eight young professionals at a round table, male and female, in business suits and running shoes, giggled uncontrollably as a waiter and waitress in blue jeans hastily tried to wipe up the melange of broken china, refried beans, blackened fish, and goat sandwiches from the floor. "And," he went on, "the help is incompetent or stoned enough to provide free entertainment. We get so many spills a night, we gotta get a service in after closing to hose the place down. It's part of the hip scene."

"And it don't bother you?"

"Hey," he stood erect and stretched, allowing his back muscles to ripple in the long mirror, "you gotta make a living." He rubbed his thumb and forefinger together. "And these people can afford the finer things. *Re*-fined, if you dig me."

Merry took out her makeup kit. "So then maybe if I go to the ladies' I could score some blow?"

The barman was heading down the bar to respond to an order. He came back and looked Merry in the eye. "Last stall on the left. The one with the autographed picture of Charles Manson on the door. Ask for Sylvia, and tell her I sent you."

"What's your name?

"They call me Ramon."

"I'll be right back," said Merry.

Ramon made the drinks and returned to where Rand was still studying himself in the mirror.

"She's an asshole," said Rand. "We got a warehouse full of shit at home, and she's gotta solicit strangers to snort a line in the crapper."

Ramon did another characteristic shrug. "It's the excitement. What's everyday at home takes on an element of danger when you're among strangers in the bright lights, big city." He twisted his face into a smirk of profundity.

Rand nodded vigorously, "Sound marketing principles like that are what make the world go around."

"Don't I know it," said Ramon, splashing Perrier into a glass and adding a twist of lime. Then he poured white wine from a jug, allowing it to gurgle into a lineup of glasses set on the tray by a waitress. More food crashed to the floor, evoking more irrepressible merriment. Ramon's eyes narrowed. He said to Rand, sotto voce, "You suggesting to me you deal in wholesale lots?"

"I'm a businessman. I take a certain amount of risk to sell large quantities of goods for more than I paid for them."

"These are tropical products?"

"Legitimate U.S. commodities. Just that you usually need a prescription to get them. Plus a special line of designer goods I'm developing."

"Maybe we can deal. My lavatory franchises here are growing faster than I could have dreamed. And, you know how it is: you stand still for a minute, allow the compass and creativity of your merchandise to be limited, the consumer moves on. Next thing you know, the scene will move to the Forties or the Upper East Side, for Christ's sake, and we'll be sitting down here packing white powder up our ass." He leaned forward again. "I kid you not; these crack and free-basing people are underpricing the shit out of me. And it keeps people at home. Or at the dens. They gotta have a place to work it up and smoke it. It ain't that easy to smoke crack in a public bathroom. The bottom could fall out of the whole saloon business. It'll be like what VCRs are doing to the movies.''

"You're one smart dude," said Rand. "Where'd you go to school?''

"UCLA. I had a football scholarship out of Samoa, but I quit the team after my freshman year. Too violent. I come from a peace-loving people. The Pacific ain't called the Pacific because it don't got waves.'' The line sounded well-worn.

Rand continued to show enthusiasm. "Business administration major, I bet.''

Ramon nodded. "With an accounting minor. I've always been career-oriented. My cousin, he was different. He majored in art history. I warned him, but he had to have what he called the 'Broad Base.' So he graduates and he has to start all over in advertising. Learn the business from the ground up.'' He leaned farther forward, as if making a long-withheld confession. "Get this. He's only making thirty-five thousand a year, and he's almost *twenty-five* years old.'' Rand shook his head in commiseration. "So he wants to borrow money from me to buy an apartment. I say, I told you so. Forget it, cuz. It's every man for himself. He had a chance to start with me at the bottom, when I had a lock on the football team in Westwood. A ready-made market of big spenders. I got a kind of paid internship in the locker room my freshman year.''

Merry drifted up to the bar, smiling without a lot of focus. "Thank you, Ramon. Thank you, Sylvia. You know what Sylvia said? 'Oh, sweet essence of the Andes.' Isn't that a trip?'' She looked at Rand. "Sorry I took so long, honey. I had to wait in line.'' She turned back to Ramon: "Another mimosa, okay?''

"You already got one.''

"Far out. I forgot. What you guys talking about?''

"Free enterprise," said Rand. "I was telling Ramon I was thinking of liquidating. If I could find the right client. For less than seven figures, I could move everything, inventory, goodwill, list of customers . . .''

"We'd have to have a tasting," Ramon interjected solemnly.

"Of course, my man, of course. Get your people together and we can make a date. Tomorrow night, same time, same station."

"See you," said Ramon. "Tomorrow." He moved down the bar.

"That was ballsy," said Merry. "You let it all hang out to a stranger. He could be undercover."

"No sweat. He'll never see me again. When I sell, it'll be through the usual markets. I just needed to test the waters and get the adrenaline up. Clears my head to deal. Even if I'm just faking."

"So, you done your thinking. Hey, that coke made me thirsty."

"No more drinks here. There's a place just like this next door where I can keep a lookout. I got a plan. You go call Megan Moore's number. If the machine answers, leave a message that you saw her on TV and she should call back because you want to spill your guts about what happened to that kid who was kidnapped from the park in Williamsburg."

"Call back *where*? Maybe I should send her my picture and Social Security number."

"I've still got that phone in the bedroom that the phone company lost track of. Give her that number."

Merry made a face. She shook her head. "I can't believe you're back on that topic. You swore you didn't kill that kid . . ."

"Shut the fuck up. This has nothing to do with what I did or didn't do. It has to do with getting our hands on Megan Moore. If I'm ever going to dump this dope and get cash to roll over into that condo deal, I wanna be sure DeSales isn't breathing down my neck. We got him thinking the dude calling Megan is the kid killer, and then we disappear his favorite broad, he won't be able to do anything else. Goes back to sound business principle, divide and conquer. In this case, I divide his attention, I walk."

"You're gonna kidnap a TV star?"

"We're gonna *borrow* a TV star. Won't do her any harm. Just keep her under wraps until I sell off my stock and the smoke has cleared.''

"But this is crazy, man. You first of all alert this supercop to keep his eye on the girl, then you say you're going to lift her.''

"I'm a step ahead of you. If he does really keep an eye on her, then I've achieved my goal: to distract him. Or we could take them both. Call that Plan A. Or, Plan B, suppose he doesn't keep her under close custody, doesn't believe it's serious, doesn't care, doesn't have manpower for round-the-clock surveillance. . . . Hey, how many celebrities get threatened every day? You think the cops can cover them all? Look at John Lennon. Andy Warhol, even. Megan Moore is a fucking nobody, a twinkie.''

Merry Pace emptied her mimosa, sucking in her cheeks and squinting down the bar, then turning on her stool to contemplate the converted office building across the street where Megan Moore owned her co-op. "I just hope that she's throwing DeSales one hell of a fuck right now so he won't be able to keep his hands off her. I want him all over her like a hot shower. For weeks. I did *not* graduate second in my class at the Empire School of Beauty to be a kidnapper.''

CHAPTER 17

MEGAN MOORE WAS LYING peacefully, eyes closed, contemplating the intersection of the paths that had brought them finally together. She was an investigative reporter, DeSales a detective. They had dedicated themselves, therefore, to ferreting out unpleasant truths about others. For the benefit of society. Eminently desirable in their own ways, they had managed to live alone into what sadly had to be called middle age. Of course she had had her marriage to Brian of Scarsdale many years before, but that no longer counted as co-habitation: a perfunctory hump now and then and weekends of houseguests and bloody marys at 11 A.M. did not constitute a relationship. DeSales, she had heard rumors, had had his own equally unsavory connections, but they had to be as far beneath him as Brian was her. If in different ways. Each, she now mused, had had difficulty finding an equal, a soulmate. DeSales had shied away from her for so many years, she was sure, precisely because he was afraid of the consequences, seeing in her his mirror equal. And she had probably been guilty herself of nipping possible fulfillment in the bud from time to time because of the threat of such intimacy to her privacy, her career,

'

the delicate balance that allowed her to proudly stand on her own two feet. In her case, it was her father's fault, and she imagined that DeSales had his own horror stories about his childhood, which he would never tell. Because he was too busy uncovering those of others.

She felt him stir beside her. She opened her eyes and let them adjust to the darkness. In the king-size bed, her powerful, wiry lover appeared diminutive, his olive, hairy body swallowed in the whiteness of the sheets. She reached out to touch him, so vulnerable, genitals shrunken, the scars on his knee and where the bullet had grazed his arm. He recoiled at her touch and began to twitch. It pained her to think he could have a bad dream after they had made love so well. He had not only had his own big pleasure, as she had always suspected him of being infinitely capable, but had worked unstintingly to bring her to orgasm too. The tingle still remained. But now his legs twitched again, and he waved an arm, crying, "Tina, Tina!" Megan tried to give him solace. She kissed his sweaty forehead and caressed his neck and arms and legs. She saw this as a subtle communication to his subconscious, to infiltrate her presence, warm and loving, into his nightmare, making it benign. She moved her hand across his chest, firm yet gentle, a gesture of imprint: neither sexual nor obeisant. A tad maternal perhaps, but how could that hurt, if it was the way she felt? It was still equal footing.

In the dream, DeSales was in a maze and then his mother was leaving Brooklyn, floating across the East River in a hospital gown, singing a song about Thorazine as Aunt Sally called her name. But she paid no heed and little Frankie was bound to the statue of Mary and Jesus at Our Lady of Peace, helpless, while the hands of the nuns and all of the women's Sodality clawed at him. Now, the hands had become Megan's, a long fingernail tracing the line from his breastbone to his navel. The voices had become her voice, professionally husky now. He blinked; he saw the Pietà reconstituted, blackening.

"You cried out," she said. "Okay?"

He nodded, eyes still foggy.

"Supercop, superlover," she said. "We'll have to do an hourlong special on that!" She giggled. She threw a leg over his and kissed his cheek.

"Yeah," he said, and there was a bitter aftertaste in his mouth. She seemed to sense it: "You're *not* okay. Something wrong? With me?"

He had to clear his throat. "Just a bad dream. I don't dream much. Not used to it."

She held his face in her hands and kissed him on the lips. The hands, the voices, returned.

"Don't dream much," she mused. "When I was in the press room, on the Brooklyn beat, we used to bet whether you did *anything*. Except catch killers of course. Now when you dream, you call out for someone named Tina."

"Mmmm?"

"Remember Rosemary? With the orange hair and the big legs? She said you were a fag. Then a story went around that you had a secret love. A beautiful black showgirl it went. Sometimes she was a thousand-dollar-a-night call girl. Sometimes she was a movie star. That's Tina, isn't it?"

DeSales felt a chill. "Wrong," he said. Again he saw his mother, the hospital gown Aegean Blue and open at the back. Exposed, Megan went on, merrily. "I liked the story about the black beauty better. I didn't like the part I heard later that you dropped her, got her a big job for the city as a payoff. But," she moved her leg farther and straddled him, at the same time switching on the bedside lamp, "at least the fairy tale—as opposed to the *fairy* tale—seems to have been right in terms of general sexual inclinations, so I was right. I could tell you had something about you." Boldly, she raised herself on her knees and looked him over. "I hope you don't mind. Once I get to know somebody, I like to see what we're doing. I like to see *you*. Makes me forget I'm jealous of *Tina*."

DeSales blinked, rubbed his eyes, put his hands under the broad buttocks and squeezed. She was all woman—soft, open, wet. Teeth clenched, he said, as gentle as he could, "Call of nature first. I'll be right back. Hey you look better in the light than the dark too."

"Hurry," she said. "It's been a long time since I felt so . . . protected."

In the bathroom, DeSales tried to reorient himself. But there was nothing there to help: the bright fluorescent bulbs, the abstract impressionist tiles, the cushioned lavender vinyl toilet seat, the stack of *Vanity Fair*s on the water tank, the built-in professional hair dryer on the wall . . .

He splashed cold water on his face and stepped back into the bedroom. Megan Moore lay spread before him on designer sheets. There was a fetching dimple on her thigh, the one imperfection, the sort of thing that might have turned someone else on. Or made him cry. This was definitely a place he did not belong. He began to pull on his pants.

"What's wrong?" she asked with alarm. He bit his lip; he wanted to respond warmly, but he hurt too much. His dream was still with him. He averted his eyes from her nakedness.

"You've heard of the one-night stand. This is going to have to be the *half*-a-night stand."

She thought he was kidding. "I know. You're pissed because I didn't provide dinner." She looked at the digital alarm clock. "It's early. We can still order out. Japanese, Chinese?" She grinned.

"Catch you later, babe. I gotta get back to Brooklyn." He was knotting his tie.

"Why? No work phone calls now for an excuse."

First she sounded merely puzzled, then she was sitting up, rigid, biting her nails.

"Isn't it *enough* to say I gotta get back to Brooklyn?"

"No. It isn't. My shrink would say I should say my feelings are hurt, and maybe they are. But I'm angry. I'm . . ." She buried her face in the pillow. She called as he was going out the door: "I know what it is, I'm not as good as your black whore." She bit her lip as soon as she said it. It was exactly the sort of thing she had not wanted to say, not even *felt*.

He shrugged. The cruel comeback was true and not true. He answered in kind. "Maybe that's it. Got a taste for dark meat. Or maybe I'm just out of place." Then, as an afterthought, he muttered, "I'm sorry," as he walked out the door, but she didn't hear the muted apology.

She counted to ten; then she did what she had sworn she would never do again, not since Sam the Sham had left her holding the bag in the duplex on the fringe of Brooklyn Heights: she screamed.

She heard him open the door to the corridor and begin to pull it closed. She leaped off the bed, shouting, "Wait." She stopped, panting, in the bedroom doorway. He paused, one foot out of the apartment. They faced one another across the long narrow room with the highly polished floors and the vaguely Levantine motif. In the indirect lighting, his features appeared more yellow than olive and he looked back at her without feeling, tolerating, rather than questioning, her panic. "You're supposed to be *protecting* me. What about the guy on the phone?"

DeSales seemed to be looking past her. He patted the pocket of his suit coat. "Got the tape here," he said. "We'll get on it first thing in the morning."

"But what about *me*? I'm here all *alone*."

"A lot of people in the city are all alone, Megan. And a lot of them are more vulnerable than you are. Hey, you got a doorman and a solid-core door and three expensive locks and a telephone and you're on the fifteenth floor and there's no fire escape to climb in off." He shrugged.

"I'm going to report you. I feel like I've been raped."

He shrugged again. There was a twitch at his mouth. "Your choice. In the meantime, if you're so threatened, stay home and order out." He slammed the door.

She lunged across the room, securing the police lock and

chain. She turned from the door, sobbing. When she raised her chin from her collarbone, she realized she was naked, exposed, on display for the mysterious dark world outside the wraparound windows. For a moment she was mesmerized, as if confronted by some giant insect with multiple eyeballs. Something from a Godzilla movie. She slipped back into her bedroom, away from the penetrating stare of the cinematic mutant that was the big city at night.

Rand Furlong said to Merry Pace, "He left already. And there's nobody watching the building. See if you can get her to meet you in the morning. On the way to work."

"If we get her, where we gonna keep her?"

"Leave it to me. I dabble in real estate, remember."

CHAPTER 18

ROZ GLARED AT DESALES and sniffed, tightening the belt around the short white terrycloth robe. It was the same old Roz; the wide-set nostrils, the long, sinewy, perfectly rounded mahogany legs, the regal big-cat bearing, the protruding buttocks, the broad shoulders framing the bust that suggested a major feat of civil engineering. The only change was in her hair. She had always worn a natural short afro that conveniently fit under the wigs she wore for tricks; now she had let it grow out and had it straightened, the 'do of the age for the Upwardly Mobile Negro Woman.

She raised herself on her toes as if she were about to say something, thought better of it, and padded silently into the galley kitchen. She fumbled with a handle on the stove, finally lit a match and ignited the burner. She put on a pot of water. Over her shoulder, she said, "To what do I owe this unexpected pleasure?"

DeSales scuffed his foot on the linoleum, some of which had already been pulled up. "Maybe I could have a drink first."

"*Right.* You haven't been coming around since way before I moved back to Brooklyn from the Big Apple. Poor baby, don't know where to go to serve yourself, make yourself at home.''

''I only heard the other day where you were living.''

''Put it this way. My income dropped, as you know. Then I was persuaded by my colleagues at the office that it was the time to invest in Bed-Stuy, next neighborhood to turn around, break out on the market. Then there was the piece in the *Times*. I could sell the loft for enough to buy and renovate a whole *house* here and have some spending cash left over.'' She was rummaging around under the sink. She looked back, flashing the headlights of her eyes. ''Not to mention the good *will*, as they say at City Hall, that a bureaucrat earns by living in one of the neighborhoods she's serving.'' She held up a bottle and peered at it. ''Cupboard's almost bare. Got a little scotch left. Not like the good old days when I was selling my ass and provided round-the-clock full-service bar, huh, Saint?''

''Right,'' muttered DeSales, looking awkward.

She got up, splashed whiskey into an old-fashioned glass and dropped in a couple of ice cubes. She stepped up and handed it to him. Again she made eye contact, which DeSales averted. ''Now, I asked you a question. To what do I owe this visit? It's been a long time since you've called my number.''

DeSales sat on the arm of a chair while she busied herself with the coffee. ''I'm working on a case. Crown Heights. A Haitian connection . . .''

She had turned, her hands behind her on the edge of the sink, and began to laugh. ''You drop me, don't talk to me for a dog's age, and I'm supposed to think you stopped by at the crack of dawn to talk about a *case*.''

DeSales pulled at his earlobe. He felt for his cigarettes, but he had left them at Megan's. He asked, ''How many other people do I know are running an agency that deals specifically with Haitian problems?''

''Probably a dozen or so, if I know *you*. And when did *Haitian* violence become important enough to attract *your* exalted attention? We maybe had a hundred violent Haitian-related deaths since I last saw you, and you didn't stop by to talk about any of *those*."

She took her cup, sat on the old overstuffed couch, and crossed her legs. Parts of the voluptuous brown body peeked out at him from all angles under the skimpy robe. It was not at all as it had been with Megan Moore. He stared at Roz, wanting to take her all in, if only with his eyes. He wanted to say, "I just wanted to be somewhere where I felt I belonged," but he couldn't get the words off his tongue. He tried another tack: "Okay, I got a case, but that's not why I had to be here now."

"Oh, yeah?"

"I wanted to talk, tell you the reason I stopped seeing you wasn't because I didn't *want* to see you. It was because I was getting heat from upstairs, Internal Affairs—somebody had been talking about us having a thing—and then I heard that you were up for promotion to commissioner of minority relations. I knew if we kept on, the snoops would find out and connect you to your . . . former occupation . . . and you'd be finished. Right or wrong, I did it for you."

She uncrossed her knees and put the cup down on the coffee table with the black-red-and-green cloth draped over it. She sat back, stretched, and for just a moment let the full force of her sensuality work on him. He felt it for what it was: a personal rebuke, a mockery. Hands clenched behind her head, she nodded melodramatically, speaking as if she were carrying on a dialogue with a third party. "He did it for po' li'l me. Terminated his own li'l minority relation so po' li'l Roz could run the whole muvva-humpin' department. How *about* that!"

He persisted with his story: "And I picked tonight to call because I just got a tip that the *press* is on to us, what we were doing, saying I got you your job in return for past favors, and I thought you should know."

"Do tell?" She got up and put a record on the hi-fi. Watching the record drop, DeSales drank thirstily, the whiskey burning his throat. Her rear end did a twitch as the needle hit, then she turned. "There was no way I was goin' for commissioner of *anything*, baby. You think you're the only honcho I played for pay with . . . for a lot *more* pay as a matter of fact?" She rotated her shoulders and threw back her head. "I can't risk the high visibility, Saint or no Saint. Especially 'cause I'm—what did you call it in your more tender moments?—*sepia*? No way, José. I'm condemned to a lifetime of pushing paper behind the scenes. And damned glad to have it."

The Supremes blared from the speakers: "Where Did Our Love Go?"

DeSales was having trouble getting his thoughts together. "Isn't that a little loud?"

Roz continued speaking to the imaginary third party. "Is the great man afraid there might be a complaint? Headlines? . . . 'Brownstone Tryst with Brown-Skinned Girl in Bed-Stuy' . . . Better than 'Call-Girl Loft in Tribeca,' which is what it would have been in the good old days. . . ." She turned back to him, beginning to sway to the music. Her eyes had flecks of brown in the sclerae, he realized, just as Watkins had as he lay expiring on his knee that morning. And her mouth, the bee-stung lips with the lavender penumbra, which had been so alien, then had treated him so well. "Ah, Saint," she went on. "Why didn't you just call, talk to me. Why did you walk?" She began to lip-synch the record. Something about love stinging like a bee. The belt on the robe came undone, the terrycloth only a cape covering her back now. Unself-conscious, she continued to move with the music. DeSales tried to say all the things he had really felt, that he had dropped her maybe because he needed her too much, because he was afraid of needing her too much, that he wanted her back, but he was in the maze again, being pulled under the river. His vision blurred and Roz had become one with the sounds, dancer and dance. The image of the ways they had made love through the years tumbled through his consciousness, as her exposed anatomy fragmented into an abstract painting.

She said, "I thought about you. All winter and spring. I made excuses for you. Your father leaving, your mother going off her rocker. Why wouldn't you mistrust? See intimacy as dangerous? But then I said, why can't the dude *call*, say sayonara, something *human*? Then I realize. You Mr. Supercool. The Saint. You keep all Brooklyn cool. Undér your thumb. Can't call and admit a little feeling, a little weakness, can't even tell a gal he's had enough. Shit, man, I say, how do I know he's any different from the guys he catches? The schizoids I had to read about in abnormal psych my last term at Hunter? Any undergrad knows it's all about suppressed urges coming out. Just the hero's in control and the killer can't keep the lid on. But they both got their mind on nothin' but the same dirty box."

DeSales drained his drink, and walked back over to the sink and refilled it. He drank some more. He turned off the record player. An exercise in control, in keeping the lid on, he knew as he did it. But what choice did he have? He said, "Terrific. I don't call you. For your own good. And I'm a mass murderer. All you broads are . . ."

"Turn us upside down and we're all the same. As long as you can keep your distance from the parts of us that don't fuck and suck. That's why you picked *me* in the first place. The last person a former altarboy and law student, *the* detective inspector himself, would ever worry about getting *attached* to was a black hooker. An outlaw. You saw me in that motel room in Sheepshead Bay where my client had just hung himself and you must of creamed in your pants. And not just because of my beautiful bod," she held the robe farther open, "but because it was inconceivable you could get close to me as a person. Especially when you insisted on paying for it long after it was exactly a professional relationship. The old dollar bill was the last barrier. Then when I wasn't a whore anymore but just a girl who worked her way through college doing the only thing her momma ever taught her. Then I had my own straight career. I was an almost-equal. Shit, you couldn't face the music. You just walked. Chickenshit!''

DeSales lowered the glass slowly. His voice was cold, distant. "Now I'm a murdering *coward*. You got any remedies, Doctor?''

"For you, maybe you oughta go into a program. Maybe the city got one that breaks down that wall between your prick and your heart. Me, I got a man who loves me for what I am. A black man. He's outa town on business now—he's a lawyer—but he knows all about my past and he's behind me one hundred percent. We're a partnership here. I bought the house; he's gonna pay for the renovation. And I finally realized what it's like to have one of my *own* people who's *proud* to be proud *with* me.''

"That's where the African shit comes from?'' DeSales indicated the black nationalist flag on the coffee table, the witch-doctor mask on the wall, but as soon as he did so he felt cheap, and he wanted to run. But he had nowhere to go. He had dug his own hole and . . .

"Maybe. Maybe I had this 'shit,' as you call it, in my hope chest, waiting for Mr. Right-On Black to come along. Whatever, I couldn't have had it on display when I had the waterbed loft—all reasonable requests granted, for a price—downtown. How many dollars you think them white johns would have put down to ball an angry militant nigger?''

DeSales shrugged and turned to the door. It was his Special Gesture of the evening.

"Saint,'' she continued, "what would *you* put down to make it with an angry militant nigger? Here I am. You can have me one last time if it'll give you any satisfaction. That's what you *really* came by for, isn't it? But you're just another john to me now. One last time. Around the world for two hundred dollars. I could buy me one of them food processors with it. Wouldn't have to cry when I chop the onions. Let me wash you up first. Here.'' She reached for his fly and he pushed her off; raised his fist—the black Madonna would shatter now—but then turned instead to the door and ran through the hall and into the street.

Bed-Stuy in the wee hours was always a chancy proposition, even when *The New York Times* had endorsed it as a real-estate investment. But DeSales had lost his wariness. A wind had come up from somewhere, blew down the avenue, past the shuttered windows and cozily intact façades of the row that Roz had chosen to inhabit. Prime real estate. But DeSales now ran away from it into the face of the wind, an uncool thing to do with ominous figures, whether thieves or undercover cops, in every other doorway. There was something wet around his eyes, the smart of pollution perhaps, and he continued to run, down other blocks, ones where the houses had been defaced by cheap siding, blocks with vacant lots, blocks with all-night bodegas and guard dogs and razor ribbon. It was the kind of neighborhood any policeman got to know well, the kind of place where the streets ran with blood on Saturday night and bustled on Sunday mornings with fat women in frilly dresses and big hats on their way to church, where the memory of the sirens that had filled the air the night before was erased by the swelling notes of "Amazing Grace" reaching to the heavens.

But now all the detective saw was an image of Roz—no, three Rozes—naked, rocking in rhythm, her voice driving him from behind.

After a while the buildings were larger, more commercial, and he was almost downtown. Near the office, his life's work. The windows and fire escapes seemed to undulate, and he heard again the incantatory refrain from Nostrand Avenue. Watkins, with Roz's accusatory eyes, fell again, mouthing the words:

> *Buffalo Soldier*
> *Dreadlock Rasta . . .*

Then he was in the coffee shop on DeKalb, sitting in a booth facing east, back in the direction he had come from. On the table sat an untouched hamburger and glass of Pepsi. The sun was coming up. The servants were making their way to the subway to work and the charwomen from the Manhattan offices were coming home.

Bed-Stuy was turning around, and DeSales for a moment imagined that Roz would materialize on the street leading an army of black women up the ladder of success. No more hookers, bimbos, broads, bag ladies, chambermaids, gospel shouters. Roz's army would be in uniform: processed hair, wide-lapelled business suits with white lacy blouses, patterned white nylons, athletic socks, jogging shoes. And briefcases, of course, if only to carry the high-heeled pumps for the conference room.

He put his head down on the table, recited silently, "Bless me, Father, for I have sinned; it has been twenty-five years since my last confession."

When he finally raised his head, he had wiped that particular slate clean. He had done his penance and now somebody was going to pay for it.

CHAPTER 19

EVERY MORNING, MEGAN MOORE had a croissant, without butter, and decaffeinated espresso in the Greek diner, now calling itself the *Café Continental,* on the ground floor of her building. At the corner booth the owner reserved for her because of her celebrity, she was able to spread out the *Times* and mark the stories that might be worth covering for next week's show. This morning had a difference. She couldn't concentrate on the paper and found herself constantly glancing toward the street to see if the limo she had ordered as a protective measure had arrived. Fat chance. The traffic report on the radio before she rode down the elevator suggested the entire area between 34th and 14th streets would be in a state of gridlock because of repairs necessitated by a broken water main on the East Side and a subway fire on the West. Although fatigued from lack of sleep, she felt a kind of peace with herself, a euphoria almost. She had beaten herself up for some hours about the debacle with DeSales, taking the blame for driving him away, giving him the paternal authority, not to mention sexual privilege, that she had given so many men. Then, near dawn, the breakthrough had come. She had taken the bull by the horns.

She looked out the window again. It was nice to see the action of the busy streets. Salespersons hustled to the old sporting-goods and marked-down-clothing stores that had once characterized the neighborhood, intermingling with the employees of the new, the publishing houses and advertising agencies that had been driven out of midtown by astronomical rents. Like Megan herself. It gave her a feeling of symmetry with her environment. Union Square had even been cleaned up. They had had to defoliate the park to do it, and add lighting that would have served well for a night game at Yankee Stadium, but the place was rid of junkies and dealers and derelicts, and the new residents could stroll it unaccosted, even enjoy in peace the weekend farmer's market.

At 5 A.M. she had taken the bull by the horns; she had decided finally that it was DeSales's problem, not hers, and he could go fuck himself. She reported the phone calls—and DeSales's dereliction of duty—to Midtown South; she called her producer and demanded her own limo and security; she had summoned up the nerve to listen to her answering machine and was relieved to find that the heavy breather had not called again but that a sweet-sounding young woman with an outer-boroughs accent was offering her an exclusive on a tip on the Greenpoint Strangler. Not bad for a night's work. She had even called the girl back at 7 A.M. and arranged to pick her up at the restricted parking zone at the upper end of Union Square in the limo, where the girl could privately and anonymously, behind the smoked windows of the car, tell her story. Where Megan herself would be free of threat from some raving maniac. Where Megan was calling her own shots, not relying on the uplift or protection of hard-assed Francis DeSales. Or any of his kind.

It was all a liberating feeling. She winked at old Joe, the proprietor who kept a proprietary eye on her, and indicated another demitasse of decaf was in order. She returned to the *Times*, her eye falling on a section she had never noticed before: a directory to religious services in the city. She looked these over, deciding that Inspector DeSales might feel most comfortable in the Ave Maria

Chapel on Long Island, a Catholic Traditionalist Center where Latin Masses were not only offered to parishioners but broadcast worldwide each Sunday. He'd feel comfortable there because, she was convinced, it was traditional Catholicism that had fucked him up in the first place. Made him an emotional cripple. Better, she decided, he should try the Metropolitan Duane Methodist Church in the Village. They offered low-cost psychotherapy Monday through Friday.

There was a tap on the window outside her booth. A pretty, if rather trashy, young blond woman beckoned, pointing at a gray-haired sickly looking man in a wheelchair. She was trying to mouth something, but with the general hubbub in the coffee shop and the rush-hour noise of the street, Megan couldn't make it out. As Joe delivered the coffee, Megan pointed at the girl and said, "I'll be right back. Keep an eye on my bags."

"Okay," said Joe, rubbing his hands and smiling, wondering if Mrs. Moore, as he called her, was doing a medical piece this week. Or perhaps something on faith healing, a subject in which his wife in Astoria, Queens, had lately taken an all-consuming interest.

Megan kept one hand on the door as she leaned out over the pavement. "Yes?"

"Ms. Moore," said the girl. "I'm so sorry. I'm Marie. Who called you up last night. About Noah Simmons?"

"Yes," said Megan. "I'm to pick you up at the Square when I finish breakfast." She looked at her watch. "It'll still be a half an hour. I'm still working on my programming for the week. Okay?"

"There's a problem. My mom's sick today. I didn't know when I talked to you. So I gotta take my uncle here for his physical therapy. To Saint Vincent's. I can't leave him alone, so maybe we better make another appointment."

Megan swung herself out of the doorway. She looked over the ailing man's face. He looked barely alive. His eyes had rolled partially back in his head. His hand twitched intermittently. He wore those club-foot shoes that always made her vaguely nauseated. She touched the girl's shoulder in sympathy. Dozens of pedestrians brushed by them, some swearing because the trio was blocking the sidewalk. Megan tried to think of an alternative.

She couldn't budge from Joe's until the limo came from the studio and she wasn't doing any interviews except in the limo or at the office. DeSales had told her to watch her own ass and she would show him she could do it. "This is a problem," she said. "Yours is a top- priority story. It could save lives. But we can't talk *here*. In the street." She chewed a fingernail. "Can you come inside? I've got a booth." She gestured to the café.

The girl shook her head, sadly, pointing at the entrance. "No ramp for Uncle Caz. And his appointment is at nine."

"I've got it," said Megan. "You don't sit with him while he's being treated, do you?"

"Nope. I read magazines in the lobby."

"Well, when my car comes, I'll have it pull up at the Seventh Avenue entrance to the hospital, and you can sit in the car with me until it's time to take him home."

The girl smiled for the first time. Uncle Caz emitted a hacking cough that was more nauseating than his shoes. A burly man with a beard and an expensive chalk-stripe suit walked right through Marie, knocking her against the side of the building.

"Cunt," he spat, and disappeared into the crowd.

The girl seemed to take this in stride, an ordinary peril of city life. She bounced blithely off the wall, looked at her watch, and said, "I better get going. And I'm parked at a hydrant. Over there."

"See you in a half hour," said Megan. "Seventh Avenue entrance . . . Saint Vincent's."

The girl was pointing at a van that had been converted for use by the handicapped. At least so it appeared, for a ramp led from the sliding side door to the curb.

"He's heavy," said Marie. "Could you help me push him up the ramp?"

"Sure," said Megan, helping her guide the wheelchair through the throng. At the open van, the two women braced themselves and pushed the chair. There was some difficulty getting it over the hump where the platform entered the van, and the girl said, ''That always happens. There's a rug that gets stuck. I'll hold him up, and you just pull the edge of the carpet from under the wheel.'' Megan did as she was told. At the moment her head came within reach of the cripple's twitching hand, he took the back of her neck in a powerful grasp, effectively stunning her while paralyzing her vocal cords. In an instant, he had risen from the seat, pulled her into the curtained vehicle, and covered her face with a cloth. The cloth was saturated with a fluid that smelled of hospitals, like Saint Vincent's, like something they had given her before she had her tonsils out when she was three. Head reeling, the last thing she was aware of was Marie sliding the door shut behind her, then darkness.

CHAPTER 20

WHEN DESALES STROLLED into the office at 11 A.M., Kavanaugh was manning the computer while Shultz, blistered and peeling, handled two phones at once. The electronic map on the wall at the left was blinking like a video arcade.

"You picked a great day to come in late, Frank," sneered Kavanaugh, without looking up from the screen. "The shit is hitting the fan. In every possible direction."

DeSales, eyes bloodshot and skin drained of color, showed no particular interest in the other men's activity.

"Thought you were taking the day off, Dutch?"

Shultz opened his mouth to speak, covering the phone with his hand, but Kavanaugh beat him to it. "Emergency. Chief doesn't show up. We had to drag Shultz out of his sickbed." He winked. "Poor bastard, suffering from tropical excess."

"You can slap my wrist, Bernie," said DeSales. "I had a night on the town, went home briefly to shower and change, and I stopped by the library on the way back. Realized there were some things I didn't know."

"There's a lot you don't know. First of all, Watkins . . ."

DeSales was standing by the window. One of the car washes was out of service. An Oriental woman carried a bouquet of roses up and down the line of cars approaching the bridge. Black urchins were peddling copies of the *Post* to stalled motorists. He didn't need binoculars to read the headline about Watkins, he'd already seen it. His voice was hoarse as he interrupted, "You work up the papers for the widow and kids?"

"I was starting to when all this other stuff came in."

DeSales held himself erect, dark-suited, hands clasped behind his back, as he had seen the Jesuits do when he was at Georgetown Law. "And how many kids were there? I only read the headline."

"Four. Between four and ten years. Two boys, two girls."

"And the wife's name?"

"Cheryl."

"And there was an Anglican priest for the last rites?"

"Yep."

"Good."

Kavanaugh began to speak again, but DeSales waved him silent. A phone rang, and DeSales took both of them off the hook. "Draft the usual letter to the widow. I'll drop by and pay my respects later."

"It better be a lot later. Wait'll you hear . . ."

DeSales raised his prefectural arm again. "I'm hungry. Like that fat private eye on TV, I refuse to work unless I have a full stomach. Dutch, run down to Junior's, will you? I'll take a pastrami on a roll with coleslaw and Russian. And cheesecake. Bernie? It's on me."

"I always get the corned beef on rye. Mustard. Jewish soda. Celery, I guess." He rubbed his stomach and typed out another command.

"And whatever you want, Dutch. Maybe a Solarcaine blintz."

Shultz made a face and stepped gingerly out of the room. He turned and cackled, like someone demented. DeSales and Kavanaugh looked curious. "I was just thinking of you, Frank. I'd like to see you in those tight pants someday with second-degree burns on your balls." He slammed the door.

DeSales adjusted his belt buckle. "You know what a *schizoid* is, Bernie?"

"You referring to Dutch?"

"Purely an academic question."

Kavanaugh scratched his head and looked at his superior as if he, then, were the mental case in question. "Something like split personality, right?"

"Not exactly." DeSales removed a crumpled piece of note-paper from his pocket. "This is one of the reasons I had to go to the library. I was thinking we needed some professional opinions on the kinds of killers we're dealing with." He began to read in fits and starts, almost to himself: " 'Schizoid tendencies spring from such a deep distrust of others, and feeling of weakness, that the people who have them compensate by having an overwhelming desire for power and superiority.' Know why?" He didn't wait for an answer, didn't even take his eyes from the paper. " 'Their greatest fear is humiliation, which they equate with the position of being loved, as the love might at any moment be withdrawn. They are convinced that they are unlovable, and extreme hostility festers within them as a result.' Remind you of anyone around here, Bernie?"

"Frank, you cracking up on the heaviest day of the year?"

DeSales resumed reading: " 'Schizoid people may be safe if they can attain high power or accomplishment. They may sublimate their aggression in stern, demanding, professional endeavor.' Sound familiar?"

"Sounds like one of those shrinks we bring in to handle insanity pleas."

"You got an opinion about it?"

"Same as always. Cops can't fuck around with that shit. It's beyond the law. Speaking of what we're dealing with today, it's like this religious crap, all this hair splitting about definitions and rules, and then splitting off into factions. Give me old Father

O'Neil, who read the gospel, told us to vote Democrat, and passed the hat; or this guy in my parish today. He gives us seven or eight minutes on condoms and ten minutes on abortion, then he passes the hat. And everybody goes home thinking he's got his money's worth.''

DeSales put his arm around Kavanaugh's massive shoulders. ''You got it, Bernie. No more hair splitting or splitting off. Yesterday I was worried about severing cases. Today I'm just going out and take 'em as they come, starting with getting the guy responsible for me sending Watkins out on the street to get killed. We'll take his flesh off one strip at a time. Who knows? We get one of them, the others may just fall into place, come together. I'm not drawing fine lines about any diminishment of responsibility. This is a stern, demanding, professional endeavor.''

''I don't know where you been all night, Frank, but it sounds like the good old days to me. Rambo stuff. The Italian Stallion's back at the reins.''

''That's a mixed metaphor, Bernie,'' said the Jesuitical detective.

''As I said,'' Bernie Kavanaugh went on, ''we got four files here, four separate problems. The first you know is the closing-out stuff on the late Otis Watkins. The second concerns his murderer.''

DeSales peeked at the display terminal.

''Winston Murray, a/k/a Haile Selassie. The zombi.''

''We found him in the hallway of an abandoned building on St. Mark's Place.''

''Dead or alive?''

Kavanaugh had taken a serious bite out of the hugely overstuffed sandwich and come up with rye crumbs and mustard on his lips. He chewed vigorously until he was able to mumble: ''A moot point. The docs say he's alive, but he says he's dead.'' He picked up the pickle from the plastic wrap.

''What do you think?''

''A tossup. I do not, however, believe that he is—as *he* says—

a reincarnated deity. I believe he's more or less permanently whacked out of his mind." Kavanaugh bit off half the pickle and chewed some more. "In other words, his brain is fried."

"Does he know who did him?"

"Lots of white devil and Babylon shit. He the schizoid you were worried about?"

DeSales scooped coleslaw onto the roll and then poured pink dressing from a tiny paper cup. "Forget I mentioned that. I was . . . well, I was . . . hungry." He bit into the sandwich. "But nothing specific from the kid."

"He says he'll talk to the dude who contacted him yesterday. Tall black guy with a gentle manner and a Babylon suit."

"Watkins?"

"Right."

"He doesn't know he killed him?'"

"Oh, he *knows*. He just doesn't think it's a significant detail."

"Get another black guy to work on him. One of the chosen people."

"Jackson?"

"Why not? He keeps trying. Maybe he'll find his niche." DeSales extracted a strand of slaw from between his teeth and placed it neatly on the extra napkin. He sipped coffee from the personal cup he kept in the office, the one that said "Thou shalt not kill" in Gothic letters. "And the house that the grandparents with the voodoo store sent us to? You got a warrant?"

"That's File Number Two. The judge did try to bust my chops, wanted to speak to you, you bastard not showing up, but I convinced her you were in the field doing undercover work. Under the covers."

Privately, DeSales winced. He maintained the breezy tone: "I'll bet she liked that."

"She suspected the worst, but she's a bawdy old broad and seemed pleased by the notion there was an inspector around acting like an alley cat instead of an IBM executive."

"And you got the warrant?"

"Got the warrant, broke down the door, and found . . ." Kavanaugh dropped the sprawling remains of the corned beef on the paper plate and grinned lopsidedly.

"Yeah?"

"An aquarium."

"No shit. That's all?" DeSales whirled in his chair and stepped instinctively up to the wall map, as if to locate the city's fish population. "What did it have? Sharks, piranhas?"

"Nothing. Empty tanks and a sink with some chopped-up fish and frogs. Looked like a high-school biology class had gone apeshit. Our lab guys are doing tests on the remains now."

DeSales threw down the napkin, missing the wastebasket. He bent to pick it up. "What the fuck? Why should we expect that to tell us anything? Guy probably had bullfrogs and goldfish for pets."

"Maybe, but he also had a wheelchair."

DeSales whistled.

"And this wheelchair was identical to the one in the botanicals. And the one the old man in the Botanique has."

"All right. All *right*. Get on the horn to the lab, get their asses moving. Now, speaking of botanicals, what about the stiff? I dispatched a hundred pictures of the guy. Something has to . . ."

Kavanaugh leaned back, drained his soda, and made a pumping motion with his arms. He burped loudly, pointing at the computer, and then typed with his chubby hand. The machine sounded like mice on a tin roof. "File Three. File Three. We got a positive. Let me get it up." He reached over and punched the keyboard again. He read from the screen. "One Jean-Paul Pic, born nineteen forty-six."

"Haitian?"

"Haitian, we assume. He was born in Guam. And his father is a retired Baptist minister in Harlem. Church with a French name."

"And a Japanese mother?"

"Why not?"

DeSales cupped his chin and mused: "Nineteen forty-six . . . could have been a Buffalo Soldier. . . ."

"Buffalo Soldier?"

"Something else I looked up this morning. They called the segregated all-Negro brigades in World War Two the Buffaloes. Buffaloes because they were first formed to put down the Indians in the Wild West after the Civil War. I heard a song about it when Watkins was getting his yesterday. How'd you get background so fast on Pic?"

"Pic was a pharmacist. He's got a rap sheet for trying every prescription-drug scam in the book."

"That's why the fingertips and teeth were removed. His prints and choppers were on file." DeSales closed his eyes. "But one day of showing his kisser around the neighborhood comes up with a positive I.D. Hey, the guy who went to all that surgical trouble must be a screaming asshole. Did he think we wouldn't . . . Hell, why didn't he cut the head off too and throw it in the garbage? It doesn't make any sense."

"Unless it has something to do with a voodoo ritual, like Desmond said. Anyway, you may get a chance to assess his brains up close, and soon."

"Yeah? How?"

"File Four." Shultz, standing behind Kavanaugh, working on his second cherry cheesecake, pointed at the screen with his free hand. Kavanaugh continued: "Colon has made a connection. Whoever is handling the drugs that blew Haile Selassie's mind has put out feelers for a big sale. If you can get the D.A. or the feds to front us some cash so Colon can pretend he's a legitimate buyer, we can set it up so this dealer walks into a trap."

"I'll do my best. Bernie. Dutch," asked DeSales, "doesn't it seem possible that this Pic was in on this scam and his partner—or partners—knocked him off so they could take all the profits from this clearance sale? Forget the voodoo."

"It makes perfectly good sense," said Shultz, supporting

himself with his elbow against the wall in the corner, unable to sit comfortably, "only before you get on the horn and start beating the bushes for cash and men and all that shit, you'd better talk to Desmond. The Professor. He's waiting outside. Has been for two hours."

DeSales pushed at the air. "He just wants to tell me about some crazy he saw in the park that he thinks could have killed Noah Simmons."

"He also knows what poison killed J.P. Pic. J.P. is what he was known as on the street in Crown Heights. And it doesn't look like we'll be able to forget about voodoo. For a long time."

"You got a Desmond file?"

"Number Five. We're just working it up."

DeSales was strapping on his gun. "Ask Desmond if he minds telling me his story in a squad car. I'm heading for Crown Heights. I want to see Colon and get this setup moving. Wait. Call the D.A. first. She's got a special account for major drug busts. We'll let her people take credit for the collar in exchange for some dough and the opportunity to get our hands on the bastard first. She can play with what's left when we're finished." He picked up the phone and put it down. "You call her, Bernie. If she's reluctant at all, call Maceo Allen and offer the case to the feds." He thought again. "And assign Jackson to Haile Selassie; tell him I'll get in touch with him at the House of Detention when I finish in Crown Heights. What's the address of the aquarium we uncovered by the way? I'll look in there, too."

"Slow down, Frank. You're all over the place. You can't do *everything*."

"Try me."

As he headed toward the door, the phone rang. Kavanaugh picked up the receiver and listened, muttering assent from time to time. Each moment his already dour expression grew more solemn. Finally, he said, "We'll get right back to you." He turned to DeSales, who stood with his hand on the doorknob. "It's the D.A., Frank. The Manhattan D.A. He's at Midtown South with

Chief Grey and the man who owns the TV station you were on with the rabbis. It seems that Megan Moore has disappeared and they have reason to believe that you were one of the last people to see her; in fact he's saying that it was your negligence which led to the crime.''

"Oh, shit," said DeSales, ''I forgot all about her.''

CHAPTER 21

DE SALES MOVED FAST. He found Desmond in the waiting room, reading a book, the round rimless spectacles on the tip of his nose. Desmond wanted to talk about Haitian poison and Japanese restaurants and a book—about serpents and rainbows or something—but DeSales took the lanky professor's arm and schmoozed him into silence. Doing his best not to appear impatient, he explained that he was on a life-or-death call and that the poison was de facto only a matter of death not life and would Desmond be so kind as to accompany Detective Shultz to a location they believed to be the poisoner's laboratory where he could provide counsel to the police and medical examiner's men until DeSales got there. It would take no more than an hour. Then they would all put their heads together and devise a scenario. To solve the crime. If Desmond would provide them with this one sacrifice, they would be so deeply indebted that he could depend on active collaboration from the department on anything within reason he might need. Desmond pushed the glasses back on his nose and allowed the pages of the book to flap in the breeze. DeSales had darted out the door before the man could decline to cooperate.

The squad car with driver was waiting outside on Tillary and they threw on the siren and took a left onto the lower level of the bridge, in front of the traffic pouring off the BQE, cutting across on two wheels. DeSales switched on the headset of his Walkman as the driver honked, bumped, cajoled, and threatened the other cars to pull over into the right-hand lane. The tape he had taken from Megan's was muted but clear. There of course were other calls before the threatening one. Megan appeared to be a person who placed a lot of phone calls but was never at home to receive them when they were returned. She was also a person, apparently, who took full advantage of Manhattan's cultural life, particularly its fashion industry and psychotherapeutic and cosmetic resources. In fact, the only one of her callers that he heard who did not have a foreign accent was a woman who could have been from Utica who wanted Megan to know that Dr. Himmelfarb was sick and the group would not be meeting that evening. Then there was a different mood on the line; it was the breather, only he wasn't really a breather at all. It was a man with a deep voice, a voice DeSales suspected of being basically Brooklyn stone, but coated with many layers of varnish. There was a good deal of ornament piled on the varnish as well, largely in the form of polysyllabic words. Megan, he said, would "suffer a leisurely evisceration" as a "caveat to her loutish Lothario," DeSales. The car shot right, into the lane reserved only for traffic headed east on Canal, into the more exotic and impenetrable reaches of Chinatown and the Lower East Side, and then cut across the bow of the lead car in the left-hand lane, going north on Chrystie. They ran the light and sped on.

DeSales switched off the cassette as he heard his sworn enemy ring off Megan's line. It was the sort of threat he wouldn't have taken seriously twenty-four hours before. Before Megan got lifted. Now he had to.

Or did he?

Listen, DeSales reasoned to himself, the guy is an absolute phony. He sounds like someone from Bushwick who went to the

Connecticut School of Broadcasting and was given his money back. And the language sounded like something Howard Cosell might have labored over for an hour or so while reciting to his shaving mirror. If he had called him up in person, DeSales would have begun laughing halfway through the recitation, unable to do much but search for a Shakespearean pun about swordsmanship to hang up on him with.

"Delancey's in gridlock," said the driver, swearing. "There's lanes down going both ways on the Williamsburg Bridge. And the Jews got *another* freaking holiday coming up." The car idled noisily, as DeSales tried to keep his impatience in check by thinking through to the end of the equation.

On the other hand, he had checked his watch and the caller had cleverly kept the time he spoke just under the time it took to trace a call. Just in case, although Megan was unlikely to be having her calls monitored. And, besides, who was to say that a guy who wrote lousy speeches and had a phony accent was any less dangerous than someone who was more "real"? In the old days, growing up on Dean Street, or South Brooklyn, anybody like that would have had his ass kicked until his nose bled. At least three times a day. By the "real tough guys" the ones anybody with common sense had to watch out for. But DeSales had spent enough time in his job finding out that the pansy weirdos who got eaten up and spit out, or shit out, in Red Hook when they were kids were, often as a result of their elementary education in the niceties of working-class American youth, the ones with the long knives and hot pokers and various other devices of torture and mayhem when they matured into adult citizens. The ones who came up out of the drains after the lights were out.

And the one piece of incontrovertible evidence was that Megan was gone.

If it wasn't a publicity stunt on her part. He remembered her, vulnerable and open, then screaming imprecations from the bed, saw from the corner of his eye her pink approaching flesh as he slammed the door on her the night before, leaving her at the mercy of the Eviscerator.

When the Chicago Bears no longer have the Refrigerator, he said half aloud, they can always sign up the Eviscerator; I'll be his agent. He started to laugh, the driver gave him a supercilious look. Then he realized he was laughing not at his play on words or the fate of Megan Moore but that he had for some moments been witnessing on Chrystie, between Broome and Delancey, a scene Roz had described to him some years before, a scene he had never seen firsthand. In the passenger seat of a new Oldsmobile station wagon, double parked on the right, the kind with the seats facing backward for the kids at the rear, was a bearded, behatted, heavyset Hasidic Jew. The visible, upper part of his body was bouncing up and down, sometimes fast, sometimes slow. His hat had been knocked askew by repeated contact with the ceiling of the car. The Hasid gave one last spasmodic jerk that knocked his hat off. For a moment, his eyes were wild behind the glasses; then, becalmed, he slumped in his seat. Slowly, a woman's head became visible above the door frame. She was smiling; her cheeks were heavily rouged and her teeth were not good. Daintily she removed a lace hankie from her bodice and wiped off her lips and chin. The Hasid, eyes at half-mast, produced some paper currency and handed it to her. She put the money in the hankie and carefully replaced it. She jumped out of the car and wobbled briskly on stiletto heels toward Delancey, joining the other hookers hailing cars. DeSales noted from the muscles in her calves and the narrowness of her hips and the swagger in her shoulders that she was more likely a he than a she.

What Roz had said was that she drew the line in certain places, had her own personal caveats: she avoided, whenever humanly possible, rough stuff, anal stuff, and the proximity of hard drugs. But most of all, she would never, ever, serve among the large corps of streetwalkers who patrolled the Manhattan approaches to the Williamsburg Bridge on Friday afternoons and the eves of Rosh

Hashanah and Yom Kippur and the like offering quick blow jobs to the diamond merchants and other religious Jews making their way home early to bovine wives and marathon segregated religious services. She would rather, Roz had said, go on welfare.

Thinking of Roz, the laughter turned to coughing. Then DeSales stifled a gag.

"You okay, Inspector?"

DeSales grunted. He needed to take charge, keep his problems further from the surface. "Turn left on Houston," he barked after he swallowed and got his throat clear. "Fuck the Second Avenue traffic coming down. Then right on the Bowery. I like to see the kids with the purple hair and rings through their noses. Much better than the winos used to be here. Then do that angle at Cooper Union so you're going up Fourth, then cut around Union Square. I don't care what the fucking signs say. The way I figure it, I got about ten minutes to do this job, or my—our—ass is grass."

The driver went the wrong way down Megan's block from the square. DeSales jumped out, flashed his badge at the doorman, and caught the elevator just as it was about to close. The door of her apartment was open; luckily the cops who were there already knew him, and they barely looked up once he had been recognized. He headed straight for the telephone and replayed the calls. He heard the woman's voice talking about the lead on Noah Simmons. He wrote down the number. He went into the bedroom and saw one of his old colleagues, Norman Chan, the fingerprint expert, on his knees next to the cushioned toilet seat dusting the sink.

Norman looked up and winked. "Only two sets of prints, Frank. Megan Moore's and what from size and pressure look like a guy's. The cleaning woman was here all day yesterday, so we figure our TV personality was entertaining a guest. The usual progress. He touches the surface of the bar, the telephone answering machine, brings his drink into the bedroom, they play games— sheets very rumpled, semen stains—then grips the sink as he looks at himself in the mirror after the act." Chan grinned. He had big teeth and happy, small, dark eyes. "You ever see her on TV, Frank? A real piece. A little *mature,* maybe," he turned down the corners of his mouth, "but definitely one I'd like to get into the act *with.* How about you?"

But DeSales was out the door.

He looked over the living room again. In daylight, the effect was different, or he had simply not noticed. Peach wallpaper, lacquered antique chests; the bar could be ebony. A good wood to leave your fingerprints on. He took one of the detectives aside, a guy named Bosworth from Midtown South, with whom he'd walked a beat twenty-odd years before. "You get anything interesting?"

"Depends what you're looking for, Frank. There's a missing tape from the sequence on her answering machine. She collected them. Unlike other people who just keep taping over. And you heard the one that's on now. Some broad had a tip on a murder. We'll have to follow that up. And Norman says she had a guy here last night. But that seems off the point, since she was hauled into the van outside the coffee shop downstairs while she was having breakfast alone this morning."

"When do you expect the chief and the D.A.?"

"How'd you know they were coming?"

"Oh, I just happened to be talking to the chief and he mentioned it, knew she was an old friend of mine."

Bosworth looked at his watch. "Should be here now."

DeSales edged to the hall door and looked out. The elevator was rising. "See ya, Boz. Tell the chief I'll be right back, that I want to see him." He ran for the fire stairs and was closing the door just as the D.A., the chief, and a muckraking investigative reporter from Megan's TV station emerged from the elevator. Only the reporter looked enthusiastic.

Downstairs, DeSales was panting from his run as he interrogated the coffee-shop people. They told him what had happened, described the blonde in the red-rimmed sunglasses on a ribbon around her neck, and the sickly guy in the wheelchair. They had the first three numbers of the New Jersey plates on the van. There was some disagreement over whether the van was a Ford or a Chevy. And then DeSales was sitting in the back seat of the police car again, talking on the two-way, roaring back to Brooklyn.

"Which bridge?" asked the driver.

"*Not* the Williamsburg," said DeSales.

CHAPTER 22

IT WAS DARK AND nippy under the El where Brighton Beach Avenue meets Coney Island Avenue. Merry Pace leaned on the phone booth, keeping her eyes open for cops or other undesirable figures, but she was sleepy and it was difficult to keep in focus. Sometimes she tried to listen in and was able to pick up snatches of Rand's heated conversation. At one point he shouted, "I told you already; it's not my current strategic direction!" Later he lounged backward and allowed with casual irony, "Hey, babe, the slip page in gross margin is over." Again and again he returned to the main point, "profitability" and something about "specialty items." Sometimes, instead, Merry just listened to the passing pedestrians speaking Russian, trying to guess what they were saying. It made about as much sense as Rand's business-school bullshit. When the D train roared on the tracks overhead, she put her fingers to her ears and looked long and hard at the backward and upside-down letters of Cyrillic script on the knish cart nearby. Finally, Rand hung up, stepped out of the booth, and immediately hurried down the street. She hustled to catch up.

"Why were you so long?" she whined. "I get the willies

around here. The spades, then the Hasids, that was enough. This is a little too far out for me. There was some old lady giving me dirty looks—she reminded me of that prune in the James Bond movie with the poison blade coming out of her boot. And I saw somebody carrying a carton of *Siberian* milk. And that restaurant over there has a *sturgeon*-kabob special. I almost blew lunch.''

Rand walked hunched forward, fighting the big wind. "I mind-fucked the guy all over the place," he said. "He didn't even know what a slip page is. A small-time retailer is what he is, but if he's got the cash, we're in business."

"Yeah?" Merry sounded suspicious.

"He'll pay fifty percent over what Big Bird or the P.R.'s in Sunset Park would offer because he needs my goodwill and general game plan to get off the ground."

"You'll do at least an eye frisk first, right?"

"I got the perfect scenario. Place, time. I'll know him and he won't know me. If he checks out and the money is good for the deposit, I bring him out here after for an inventory. He makes the final payment and I give him the keys. Then, we move the stuff when they're having the parade for the whatchamacallits, the Refuseniks."

"They'll be here already?"

"I heard on the radio. Yesterday they exchanged them for the KGB spy. Today, they get debriefed in Frankfurt. Plane arrives Kennedy at dawn. They bring them right here where all their cousins and aunts and uncles live. They'll be freaked out. Just like the other times, no one will notice a little everyday commerce taking place. Especially when it's a new business that promises to improve neighborhood services, like a twenty-four-hour pharmacy."

"But this time it's different. We got a responsibility. A *guest*. Maybe you forgot."

Rand continued to ignore her. Instead he pointed at the Cyrillic signs, the babushkas, the hot ponchlik counters. "They call it Little Odessa," he said. "Ten years ago you could have torched all of Brighton Beach and nobody would have noticed. The Russians put it back on its feet and now a developer's going to build a Florida-style condo complex down at the old Bath and Racquets Club. Three hundred million dollars. We close this deal, I'm going for a piece of that shit too. Can't lose. No way. Hey, you can't even rent a storefront around here anymore.'' He turned into a doorway, produced a key and turned it in the lock of a glass-plated door under a weathered sign that said MEAT. GLATT KOSHER.

"We did.''

"I had to grease a few palms at Borough Hall. This building is vacant only because it's still in probate court. It's a ward of the city. The guy I know is warehousing it until everybody realizes this is the next Miami Beach. He'll make a killing.''

They made their way through the jumble of unopened packing cases and plaster dust to the back of the store where the disused meat locker stood. Rand lifted the heavy bar and the old wooden door swung outward. The smell was rank. He switched on the light. Megan Moore was tied by the hands to one of the hooks from which sides of Rumanian beef had once hung. She wore only a bra and underpants; a ripped T-shirt had been placed in her mouth as a gag. There was a high stool under her backside so she could sit on it with her feet on a bench above the wet sawdust floor. A rat scurried for cover. Megan's eyes were bright, frightened, like a doe's.

"This shits,'' said Merry Pace.

"You got no taste,'' said Rand. "Nobody's hurting her, and she looks like the cover on a Mickey Spillane novel. Who's got his own Mickey Spillane cover, in the flesh?'' He laughed. "Listen,'' he said, "I got an idea. We can have some fun with her. Without doing anything we can get indicted for more than we got already. Get some of J.P.'s powder.''

Merry didn't move. She glared at him from behind the red-rimmed shades with the cord around her neck. She popped her gum with defiance. "No way, José.''

Rand took her neck in one hand and cocked the other fist. "I hit you before, Merry, and you take a punch good. It's one of the things I like about you, the way you take a punch. Maybe because you know I'll shoot you up later and that it's worth a little pain. But you don't go along with me now, I'm gonna hurt you in the soul."

"What soul?" She popped the gum again.

"The net profit from the liquidation. You're in for twenty percent, right? With that you can run a whole fucking stable of fag haircutters on Madison Avenue, right next to Kenneth."

Merry shook her head, then dropped it. "Okay," she gave in.

"And hurry up. I don't have much time. I gotta go to my brother's in Greenpoint."

"The cop? What do you want to see *him* for?"

"I don't want to see *him*. I want to borrow one of his uniforms."

"Huh?"

"The buyer? He thinks I'm a cop. A rogue, a bad apple who's been stashing the take from drug raids."

As the driver raced down Broadway, across to Centre, and onto the Brooklyn Bridge at City Hall, DeSales talked at length to Kavanaugh on the two-way. A trace was put on the phone number the woman had left on Megan's answering machine. Then Kavanaugh described how they had made a tentative identification of the guy Desmond had seen impersonating an Amish elder in the park. A priest in Manhattan who took care of the homeless had given him a shave and a haircut that morning. Out of costume. The priest knew him from previous encounters in a kind of support-group session he held for people who used his soup kitchen. He knew his name and presumed place of origin. "Jack Schwartz, about forty years old," said Kavanaugh, already hoarse. "Comes from a town near Hershey, Pennsylvania. Town begins with a P. That is all Father Dougherty can remember."

"Keep on it Bernie. Does he have a yellow sheet with us?"

"I can't get anything under Jack Schwartz."

"Try some different spellings. Maybe he's German. They got a lot around there."

"What if I don't come up with anything?"

"You raise any cash from Headquarters for the drug buy?"

"Not so far."

"Call Maceo Allen. *Now.* Suggest we'll cut in his federal buddies in exchange for a little cash and access to their files. Anybody who's killing kids at forty has got his hands dirty sometime before. Mace can hook up with Quantico and the national lines. See if he'll drop in after work tonight. He likes Junior's cheesecake. We can brainstorm."

"That all on Schwartz?"

"Check the mental institutions again."

"Okay. Now get this."

"Hold on." DeSales lowered the receiver and directed the driver to avoid Atlantic Avenue, instead to go down to Wyckoff and up to St. Mark's and Flatbush Avenue. "Go ahead, Bernie."

"This guy Pic. The druggist stiff? He's taken out licenses to open new drugstores six times in the last year."

"I thought he was disbarred, or whatever they do to pill pushers."

"He was, but the info never made its way from the *druggist* licensing bureau to the *store* licensing bureau. Usually takes at least a year. Shit, Frank, the offices of those bureaus are at least two blocks apart."

"Where were the stores?"

"Bushwick Avenue, Eastern Parkway, the place on Rogers, and a place on Thirteenth Avenue."

"In Borough Park?"

"Down the street from the Kosher Blossom."

DeSales took a deep breath. "Any more?"

"The computer system only goes through September. He could have done more before he died."

The car passed Atlantic, with the Arabic stores and barrels of spice outside, and into Boerum Hill, which was not a hill at all but a section of real estate that had been arbitrarily divided from "downtown" in the sixties. "Brooklyn Heights vicinity," the ads said. On Wyckoff they turned left, passing the idle blacks at the housing projects built in the lowland at the terminus of the Gowanus canal. They passed a corner full of prostitutes at Third Avenue, near where Roz had begun her professional career. DeSales imagined her at eighteen, awkward but experienced, and now, he had finally realized, probably very angry. They began to climb Park Slope. They hit Flatbush just after Fifth Avenue, where a three-block strip of heroin-shooting galleries had been converted, at the city's expense, into fancy commercial façades beneath signs for exclusive co-ops. The buildings were still empty and the junkies were still shooting up on the streets.

"If you get a new drugstore application, it could be the place this guy's working out of now. The guy who killed Pic and is holding the auction for his prescription pill business."

"Friedman doesn't think it was murder."

DeSales spat out the window as they wheeled around Grand Army Plaza. "I've heard enough, Bernie. Keep at it. I have a date with Colon in Crown Heights and then I'm going to the drug factory on Rogers. Can you get Friedman or one of his men there? And the kid who calls himself Haile Selassie? I won't have time to go by the jail."

"Great minds run on the same track, Frank. I have them lined up rarin' to go."

Hector Colon was standing in front of the Base of the Rainbow armory on Bedford. When the car pulled over, the driver got out, made Colon stand against the wall, and half-heartedly rousted him. They were cousins. Then he prodded him with his nightstick until he climbed into the front passenger seat of the squad car.

"We're on," said Colon, not looking back at DeSales. "All I need is twenty-five thousand in cash as a down payment. And my good looks."

"You'll get it. Where do you deal?"

Colon giggled. "In the park. The Nethermead. They're having some kind of Halloween masquerade party tomorrow, for the kids. The guy's got a sense of humor. I'm supposed to just be there in a cowboy suit with a Ronald Reagan mask. He says he'll make me, and then we can exchange confidences and money behind a tree or something."

"What's he offering as collateral?"

"Samples of the merchandise and the address of the stash and his rep. It counts on the street. He got Big Bird as a reference, Antonio Caballo from East New York. He fucks around with me while using them as references, he's dead."

"What *is* his name?"

"Calls himself Deep Throat."

"Original. And why the fuck did he pick that thing in the park? There's an army of cops there. To protect the kids from the weirdos."

"It's easy. He says *he's* a cop and he'll be on duty, in uniform, in the Haunted Ravine all day tomorrow."

DeSales tugged at his earlobe. "You'd better be at my office tonight, Hector. We'll be holding a powwow."

"For my brains or my *salsa*?"

"For your hairdo."

CHAPTER 23

RAND TOOK THE SCALPEL out of his attaché case and held it under Megan's nose, as he had seen Roman Polanski do to Jack Nicholson in *Chinatown*. He yanked the gag out of her mouth. She moved her lips, without sound.

"Hi, Megan," he said. "You can call me Randy."

She had the dry heaves for a moment, caught her breath, and coughed. She stood erect on the bench, taking her rear off the stool, to give her arms a rest. Rand inspected her closely. Choice or Prime?

When she was finally able to speak, her voice was cracked, thin: "Where am I?"

"Behind the Iron Curtain." He laughed, in the meantime shoving the blade a little farther into her nostril, causing her to reach higher, moving her wrists against the meathook. Her lacy bra climbed up into her armpits. One breast popped out, then the other. Rand menaced the soft flesh, poking here and there. Megan flinched, then fell back against the stool, drained.

"Sure," she said. "Anything you say. What do you want me for?"

"Let's just say you're a hostage."

"To what?"

Rand raised an eyebrow, searching with pleasure for the right word. For the moment, he couldn't find it. "A cause."

"What cause?"

"Fortune," he chortled. "You're a hostage to *fortune*."

"You're the jerk who called me on the phone. The happy eviscerator."

"And you sound to me like someone who's looking for a quick hysterectomy." He traced an oval, pressing the blade in, making the flesh whiter, then red, from her rib cage to her navel. He engaged the satin underpants there, briefly flicking them out for a peek.

"Okay, Randy. I can skip the surgery. I'll do whatever you want."

"Sounds better." He continued to agitate the tip of the weapon inside her pants, uncovering the top of the thick, curly pubic hair. The locker door swung open.

"Hands off," Merry said. "You promised." She carried two glass containers of powder, one white, the other like red clay.

Rand looked like a child caught with his hands in the cookie jar. He moved quickly to erase the embarrassment. He placed the scalpel back in its place in the case and roughly shoved Megan's feet off the stool. He took the jars from Merry and placed them at his side. He put on a pair of sheer latex surgeon's gloves and scattered a quantity of each substance on the bench. Then, facing Megan, who remained sitting on the high stool with her legs dangling, he hesitated. But only briefly. He grabbed her elbow in his right hand, said, " 'Jerk,' huh?" and indeed jerked her as hard as he could off the stool. She dangled against the wall, rope digging into her wrists at the hook, only the tips of her toes brushing the sawdust floor. Merry made a noise, halfway between anger and disgust, behind him. He paid no heed, either to the half-naked, strung-up captive, nor to his collaborator. He was all business. He dragged the stool over next to the bench and covered the seat with the mixture of powders. He rearranged the furniture so it was in roughly the same position vis-à-vis Megan Moore as it had been when they entered. Still, he made no effort to help her regain the support she had had before, either to sit on the stool or stand on the bench. Instead, still coolly professional, he half turned to Merry, indicated the case, and said, "Scalpel."

"Whadda I look like? General Hospital? Whaddaya want the sticker for. Again?"

"Incisions. Like with J.P."

Merry had to think about this. She looked almost stunned behind the sunglasses, then merely puzzled. She put a long green fingernail to her lip. "Oh, *those,*" she said with relief. "I thought it was butcher-block time again. Never, like I said, *never,* do I do *that* again." She shuddered. She fingered the scalpel, then put it back. Instead she brought out of the leather case a package of hypodermic needles and a full syringe.

"You don't need a fucking pigsticker for this job. You just wanna make pinpricks."

She broke out a needle, then another. She found another already prepared syringe. "I'll take care of this," she said. "You keep your hands off of her." She approached Megan. "Be cool, honey," she said, "and this won't hurt that bad." She took each of Megan's feet and made a succession of shallow punctures on the soles. Blood began to seep out of the wounds.

"Do it to her ass, too," said Rand. "Pull down her pants. Like J.P."

"No way, José," answered Merry. "We agreed we do nothing they could say was some kinda sex thing. We get caught, we gotta cop a plea. The only way is to show we didn't mean no harm. J.P. was different. He was into it, strung out, he would've let me scratch his eyeballs if it would've added to the trip. Remember he was a zombi, you said, as well off dead or alive."

Megan had begun to struggle with the ropes. She couldn't see her feet, but obviously the cuts had upset her. She was crying. "No harm! Are you crazy? What are you doing to me? What's the stuff on the bench, on the stool?''

Rand was pushing the bench closer to her feet, so she could choose to stand on it and relieve the strain on her arms. He moved the stool out of reach. ''It's her choice. No punctures in the ass, no seat.''

''What *is* the powder?'' Megan croaked.

''Better than mescaline, better than XTC, better than Spanish fly,'' breathed Rand. ''Stand on it, with those cuts, let it get into the bloodstream, you'll first get high, then maybe a good night's sleep, and when I get back here tomorrow, you'll be another person, you'll be begging me to take you higher. And *lower* too. Hey, you could say I'm the original sixty-minute man. I'll make your friend DeSales look like the pansy that he is. The wop pansy. Supercop, Superwop—that's pretty good . . . You'll want to do a TV special on me, how I make you feel good. And *bad*. But first, I made a deal with Merry. You gotta ask for it yourself before I touch you. And you *will*, baby, you *will*.''

''Don't hold your breath,'' Megan Moore said out of the side of her mouth.

Rand cocked his fist, but Merry grabbed him by the arm. ''You want some ass, Rand? You wanna penetrate somebody? Well, save her until business is taken care of. Tomorrow. Me, I'm tight as I can get.'' She handed him the other needle and the two syringes. ''I need a double dip.'' As quickly as she said it, she had the mauve sweatpants and bikini bottoms down around her ankles and was bent over, her buttocks, covered with scar tissue, facing up toward Rand. He poked her in the upper right quadrant of her right cheek, changed syringes, and then jabbed the second into the upper left on the other side.

Merry stood up, leaned on the wall, breathed deeply, scratched her crotch, then pulled the pants back up. ''Thanks, babe,'' she said. ''Now run along to Thaddeus's. Before he gets off duty and finds you messing with his uniforms.''

''Right,'' said Rand. In playing doctor, he appeared to have forgotten Megan's presence. "And I have to ditch that phone and clean out the loft over the store. Cover our tracks. Brave New World Day tomorrow." Merry opened the door and stepped out. He began to follow her. He stopped and looked back at Megan, desperately swinging her feet about, resisting the urge to rest them on the powder-covered bench. "Brave New World for you tomorrow too, Megan. Sleep tight."

The heavy door swung shut. The bolt was slid into place. The lights went out. And Megan Moore felt it strange that she was less frightened by the powder or Randy's threats than she was by Merry's gesture; the quick dropping of drawers; the supplicant posture, begging for the needle; the perfunctory scratching of the sparse fair-haired pubes before strangers; and the glaze that had covered her eyes—as if someone had disconnected her from the rest of the world, pulled the plug.

CHAPTER 24

DE SALES SAT ON THE EDGE of the old-fashioned zinc lab table, near a pile of hosing. Desmond and Friedman, the medical examiner, sat nearby, on old empty crates. Behind them, guarded by three uniformed patrolmen, there huddled a young man with a terra-cotta complexion, freckles, and hennaed dreadlocks. From time to time the young man shook frantically, rattling his chains; then he would burst into song, a plaintive dirge:

Redemption song . . .
These songs of freedom
Was all I ever had . . .

DeSales gestured at the dirty jars, sink, and assorted paraphernalia. "Besides our incommunicative Rastafarian Prince over there, what do we got?"

Friedman had a drooping salt-and-pepper mustache that he often had to brush back from his lips. He spoke in a gravelly voice: "Scrapings mostly. Prescription stuff: secobarbital sodium, amobarb, propoxyphene hydrochloride, dextroamphetamine sulfate, lots of aspirin and caffeine mixed in." He raised a bushy eyebrow.

"Translate," said DeSales.

"Downers, uppers, painkillers, Tuinal, Dexedrine, Darvon, like that. Drugstore quality."

"And the tanks?" He indicated the disused aquarium against the wall.

"There's not much in there. Certain amount of waste, decaying plant life. I found the most interesting results in the drain to that sink there." He pointed at the depression in the lab table from which the hose, like a jungle snake, emerged.

DeSales offered his Benson & Hedges around. Friedman and Desmond refused. Friedman instead took out a cigar and began to chew on it, unlit.

DeSales continued to press: "Yeah?"

"And in the toilet drain as well. *Datura*, for example. It's not something you'd expect to find in Brooklyn, a useless tropical plant . . ."

Desmond spoke to DeSales, as if in a confidential aside. "In Haiti they call it the zombi's cucumber. *Datura stramonium.*"

"Whatever they call it," said Friedman, "it *can* be toxic in intense quantities. Stuporific."

"And this was the cause of death in the Botanicals?"

"Not so fast. There's more. Both in this dump and in Pic's organs. Tetrodotoxin and all the bufo's: bufogenin, bufotoxin, bufotenine. All capable of the sort of death the guy went through. Respiratory failure, pulmonary edema."

"How about him?" DeSales pointed to the corner. The boy registered his skewed awareness by resuming his song:

> *How long shall they kill our prophets*
> *While we stand by and look?*
> *Some say it's just a part of it,*
> *We've got to fulfill the book.*

Friedman shrugged. "It's not that easy to say scientifically exactly *what* symptoms Pic exhibited before he died. Without an eyewitness. But the kid *is* experiencing accelerated heartbeat, the shakes, and diminished oxygen supply. And these are consistent with these toxins. That's all I can say."

"There could be more to the story," added Desmond. "They're not only toxins, they're psychoactive drugs, hallucinogens. There's a tradition—especially in esoteric religions—of using them for spiritual purposes to get high, out of this world."

"This I know little about," Friedman shrugged. "But it's not impossible that Pic was medicating himself."

DeSales dropped to the floor and paced around the lab equipment. "Who scratched his ass and feet then?"

"The wounds occurred over a long period of time. Not unlike the needle tracks you see on a junkie. Maybe self-inflicted. Or he could have had a friend. The needle-holding hanger-on is a fixture in certain corners of contemporary culture."

"It makes perfect sense," said Desmond. "The tetrodotoxin and bufotoxin come specifically from the innards of puffer fish and sea toads. That's obviously what they were keeping in the tanks, wherever they got them in the first place. And the substances are not just any old drugs, they're topically active. The Haitian *bokors* use them to make zombis, by sprinkling the mixtures where a person with an open wound might get infected. That's the significance of the cross under Pic's ass at the Botanicals. It was in the entranceway to the Temple, remember, where everyone would have to walk. In Haiti, where people go barefoot and have lots of festering skin sores. It *was* this powder, right?" He looked at Friedman.

"Right."

"Now these can be soporific or deadly, but they've also been used all over the world, like I said, for their hallucinogenic properties. They make people high. Like our friend in the corner. But it's a very tricky business, and the line between euphoria and toxicity is fine. There were priests in pre-Columbian South

America who rubbed the stuff on their genitals and it made them think they were flying.''

DeSales laughed.

Friedman pulled his mustache down over his lip, squinted, and brushed the few remaining strands of grizzled hair over his pate. ''Mind if I ask how you know so much?''

''I've done a book on the history of religious violence. In the course of my research I came upon this book, *The Serpent and the Rainbow,* by Wade Davis. It tells how a young American went to Haiti and discovered the ingredients of zombi poison, among other things. It covers the social and spiritual implications of these drugs. Pretty well, in fact. I didn't use it in my book, but when this business in the Botanic Gardens came up, I knew it was strikingly familiar. I just didn't know from where. Then the other night I was reading a food-and-wine magazine . . .''

The kid wailed, stood up, and began to gyrate in the corner, a man possessed. He began another song, stomping on the floor:

> *Ex-ee-dus*
> *All right!*
> *Movement of the people!*
> *Are you satisfied*
> *With the life you're living?*
> *We know where we're going.*
> *We know where we're from.*
> *We live in Babylon.*
> *We're going to the Fatherland.*

The cops had to wrestle him into submission until there was only the sound of his chains.

Desmond waited until the struggle was over. ''Anyway, there was this article by a well-known chef about how he once went to Japan and ate *fugu* in a kind of culinary speakeasy. This brought it all back. See, the fillets of the puffer fish are a harmless delicacy, but the more daring Jap gourmets insist that a sauce made from the

lethal livers be added. It's the ultimate aesthetic experience for the
fugu freak, and a lot of them overdo it. It starts with euphoria,
tingling of the lips, sense of warmth, but you go too far, you've got
an O.D., like Pic. Or a basket-case zombi like,'' he jerked his head
toward the corner, ''over there. The death rate among *fugu* chefs
in Japan is startling high.''

DeSales smoked. Friedman took the cigar out of his mouth
and looked at it as if it might transmit a message. DeSales said, ''I
still don't get one thing. The lacerations. Self-inflicted? You guys
mean Pic had access to these drugs, could have mixed them as he
wanted and ingested them in some controlled form, like capsules or
a measured drink, and instead he cuts his ass or feet open, then sits
in the stuff or walks in it? The way a Haitian black-magic guy
might try to sneak the drug into a victim? That's *sloppy*.''

Friedman assented, nodding. ''Maybe it was the *danger*. It's
a daily bit we deal with in addiction therapy. Look at these people
using dirty needles now, when they know it can give them AIDS.
It adds to the kick to be fooling with death. And besides, don't
forget that what we've found around here suggests that this guy
wasn't just re-creating ancient jungle rituals with natural drugs
from plants and frogs and fish, but he had an arsenal of synthetic
modern pills that he was also using. Haile Selassie here might be
a Rastafarian voodoo creation, but he also bears a close resemblance to certain Hell's Angels I've treated after a long weekend of
red devils and Budweiser. It's an O.D., brain damage even, but the
chemical was that much more complex, intense. A cocktail, if you
will. Like one of those drinks with seven different kinds of rum.''

''The kind you get on a Caribbean vacation,'' cracked
DeSales. ''The ultimate Island Experience.'' Then he flicked the
cigarette into the sink and looked thoughtful. He started to say
something, but Desmond interrupted.

''Here's something out of the blue. I read an article the other
day about autism. The poor kids who suffer from it often hurt
themselves a lot, and the study theorizes that in cutting themselves,
lacerating themselves, they may actually be doing some self-

medicating—because the penetration of the skin releases hormones in the body that are something like morphine. This has the opposite function from traditional perceptions. Instead of the kid being a simple klutz or pathologically self-destructive, maybe he's actually numbing the unbearable pain that is chronic to his condition."

"I heard about that study," said Friedman. "Done in Japan. By a woman psychologist."

"What if she's right? Think of the other 'exotics,' like the Hindu fakirs who lie on a bed of nails, the guys who rend their own flesh?" Desmond closed his eyes and covered his brow with his hand, recalling a vision. "I remember a painting I once saw in a museum in Italy. There was this Catholic saint flagellating himself, blood streaming down his back. Think of that from this new perspective: they're getting high on the pain, releasing hedonistic chemicals in the body."

DeSales turned up one of his thin lips. He looked knowing. "Sure sounds like the Italian Catholicism that I've had the good fortune to encounter. But can we say that, that religion is a way of getting stoned?"

Desmond was wide-eyed now, as if he had erased the bloody memory of the painting. "Getting stoned, masochism. Remember, masochists who do not go so far as to break their bodies open still get a kick out of being hurt. Even emotionally. And who was the first martyr? Didn't he get 'stoned'? To death?"

"And this tells us something about these religious people we keep stumbling over in these cases?"

Desmond sat back, furrowed his brow. He took off the glasses and wiped them with his tie. "Life is inherently painful, unhandleable for these people. So they turn to the opium of the masses."

"And you think our friend in the Botanic Gardens was practicing some African religion while incidentally," he swept his arm around the makeshift laboratory, "dealing drugs?" DeSales reached into his pocket and took out his box of Benson & Hedges. It was empty. He tried without much success to crush it in his fist in one motion. He looked disgusted at his impotence. He dropped the wrinkled packet onto the floor.

"I don't know what he thought he was doing in terms of religion," said Desmond, "but the guy who put him there did."

They headed for the door. The cop lifted the shackled putative Rasta man, a.k.a. Winston Murray, from the floor by his arm and pointed him in the direction of the stairs and the House of Detention.

"Ex-ee-dus," the boy crooned. "Movement of the People."

CHAPTER 25

MEGAN MOORE FELT the pins and needles in her hands, then her wrists. The strain on the muscles in her upper arms was becoming unbearable. She visualized the dreaded mounds of powder beneath the bloody soles of her feet and remembered a poem she had had to write a paper on at Vassar. Something about being half in love with easeful death. Keats. And she realized now that she, too, had begun to be seduced by the sense of ease, of letting go, of giving up her torn flesh to the poison. Whether it would lead to death or merely to putting herself at Randy's disposal remained a moot point.

Then, with a groan, the heavy door swung open again, and the locker was flooded with light. Momentarily blinded, she could make out only the apparition of one figure. The figure materialized, defined itself, in the person called Merry. Indeed alone. No Randy. Megan exhaled with relief, allowed her muscles to go limp, and felt her feet slowly drifting, as if riding a deflating balloon, to the powdered bench.

But Merry got there first, catching her ankles and holding

them up. The girl cleared the bench of powder with a dirty cloth. She balanced Megan's uncut heels on the edge as she freed her hands from the meathook. Again she was falling, scraping against the wall, but Merry got her arms around her, fell to her knees in the sawdust, and managed to lay her out on the bench. Although her hands were still bound together, Megan felt as if she had shed the most unbearable weight of her existence and she looked at Merry, weakly grateful even though the young woman was now engaged in lashing her prisoner's legs and upper body to the bench with the rope that had been on the hook. The blonde knee-walked toward Megan's head and looked at her sympathetically, even maternally. The eyes behind the tinted glasses were unworldly, as was the patronizing smile, and her voice sounded as if it had been directed from a faraway air duct. Merry was speaking, but her lips were not moving a lot. "Too much, *too* much," she kept repeating.

Megan realized she might be looking at her last chance for salvation. She tried to say the right thing. She came up empty, then looked again into the girl's spaced-out eyes, and uttered, "Thank you, Merry."

Merry seemed to appreciate this. "Rand's on a power trip," she breathed huskily. "He didn't use to be like this. Honest."

"I'm scared. What's he going to do to me?"

Merry sat back on her heels. She threw her head back so her bleached hair hung flush to the ground without touching her shoulders. "Nothing, I hope. He's all hot air, never hurt nobody before."

"But you called me about the boy who was kidnapped and murdered in Greenpoint."

"That was bait. Only. And Rand likes people to think he's a lot badder than he is."

Megan decided that Merry had come in to kneel beside her in need of intimacy. The confessional mode seemed to comfort her. She pressed on: "But there was someone else I heard you mention who's dead. J.P.?"

Merry smiled gleefully at the ceiling, keeping her eyes closed. "J.P. *is* dead," she said. "But Rand didn't do that one neither. J.P. did himself in. Rand just disposed of the remains."

"Why?"

"You bury your friends, right? Give 'em last rites, right?" She tittered at the pun. She touched her eyebrows, cheeks, lips, unseeing—as sunbathers often do. "Actually, as Rand says, it was a piece of business. We're doing some illegal trading here and it was necessary that we dispense with J.P. in such a way that nobody would know who he was. So we could finish our business. If J.P. had waited until tomorrow to die, we would of just called nine one one."

"What's tomorrow?"

"Tomorrow we go straight."

"And the business was the drugs he just injected in you?"

"Not *exactly*. That was my personal highball, a little speed, a little coke, a little morphine to slow it all down. *Lots* of vitamins. I'm into health, you know."

"Rand concocted that for you? He must be very fond of you." Megan tried to keep the irony out of her voice.

Merry stood up, nodding. She stretched with apparent contentment and began doing a little dance step around the room. She finished with a pirouette and curtsy. Then a cloud passed over her features. "He likes me when he needs me. Now he thinks he needs *you*. That's why I came back. Not because I'm jealous so much as I don't want you or him to get hurt. If you get hurt, he gets hurt, I get hurt. See what I mean?"

Megan thought she did. She braced herself and tried to keep the conversation going. "Well, he certainly seems like an *interesting* person; sophisticated, creative, and all that."

Merry opened and shut her eyes. She broke into girlish laughter. "See, he fooled you too. He fools everybody. Says he went to Harvard Business School, uses all those big words and technical terms. He's from Greenpoint, can you believe it? He's a Polack, like me. Only I come from Jersey. Jersey City. The part

under the Pulaski Skyway. Rand used to joke that that's why he's
always on top of me. . . . Get it?''

Megan gave an obligatory chuckle. Her neck was now stiff
against the bench.

"Two Polacks. I used to be Marie Kuzma. Which had already
been changed from Kuzmitsky. Can you believe it? Why *bother*?
Rand was Casimir Ronald Pulaski. Changed our names so we'd
sound American. Like you. You change your name?''

Megan shook her head, testing the muscles in her neck.

"A lot of people do. But I guess you're not the type. You
were born with the silver spoon in your mouth. It took me five
years to get my silver spoon, after I was Merry Pace, and it turned
out to be a coke spoon.'' She produced the implement on a chain
hanging around her neck from inside the sweatsuit.

"Why do you use the drugs?'' Megan asked in her kindest,
most concerned voice.

Merry thought about this a while. She sat on the end of the
bench. She took off the glasses. Megan saw that she was not only
stoned, but she had funny eyes to begin with. One iris, the left one,
was off color, and looked ever-so-slightly away from her subject.
Megan, when she had been a housewife in Scarsdale, had had a cat
with an eye like that. She called him Uncle Wiggily. After the
Salinger story.

Merry said, hesitating, "Nobody ever asked me that question
the way you just did. Like you cared? You do *care*, don't you?''

Megan forced herself to maintain eye contact. She nodded her
head and smiled as warmly as she could, considering she was
half-naked, flat out, and tied up on a hard bench. Merry seemed to
take in at that moment at least a portion of her discomfort, reached
forward and readjusted the bra, covering her up. Merry whispered,
still leaning over, "You care, but nobody ever called you Polack,
did they? Never told jokes about you for a whole party. Never
didn't give you a job because of your name.'' Merry's breath was
spearmint.

Megan thought, with a sinking feeling inside, that it was far more likely that Merry's funny eye and general air of not exactly having her feet on the ground had lost her the jobs, not the name. And Rand could have been a Rockefeller or Kennedy and would have still ended up a sleazy crook. But that didn't make her own predicament any better. "Merry," she pleaded, "let me go. I don't want to be hurt either."

Merry didn't hear her at first. She appeared to be practicing baton-twirling, then did a little tap dance. "That's what they expect girls to do to get ahead when they're Polacks in Jersey City. Twirl the baton. Tap dance. Fuck. Best you fuck a fireman. The Polish like firemen, I never figured out why. You can bet your ass Rand didn't want to be a fireman, spending his days off fucking graduates of Lily Kowalski's Performing Arts Academy. Lily Kowalski was Miss New Jersey Lions Club once. So Rand came to the City like I did. Like, I went to beauty school in the day and waitressed at night, Rand tended bar, did some dealing, in daytime. And he went for accountant at Baruch at night. But he got screwed."

"How?" Megan had resigned herself. Maybe the longer Merry talked, the more likely she would be to cut the ropes.

"He was doing some really small-time stuff with these doctors. They all just got out of med school and owed the shylocks and they would answer an ad that Ronald . . . I mean Rand . . . placed in the *Village Voice*. For docs to write scrips. They did, but it was Rand who did time. Probably because he was a Polack without an M.D. after his name, you know what I mean?"

"Sounds like a good time to get out of the business," said Megan, not without sympathy.

"Right," Merry agreed, floating around the room now like a child who had to go to the bathroom. "But he met J.P. at Lewisburg and they hit it off right away. J.P. had the . . . or used to have . . . the druggist's license, the credentials. He also, being a spade, knew better connections for moving the inventory. Rand had the idea of opening the drugstores. But," she paused and sucked her thumb for a minute before going back into a vigorous drum-majorette routine, "but there was a problem. People noticed. I mean you go to these brownstone neighborhoods with all the lawyers from Manhattan and you got zoning freaks, ecologists, busybodies, whatever. What you got especially is people who don't seem to distract easy. They want to know what you're doing there. When they find out they call up some bigshot to complain. Too many drugstores, they might say, not enough fresh pasta stores. Like that. Or no Landmarks Commission design approval. You go to, say, down by the docks or some shithole where there's garbage dumps and no people, the cops have their hands out. You run into an honest cop, which is unlikely, then you get busted. There's other neighborhoods—Howard Beach, Bensonhurst—the wiseguys control the action. You can't give perms in your kitchen without paying a percent."

"So Rand had a good idea?"

"Well . . . it seemed good at the time. We noticed when we were doing a small deal in Bushwick that these Black Muslims and P.R. Pentecosts was having some kind of fight. All they thought about was one another. You could of put Macy's on the corner and they would of not noticed. So we started to take beat-up storefronts in these down-at-the-heels religious neighborhoods. That worked okay, but you had to wait for these people to start fighting, or know they were fighting in the first place. You run out of neighborhoods after a while. Then Rand saw what happened when this Jew was supposed to have snuffed this little rich kid in Greenpoint and he decided he could make things happen himself. About the same time, J.P. was fading out of the picture and we had to make a killing fast."

"And Rand cuts the beard off the Hasidic guy in Borough Park."

Merry blinked. "How'd you know?" This display of omniscience on Megan's part seemed to rattle her. She began to fidget, move toward the door.

Megan saw she was losing her. Too smart for her own good, too inquisitive again. She made a last plea: "Merry, I said I didn't want to get hurt. *Help* me, please. You want to. Why else would you come back after *he* left me for the night?"

Merry's good eye flashed intelligence. She looked at Megan with sadness. "That's right. I forgot. It's getting too heavy now. J.P. hurt himself, but somebody's going to get hurt and I'm to blame."

"Let me go."

"I can't. What if *he* finds out? You think *you're* scared?"

"Tell the police. When they have him, then he can't touch you."

"Sure."

"You can't leave me here. Like this."

"Why can't I? It's better than hanging on the hook with the chance of freaking out on that powder when it gets into the cuts."

"Thanks."

"Here," said Merry, removing four red pills from her pocket. "I brought you some Seconals. So you could sleep. I'm sorry I forgot a blanket but it feels warm in here." She shivered. "It is warm, isn't it?"

Megan intoned: "Tell the *police,* Merry. It's not only my only chance, it's yours."

But Merry was leaving. "Right, I'll think about it."

"How will I know?"

"Swallow two of these. You'll forget about what you know for a while." She placed the pills on Megan's tongue, then held the can of soda to Megan's mouth so she could drink. "When you wake up tomorrow, either Rand is here or the cops. That's the *best* I can do."

CHAPTER 26

DR. FRIEDMAN LIVED in Midwood, farther out than Park Slope, so he was being dropped off first after they left the aquarium on Nostrand Avenue. The doctor slumped back in his seat and asked, "What ever happened with those Hasid cases? The little boy in the bed-frame box in Williamsburg and the guy with the Succot plants and scissors in Borough Park?"

"We're still working on them," answered DeSales. "In fact, we don't know if it's a coincidence or not, but the same guy who leased the building we just left also took a place across the street from the Borough Park restaurant, so *that* may be related to *this*. God knows how or why. And Desmond here's been working overtime; he spotted a guy in Prospect Park who resembles the Greenpoint kidnapper. We've managed to trace him to a homeless shelter in the city. Tentative I.D. makes him a drifter from Pennsylvania who likes to dress up Amish."

"So he's *not* Hasid then. Phew. That's a load off my mother's shoulders." He turned to Desmond and looked oppressed, knitting his bushy eyebrows. "My mother *lives* with us. She's eighty-five and remains what they call a constant presence."

"Your mother's religious?" asked DeSales, surprised.

"No chance. My mother's been a Trotskyite, a Stevensonian liberal, a supporter of Eldridge Cleaver. She gave up on politics after she had to choose between Gerry Ford and Jimmy Carter. Now she's obsessed with the Mets and AIDS testing. Thinks it's a violation of First Amendment rights. But religious, *never*." He turned to Desmond again, as if the Professor's presence required explanatory footnotes. "We keep kosher on the High Holy Days, but it's more tradition than religion."

"So why the interest in the Hasids?"

"She *hates* them. My grandfather came through Ellis Island from Russia so we could be free, not just to be Jews but to mingle openly, not be cut off from the rest of the culture. Freedom, she says, includes freedom to be clean and not wear woolen suits on the Fourth of July. She says the Hasids allow the rest of the country to be content with an image of Jews as arrogant, unwashed separatists. This is bad for Jews and also bad for America. Particularly, it's bad for the Friedmans. My brother, see, has a son he named Forbes. After the magazine. The Capitalist's Tool, right? Forbes Friedman. My mother's grandson. He goes to the best private schools in the city when he's little. Then when my brother retires to the North Shore, on the Island, the local schools aren't good enough for Forbes. So Shelley and Harry send him to boarding school in New Hampshire where maybe his roommate will be a Forbes, a *real* Forbes." He poked Desmond in the ribs. "Guess what happens then?"

Desmond shook his head. Friedman went on: "Forbes does a year at Brown. Ivy League. Then he joins the Lubavitchers. Shelley has a nervous breakdown. Harry goes to his country club and the guys in the locker room call him Tevya; he walks in the room, somebody whistles 'If I Was a Rich Man'! My mother wants to hire a deprogrammer. Forbes, now called Moshe, won't speak to any of us. Last time I saw him was on a street corner in the Village. He was button-holing people, saying, 'Are you Jewish?' "

"That's too bad."

"What does it mean?" Friedman asked Desmond, pulling on his sleeve. "The young people today. I have two daughters and a son, all teenagers. Some of their best friends aren't Jews." He snorted. "So, if you don't have to worry about drugs or drunken driving or rapists, you gotta worry they'll get religion. They should have TV commercials warning against it. 'Do not get in a Mitzvah Tank with this man.' Hare Krishnas; charismatics; this guy I read about in Oregon, the Indian with violent sex orgies and sixty Rolls-Royces—my mother read that sixty percent of his followers are Jews who went to graduate school. And the Christian right wing. They got nuclear weapons already. What's the world coming to? Even the *schwartzes*, you see that poor kid out there today. Thinks he's some kind of Messiah."

Desmond hesitated, then saw the man was essentially serious, required an answer. He shrugged. "They're all *afraid* of freedom. Don't want it. Freedom is the world. So they circle the wagons against the world. Siege mentality. I suppose it's a form of paranoia, but the rigid structures of these movements give them a sense of comfort, of security."

"It's like being a member of a street gang, no? Or the Mafia."

"You ever hear of," asked Desmond, "a work called *The Gang*? By a guy named Thrasher. Published in the nineteen twenties?"

"No."

"He says street gangs are largely an immigrant phenomenon. They represent ethnic groups in transition, waiting to be 'assimilated' into 'normal' society. These people today are like street gangs turned inside out, or around. They're rejecting assimilation and the sense of American Normal."

"From Murder Inc. to the Messiah," said Friedman. "Definitely a step backward."

"Who's to say?" asked DeSales. "The FBI guys at Quantico work on the assumption that there's more violence today because we're a more transient society. Crime adjusts to the environment. The more stranger-to-stranger contact we have, the more space there is for criminals to move into.''

''I didn't ever think I'd hear you supporting a fundamentalist revival, Frank. A deassimilation.''

''I didn't. I only said what I hear from the FBI.''

''Good old Brooklyn, always a hotbed,'' said Friedman, getting out of the car and heading across the spacious lawn, through the elaborate planting to his rambling Victorian frame house.

''What's *your* religion?'' asked DeSales as they headed back toward the park on Ocean Avenue.

''None,'' said Desmond.

''I mean, how were you raised?''

''Mixed-up. German Catholic and Anglo-Irish Protestant. When my parents started to argue about it, they just gave up on the issue entirely, so I wasn't even confirmed in a church.''

DeSales was quiet for a while. Here, buildings that had been boarded up only a few years ago were making an attempt at a comeback. Church Avenue was thronged with people. Most of them were black, but they had a comfortable, even prosperous, look about them. It was easy to imagine that they were carrying their loaded shopping bags back to expensively renovated prewar apartments they had bought through the Redevelopment Council. DeSales remained introspective, not interested in the world outside the squad car. He spoke again: ''You talk about freedom and paranoia and stuff like that. You in psychotherapy?''

''Just group now, but I've done couples for a few years and I was analyzed a long time ago.''

''So *that's* something you believe in. Like religion.''

''Not exactly. When it doesn't work for me, I don't think of the God That Failed or anything. More like the Little Engine That Could. Or Should. How about you?''

''I'm shopping around,'' said DeSales.

. . .

An hour later, Francis DeSales studied the map of Brooklyn on his office wall. There he rediscovered something of which he had first taken note some years before. The borough, reduced to its outline, resembled a man's head in profile. He still found nothing particularly intelligible or significant about this—like most things it merely reinforced his sense of the empty randomness of the universe—but it did seem striking how well the details of his original observations, upon close inspection, reinforced the pattern he had discerned. Bay Ridge was a prognathous jaw. The waterfront at Bush Terminal looked like so many filed-down teeth. The old Navy Yard, with its branched pier, constituted eyeball and eyelashes above the nose of Red Hook. Williamsburg was a furrowed brow. Greenpoint was a 1940s pompadour. All looking wistfully toward Manhattan. Above the head, graveyards and foul creeks demarcated the border with Queens.

Pressed to make an I.D., DeSales mused, one might say that Brooklyn looked like Dick Tracy or Fearless Fosdick, A detective searching for meaning in an enigmatic urban sprawl that cried out to be made intelligible.

He turned and faced the room. It was populated by Kavanaugh, Shultz, Colon, Jackson, an unhappy-looking and emaciated Maceo Allen, and a large cheesecake from Junior's.

Allen said, "Let's get on with it. I've got a long commute."

"You sold the apartment uptown?"

"Wife wanted to move to Connecticut. Near Westport. We got a good price on the apartment, found an affordable house, and we're saving fifteen thousand a year on private schools because the public schools there are safe and sane. We're also, except for domestic help, the only nonwhites in the community. Mixed blessing."

"That's why you're not eating?" asked Kavanaugh. "Getting in shape in case the Ku Klux Klan is waiting when you get off the six-o-five?"

"My condition, I'm unhappy to say, is the result of too much cholesterol and too many martinis over the years. Doctor's orders. Clean up your act or die.''

"Gee, that's too bad,'' said Colon.

"The only thing not too bad about it is that you can bet it's going to happen to fat-ass Bernie within a few years. Then we see if he gets his rocks off making racial wisecracks anymore.''

"In the meantime,'' said Kavanaugh, mouth full, "all the more cheesecake for me and Dutch.''

"Open up the file,'' said DeSales. "The faster we do this, the faster you get home.''

"We ran the data through the National Crime Index and I think we found him.'' Allen pulled some papers out of his overstuffed briefcase. "You guys had the wrong spelling and the wrong first name. It's not Jack Schwartz. It's Saul Jacob *Swartz*. S-W-A-R-T-Z.''

DeSales looked at Kavanaugh. "How did you miss this, Bernie? I told you to try alternative spellings and first names.''

"My computer doesn't have the same search mechanism his does.''

"And,'' Allen smiled for the first time, "it doesn't have the same operator either.''

"That monster you got, a monkey could hit the keys and it would do the job.''

"Please,'' said DeSales.

Allen looked at his papers. "We have this Swartz on record because he caused a stir in the District of Columbia a while back. He attacked a kid in the men's room of the Lincoln Memorial.''

"How successfully?''

"Not particularly; made this six-year-old take his pants down, started to beat him. Then the kid's father came in and restrained Swartz, calling the police. When they did get him to trial, he was declared unfit and sent to the psycho ward, St. Elizabeth's. . . .''

DeSales butted a cigarette in the heaping ashtray and walked back to the wall, behind Shultz and Kavanaugh. He stood next to Colon. "Wait a minute. I'm losing my touch. Before we hear the sad details of this creep's life, do we have anything concrete linking him to the guy Desmond spotted? Or to Noah Simmons?'' Allen threw a grainy black-and-white photo on the table. "I had this sent up on the wire from D.C. I also took the trouble on my way over here to drop by and see the priest at the mission. I.D. positive. This is the guy who used to think he was an Amish elder and showed up yesterday in need of a shave and a haircut, wearing old army clothes. Known as Jake. Only, of course, this is some years ago.''

DeSales picked up the picture, glanced at it briefly, and circulated it among his men. It was not the kind of face he needed to dwell on: a young man with the lopsided cheekbones and dead eyes of the terminally abused. With a bad case of zits. The kind of a kid who ran from a fight, but tortured cats and made younger kids pull down their pants. There was one in every neighborhood.

"And,'' Allen continued, "I pressed the priest a little more than your boys did. Maybe he's just afraid of the federal government, is Father Dougherty; maybe he has some well-earned scorn for the NYPD; maybe the NYPD handles him with kid gloves.''

"Midtown North handled that, Mace,'' said DeSales. "You know it's out of our jurisdiction, our quality control.''

"Of course.'' Allen winked conspiratorially. "If my men and yours, and *my* computer were in charge, crime would disappear from the streets altogether. Maybe. Anyway, the *padre* allowed us how Swartz used to camp out on the West Side Highway when he hung out in the neighborhood.''

"At least there's no kids up there . . .'' Kavanaugh began.

Colon interrupted. "Wrong again, Bernie. I grew up in Hell's Kitchen. I got family back there now. All the kids, the rollerskaters, skateboarders, break dancers, badasses, hang out up there. It's like a playground except, because it's officially off-limits to anybody, it's out of everybody's jurisdiction. There's even a bum's shantytown up there and the gays from the trucks under the highways sometimes come up for a little action. And the dealers. My nephew Espirito calls it the Wild West.''

DeSales said, "Call Midtown North again and try to get somebody who's awake to check it out."

While Shultz dialed, Allen went on: "I do intend to spare the irrelevant details. I want to get to what makes this trip worthwhile to me. The drug bust. But this guy Swartz is a classic loner, outsider, with self-destructive and antisocial tendencies. Mother died early. Grew up in a kind of Tobacco Road setting without much supervision by the father, except for regular applications of the strap. Had a sister, and when the father split, the sister was picked up immediately by concerned neighbors, but nobody would touch our Jacob with a ten-foot pole. So his grandparents took him for a while, but they were strict Christian fundamentalists. Church of Universal God. Hellfire-and-brimstone sect. No drinking, dancing, sex, whatever. He didn't last long there. Got himself shunned by the church for some unstated sins. This made him a complete outcast in the community, which he probably was already." The FBI officer scratched his nose, then the woolly hair, which was now salt-and-pepper. His trousers were too big for him and he had to pull them down where they had ridden up on his thighs. He interjected, "Ever notice how these misfits who are officially cast off or imprisoned by social institutions are already de facto out of it. The institution is always behind the reality."

"Present company included," said DeSales.

Allen pursed his lips and continued. "They sent him away, to a trade school for orphans. It was mostly black, and the black boys treated him sort of rough. He retaliated with a switchblade and ended up in reform school, where I guess he finally got used to bending over in the showers. Since he got outa there, it's been downhill all the way."

"Starting at the lowest point possible to begin with."

"The reason he's in New York is that he made one move to get out of the drifter's world. He got married to a woman he met at a carnival. She was a Brooklyn gypsy. They had a child and Swartz abused him sexually, then beat him; the wife called in her brothers and they damned near killed Swartz. Father Dougherty says he's got a lot of scars you don't see in that picture, and a funny way of walking, like somebody's been punching him in the nuts for a long time, and a tendency to talk to himself . . .''

"That fits with Desmond's description."

"This family stuff landed him back in court here. I don't know how you guys missed it, but there was an order put out to keep him away from wife and kid and he was remanded to Bellevue for a while. Been quiet the last two years, though. Think about it, a guy like that wandering, homeless, through the wonderful world of bus terminals and hobo camps and children's playgrounds and national monuments. Nice. So that's it." He began to put papers back in the briefcase.

"So if we don't get our hands on him on the Highway, you got any profile might help us anticipate his next move?"

"Our Behavioral Science Lab at Quantico routinely does these things. On demand, for me at any rate. But I didn't even bother to send it in. I just got back from a seminar on freaks who kill young boys—in London—and I think I have a pretty good line on this guy."

"Yeah?"

"We were studying two mass murderers. This guy Gacy from Chicago and a guy in London named Nilsen, Dennis Nilsen. They each had a taste for teenage boys primarily, took them home, got them defenseless in some way—usually with drink or drugs—and then tortured and killed them, buried the bodies in the basement or backyard or hacked them up and flushed them down the toilet. It was an important seminar because this sort of thing is stacking up as the crime of the last quarter of the twentieth century. Think of the guys who have been caught in the last ten years having killed dozens of boys and gotten away with it. And, for a long time."

"But," said DeSales, "that's different from this case. In a number of respects."

Allen held up his palm. "Hold on, Frank, I'm aware of that and I'll get to it in a minute." He pulled a notebook out of the briefcase and turned some pages. He put his nose against a page and squinted at his scrawl. "Here it is. Schizoid types. Abused and/or abandoned by father or father figure. Driven as an adult to master, to control environment, because childhood experience was so out of control. It's weird: the killer identifies in his subconscious both with the abused child that he was and with the abusing—and withdrawn—parent. So he's alternately attracted to, and scornful of, the boys who remind him of himself. He identifies with them, wants to love them, but the form of love is usually punishment. The punishment begins with mastery. It's speculated that one of the reasons Gacy and Nilsen kept these boys' corpses around the house so long is an ultimate refusal to discard *themselves,* whom they've just killed symbolically in the person of the literal victim." Allen fidgeted in his pocket, brought an immaculate handkerchief out of the chalk-stripe suit, and wiped his brow. "Now I know this is a mouthful and I know that our man Swartz is only alleged to have kidnapped *one* helpless child. And he killed him before he had any opportunity for the sexual play or torture that these guys had. But the transcripts from St. Elizabeth's are remarkably similar to courtroom psychiatric evaluations of Gacy and Nilsen. Personally, I think the only difference is that Swartz is too much of a coward to mess with anybody who reminds him of the teenagers who picked on him wherever he happened to be, and probably his big traumas came before puberty—with his father—so he picks on defenseless little kids. But the big difference is in his organizational abilities."

"Say what?" Colon looked uncomfortable.

Allen laughed without humor. "It's Quantico lingo for the types of killers we've studied. The Gacys and Nilsens of the world are on the surface remarkably well organized. Jekyll and Hyde, if you will. They're not split personalities per se, but they have a neatness and drive which enables them to hold down jobs, even with success, for long periods of time, though they will blow it occasionally. They have homes or apartments that they keep up fastidiously. This provides them, both literally and figuratively, with the structure within which they can actually get away with murder. And they're helped along by the proliferation of runaways and abandoned children in this country whom they can prey on. There's just enough freedom—or anarchy—around for them to exploit.''

''And Swartz?''

''Here's a guy who only fucks up. His sociopathy is forever incomplete. He's so shunnable that he never gets a job, has no home. You could say that he would have already killed a lot of kids if he only had his own place to take them. Instead he's left with random unconsummated acts of passion.''

DeSales looked intent. ''You mean he's a schizoid who can't get out of the closet because he doesn't have a closet of his own?''

Allen grinned. ''That's a nice way of putting it. But here's another. The costume fetish. The Amish business is only the most recent, as I understand it, of him pretending he's something he ain't. Gacy and Nilsen both had this in, once again, more organized ways. Gacy was an honorary cop and played the clown in parades. Nilsen was always in some uniformed job or another. Swartz has pretended to be a Green Beret, a priest, an Amish elder who was mistaken for a Hasid. It's all denial of self. They can't stand who they are, what they are, and they dress up to disguise themselves. At the same time, whenever they can, they're murdering, destroying their own self-images: the 'bad boys' who never won their father's love.''

''Fascinating, as usual. But what do we do with it?''

Allen shrugged his shoulders. ''I didn't promise you a rose garden.''

''I know, I know. But maybe you noticed something less, well, theoretical in the file. Something concrete. Like the swimming pool in Greenpoint or the yeshivah?''

Allen snapped his fingers. ''There is, now that you mention it. This guy Nilsen, the London mass murderer?''

''Yeah?''

''He had a kind of fetish about his corpses. He always gave them a bath. In fact,'' Allen raised both eyebrows like Groucho

Marx, "he liked to get in the tub with them from time to time."

"And what has that to do with Swartz?"

"Figure it out. He takes the kid to a locker room. At a swimming pool. And it happens that one of the biggest problems they had with him at the institutions was about baths. He wouldn't take one, but when they got him in the tub, they couldn't get him out. It turned him on. Now, one of the speculations about Nilsen, who was vociferously antireligious, is that he was indulging in his own homemade purification ritual."

Colon interjected, "The Hasids do it to their women. Make them take a ritual bath regularly 'cause they think they're basically unclean. Women."

"That's why Megan Moore had it in for that rabbi the other night, but let's get back to Swartz."

"Just don't get caught alone with him at the baths." Allen chuckled, standing up. "Now," he took a bulging envelope out of the briefcase, "I want my goodies. Here's the twenty-five grand. Give me the battle plan for tomorrow. The FBI needs to position itself to reap the glory."

"Hector," said DeSales, pointing a finger.

Colon took the Reagan mask and cowboy costume, chaps and spurs and suede vest included, out of a shopping bag.

"Dutch."

Shultz took out the map of Prospect Park and spread it on the table.

"This is the Nethermead." DeSales pointed down, then traced his finger along a narrow meandering line. "And this is the Haunted Ravine."

CHAPTER 27

THE WOMAN HAD ON METAL bracelets and earrings and necklaces that clanged together as if she were some kind of Salvation Army Santa Claus calling for attention. She wore a hot-pink sweatsuit. She had the earphones over her ears so others had to listen to her noise while she could listen to somebody else's. And she wasn't even really running. She merely sort of lifted herself off the toes and balls of her feet so she wasn't exactly walking and she wasn't quite a jogger either. But the movement caused her ass cheeks to wiggle and her tits to jiggle enough. She was getting the attention.

Swartz's place on the bench on Prospect Park West was maybe ten yards away, but he could tell that she probably stank of perfume and that the high color in her cheeks was really makeup, designed to show off the red headband that held her hair in place. No sweat for this one. Another phony.

He spat on the sidewalk. More of the phonies were running by in fancy shirts and satin shorts and hundred-dollar shoes. Their Saturday morning in the park. You'd think they had a patent or something on the Only Way to Live. Yuppies, they called them.

He wanted to go after them with one of the knives he had lifted from McTavish after the crazy Scotchman tried to throw him out. He let go another hawker.

The dike who thought she was commanding an aircraft carrier made a grunting noise, then moved as far away from him on the bench as she could. She wore tan Class As and a cap with blue and gold braid on the peak. Her hips were about three feet wider than her chest. She looked like a toy he had once, the only toy he'd ever really enjoyed. It was this Shmoo, from Little Abner in *The Sunday Patriot,* that you could hit as much as you wanted and it would still keep bouncing back up again to take another punch. The Commander gave him the look and he decided he'd better move on. Another phony. In their costumes, every day was Halloween.

Swartz shuffled toward the Plaza, heading into traffic. Cars swerved to avoid him, leaning on their horns. One, a gypsy type, yelled out the window, "Fucking hippie freak."

The thing was, Saul Jacob Swartz had an idea. Somewhere over the years, he had lost track of himself. It was as if somebody had given him the Shmoo that one Christmas and he had slammed it until it was him rather than the toy that had been knocked silly, not waking up until today. He finally dodged out of the traffic, under the arch that looked like the place the army had marched under in Paris in the World War II movies, but had a plaque about the Civil War and he knew that was right too. He had been fighting a civil war himself all these years and he had forgotten that all he needed to fit in was a home to return to.

A place to have guests, to have the kids in the neighborhood visit. His father had never let any other kids in the trailer where they lived. The tables were never pulled in and there wasn't room. And his grandparents *never* had visitors. Visitors would have gotten their dirty feet on the rugs and their dirty clothes on the furniture and Grandma never let anybody in until Grandpa had died and then you wouldn't notice anybody there anyway because you had to look at Grandpa in the casket dressed up by the undertakers. He wore a polka-dot tie, with pancake makeup and rouge on his cheeks. No gumboots. Not like he was real.

Swartz remembered where he was going and followed the crosswalk to Plaza Street. With the light. He stayed away from the big doorman buildings, hugging the fence on the dog run, past Vanderbilt, Butler, to St. John's, where he knew the buildings were mostly abandoned and he could get himself a sort of starter apartment, squat a bit while he looked for something more permanent. He could get custody of his kid.

He turned into St. John's Place off Plaza and did a double take. He couldn't remember when he had last been there, summer or winter. The seasons, years, had run together. Like a creek with waterbugs. Things had changed. On the left, the big welfare apartment houses with the ripped-out mailboxes and graffiti and the rat-poison signs in the lobbies had newly sandblasted façades, glassed-in entranceways and doormen. There were large clean signs on each building: THE MEWS AT GRAND ARMY PLAZA—BEAUTIFULLY RENOVATED CO-OPS. On the right side of the street, the smaller buildings, which had had jagged holes for windows and bricked-in doorways, were being restored. There was a sign there too. It was centered discreetly over the center house, which appeared to be ready for occupancy. SAINT BROWNSTONE'S AT SAINT JOHN'S, it said. THE CONDO WITH THE DIFFERENCE. SEE OUR MODEL NOW!

Swartz sensed first the silent emptiness of the street and then realized there was a police cruiser up at the next corner, Underhill, with lights flashing, as if deliberately setting up a barrier between St. Brownstone's and the ghetto beyond. Where Brooklyn descended into Bed-Stuy and became piles of garbage and burned mattresses on the sidewalks and dusty men in the doorways. Encouraged by this sense of sanctuary, he made his way cautiously toward the model house. There was a hand-printed cardboard sign on the door: "Sorry we're not here to guide you through the first unit of St. Brownstone's but our staff is honoring the Jewish

Holiday. See you on Sunday!'' Swartz checked Underhill, but the cops over there were looking at smoke gushing out of a sewer hole. Back toward Plaza, the people they called yuppies were going home, carrying bagels and the *Times*. He turned the knob and the door swung open. It was a small apartment, really, not much bigger than the trailer in front of the barn off Route 22, but it was certainly plush. The wall-to-wall carpeting was deep enough to sink into; the kitchen had exposed brick; there was a fireplace and a living room with a round glass coffee table and a big leather couch. And the place was empty of people.

He was in the bathroom. It was at least as large as the living room. He could see himself in the wall-size mirror. It was the first chance he had to look at himself since he had fled McTavish's hut, taking with him the crazy bastard's knives and the outfit he was wearing. McTavish should have been dead a long time ago.

Swartz was startled to see that he *did* look like a kind of hippie, a hippie Uncle Sam or Abe Lincoln, with the long hair and the stars-and-stripes hat and the colors on his face. He remembered for the first time in a long time the day he tried to find out about the past at the Memorial in D.C. and instead had been swallowed up by the Institution. Like Jonah by the whale. Now he had become what had eaten him up. Saul Jacob Swartz was American History, only damaged, like the little kid in the picture with the musical pipe and the bandages and the crutch.

The one in the picture he had seen at Valley Forge, at the beginning of the tour that had ended in Brooklyn.

Then he saw the bathtub, gleaming white porcelain, deep and pure. He turned on the water and let it run until it was warm, watching it swirl down the drain.

At Saint Brownstone's. His smile was lopsided and afflicted. A place where a man could entertain.

Voyez vous les Zombies là
Les Zombies et les loups-garous

The children, an assortment of fidgeting pumpkins and spacemen and ghouls, marched about her in a circle. "Now repeat after me," Mona Desmond called:

Madame Zombie elle est méchante

Those children who had paid attention in the nursery-school music class—there were not many of them—repeated with glee:

Madame Zombie elle est méchante

Mona waved her finger, encouraging more responses.

Mais sa soeur est plus méchante

The children sang:

Mais sa soeur est plus méchante

Mona did a little dance. The children who could not pick up the words hummed. The others kept up their garbled French:

Mais sa mère est la plus méchante

Then the kids were shouting. When the next part, about the werewolves, was over, they lapsed happily into bedlam. There was talk about headless horsemen and Dracula and Thruster Renegades. And a lot of chasing.

Mona had to finish her preparations for a pitch to the client on Monday, so she gathered her coat, changed her heels for her running shoes, putting the former in the shopping bag she carried in the same hand as her briefcase, and went over to kiss her boys good-bye. Nick was trying to sit dutifully on Tim's lap while he had his shoelaces tied. As usual, Nick was doing his share of squirming. Tim gently but firmly held him in place as he double knotted the lace of the flailing sneaker. The sight of the tininess of her son, his curls, his flawless complexion, his puppylike squirming in the lap of the very large weatherbeaten man she had married, gave her a kind of thrill. She had it all: motherhood, marriage, career.

Nick was saying, "What are we going to do if one of the monsters tries to grab me? One tried to grab Christopher last year."

Desmond crossed the index and second fingers of each hand, and made a demonstration of waving them in front of an imagined attacker. "Just like we said, do this and he'll back off."

"Is that all?" Nick looked skeptical.

"I'll tell you what," said his father. "Let's get ourselves appointed honorary Ghostbusters for today." He produced two Ghostbusters badges from his pocket and pinned one on Nick's costume and one on his own jacket.

Nick's face lighted up. The freckles seemed to shimmer in the reflection from his eyes. "Great idea, Dad. I love you." He threw his arms around his father's neck and scrambled onto the floor, squirming again as his mother planted a big kiss on his forehead.

"Take care, Lamby," she said, then pecked Desmond on the cheek. "You too, big man."

"No sweat," said Desmond.

Nick had pulled the robot mask down over his face and now looked like any other four-year-old wearing a shiny metallic box over his body and multihued visor over his face. Desmond paused, holding Nick's arm and adjusting the visor for him. "Remind me again, Nick. Which one of the Transformers are you?"

Nick was indignant. *"Daddy,* you saw the movie with me. I'm Optimus Prime, the leader of the Autobots."

Desmond had indeed seen the movie, but had lost track of the plot within minutes and the characters soon thereafter. It had been one of those rainy Saturday afternoons when fathers sit in darkened rooms with their sons and dream of other times, other places, while still deriving warmth and tranquillity from the proximity of the alert creature they helped bring into the world.

"Oh, right." Desmond pretended to remember. He narrowed his eyes. "And is an Autobot a good guy or bad guy?"

"*Good!* He can lift four million pounds and his waser rifle can burn a hole in a Decepticon fighter and he has a spare station and Roller. Roller is the buggy that slips behind enemy lines. C'mon, Dad, let's go."

The three of them stepped onto Prospect Park West. Desmond and Nick headed for the 3rd Street entrance to the park. Mona began to walk back to the Plaza for the subway to Manhattan. She wondered what she had been worried about, chiding herself for being overprotective and hassling Tim about the Haunted Ravine business.

"Good-bye, Mom."

She turned to wave good-bye and, in doing so, noticed that one of the new red-and-white sneakers was still untied.

"Your shoelace is undone," she pointed.

Tim blew her a kiss and waved her away. "He'll live," he said.

CHAPTER 28

DE SALES FELT LIKE a general. Patton maybe, or MacArthur. This fantasy had been prompted by the plaque informing him that he was crossing a woodsy depression called the Battle Pass, where a major incident had taken place during the Battle of Long Island in 1776. On his way to the high ground overlooking the bridle path and ravine, the military analogy was heightened by the phalanx of armed Urban Park Rangers on horseback who were lined up on the drive between the ravine area and the Nethermead. It was neatly wrapped up by the fact that he was deploying a dozen of his own men, in and out of uniform, through the rough terrain, backed up by a communication center in a police van. The key element, he had decided, was to form a series of concentric circles around the focal point, the purported dealer in the Reagan costume. He had also decided that he needed the youngest and fastest men for pursuit. Since he was neither of these, he had decided to wear the disguise. Around him would be Colon and Jackson, each in casual clothes pretending to be attached to one of the families. The next line of resistance would be the uniformed police whom he had arranged at lookout sites wherever a gap might exist. Half he sent to elevated lookouts; the other half near tunnel entrances, the crumbling stone stairs near the big bridge, and at each end of the bridle path. All the roads and paths entering the area except one—through which the parents and kids would enter—had been barricaded. On the periphery of the area, the mounted rangers would spread out. The place would be sealed up tight. Especially with the western and southern approaches shut off either by water or by the new fencing around the construction sites where they were rebuilding the ball fields and the old fence around the Quaker cemetery. Once they got their hands on the guy, he wasn't going to slip out anywhere.

Then the FBI agents, mingling patiently with the crowds, like vultures waiting for carrion, would pounce.

They had paid for the privilege.

Tim and Nick joined the stream of people winding through the Long Meadow, heading for the feeder path to the Nethermead. They passed the pools on the left and the waterfall and ugly tall fences that separated them from the playing fields on the right. But there was no hurry, no rush. Nick pointed at the costumes with glee, then punched his old man—the designated code—on the knee and the two snapped their fingers, did their little dance, and sang together:

> *If there's somethin' strange*
> *In your neighborhood,*
> *Who ya gonna call?*
> Ghostbusters!

Nick laughed heartily.

Then he crossed the fingers on both hands and directed them toward the beckoning wood.

Swartz was confused. All his normal routes through the darker fringes of the park were closed down, inaccessible. And he had forgotten about the fencing around the fields where the kids played football and baseball and soccer and which were now just a big mudhole. And then his heart had almost stopped when he had climbed under the cemetery fence and then walked through the hillside of unremarkable tombstones and back under the other hole in the fence and through a thicket of trees and there in front of him was the powerful black horse and the rider in frock coat. The rider with the long sword and no head, only a flat, blood-splattered stump for a neck.

Then he remembered why he was there. The Halloween Extravaganza.

From inside the chest of the Headless Horseman, a tiny voice spoke: "What are you doing up here, Eddie? The graveyard exhibit is over above the ravine, just after you go under the drive. You better hurry up. They're setting up now; the kids are going to start walking through." He pulled back the black sleeve and peered at his watch through the eyeholes cut just below the bloody cross-section of neck. "At noon, I start swooping around waving the sword and thundering up behind people."

Swartz nodded his head, wondering who Eddie was, if he was another historical figure, then swept back the greasy locks of his wig and touched his white cheeks and blue eyelids as if he were making sure he was all there. He knew where the ravine was. He set off, skirting the edge of the open meadow, which he had only seen used before by blacks and Puerto Ricans who picnicked there and washed their cars on summer weekends. A section of the open area had been fenced off and he saw buckets of floating apples lined up with carnival games. He was taken back to the Carlisle Fair again, then carried away immediately, as if by a witch on a broomstick, to another Halloween. It was a party in a chilly damp grange hall where he had entered his first apple-bobbing contest and the older boys who were in charge held his head under the water so long that he thought he would drown. So he flailed away at them desperately, spilling the bucket over the floor. This had given Herman Hefflefinger, the football star, cause to take him out into the parking lot and club him to the asphalt with his fists in front of a cheering circle. Then when they had left him to walk alone back to town, he had instead found some soap in the boys' room you entered from outside the basement and he had soaped the windows of as many cars as he could, including Hefflefinger's, and that was when the police started coming around. That was when he had been afraid to go to school without the switchblade. Then, another witch-flight, and it was the weekend he had taken off for D.C., on his historical tour. He had hitched from the Harrisburg bus terminal to Carlisle, where they had the grave of Molly Pitcher, and then down to the Battle of Gettysburg, and on to Valley Forge, and then a trucker had taken him all the way to a bridge along the Potomac and he started to walk to the Lincoln Memorial and he was shocked to find that the nation's capital was all niggers. At the Lincoln Memorial he had caught the young punk in the boys' room writing "fuck" and "suck" all over the mirrors with the soap and had started to punish him and the kid's father; then the cops had come in and the tables were turned again and somehow it was he, Swartz, the innocent traveler through American History, who got punished instead of the bad boy.

They put him in the nuthouse that time. And that was where it was like Job and Jehovah and he found out how, if he persisted long enough, his suffering would end in a kind of sweetness.

He had only felt the sweetness fully once, with the boy named Noah, and he had never had time to enjoy it because *they* were after him again. He had wanted to with his own kid, but the Gypsies had put the evil eye on him.

CHAPTER 29

MERRY PACE WAS REVIEWING the new set of cassettes that had arrived at Video-Rays the day before when she and Rand had been in Brighton Beach. She chose a French import first, something called *In the Heat of Saint-Tropez*. She had already dropped a Darvon and found herself feeling a little fuzzy as she opened the case and inserted the tape into the VCR. So, before she pressed the play button, she found a vial of coke, laid out some lines on the tabletop, and snorted them off. Like a vacuum cleaner. This picked up her clarity considerably, and she turned on the TV and hit the button and the movie started. She was standing there, feeling a little silly, a little guilty for having been nice to Megan. Rand was going to raise hell when he found her lying on the bench, off the hook. Merry giggled in spite of herself. It would ruin his Mickey Spillane trip.

The movie started. After the credits and one of those hysterical European rock soundtracks, there was a shot of some guys digging a hole in the sand of a beach while another guy with a handheld movie camera was shooting them and a director with a beret on was giving orders. A movie within a movie. Original. This was all in

French; they hadn't bothered to dub it because you could get the idea without knowing the words. Then a tall woman with not much in the way of tits and a broad ass took off her bikini and got in the hole. The diggers dutifully refilled the hole until only the woman's head remained above level. She looked a little grim. One of the diggers was an Arab with sores all over his neck and the other was Swedish maybe, blond, with an earring. The director and the cameraman were short froggie types. When the last spade of sand had been dropped, the director came over, opened his fly, and knelt down in front of the woman. He stuck his cock in her mouth and manipulated her head by moving her ears with his hands. Then having put his hands out on the sand behind her for balance, he proceeded to fuck her head. Merry had seen many scenes like this before—except for the beach-burial angle—and participated in not a few, but she had never thought about it that way. The guy was fucking the girl's head and didn't even have the decency to take his pants off. This was why they called it *giving* head. He came pretty fast, all over her face, and was followed in turn by the cameraman (the director held the camera), and then the two diggers. Then having head-fucked her and ejaculated in her ears, hair, eyes, nostrils, mouth, they hopped in a car and drove away, leaving the woman behind, still buried. The camera that was doing the real filming switched to a long shot. A fat old bum was staggering along the beach. The camera zoomed in on him, then on the woman's head. He got the idea immediately, so he dropped his pants and squatted over her. After some disgusting business with his ass and his fat belly, he also fucked her head. The starlet kept her eyes closed for this one.

Merry Pace couldn't swallow.

She switched off the tape. She had had enough. It wasn't just that the scene in the film reminded her of Rand. It was that she was in the business of renting films like that to people who weren't much better than the bum on the beach in the movie. She was part of the system. So she decided to walk. And she did. She tossed the cassette back in the box it came from, went back upstairs, and took a decent share of pills and cocaine and packed the stuff in her shoulder bag. While doing so, she took a Diet Pepsi out of the fridge and sipped cautiously, making sure she wasn't going to gag or throw up. It felt okay, so she did one last Darvon and headed back downstairs and out the shop door onto the avenue. She didn't bother to lock up. She wasn't coming back and she actually hoped some smart dude would help himself to Rand's stash and his Universal Gym equipment. She almost went back in and got out the box of X-rated cassettes to take them up to the Catholic rectory where she could donate them to some charity for horny old monks. But instead she drifted calmly in the direction of the precinct house. There was a uniformed female officer at the desk, a black one.

"I want to report some crimes," said Merry Pace.

The cop looked skeptical. "Any particular ones first?"

"Not necessarily. Kidnapping, drug dealing, maybe murder. Like that."

The officer looked imposed upon. She dialed a couple of numbers without success. She shuffled some papers. She said, "You picked a lousy time. We got nobody available right now. Stepped-up security all over the borough. Everyone's on overtime. Lookit me; I worked three out of the last four shifts. Slept on a bench. Come back later?"

Merry shook her head. "I don't think that's a good idea. Once I start something, I like to finish it. And this could be urgent."

The cop held her head in her hands. "I'll do the best I can."

Merry had an idea. "I think the best person to handle this would be that guy they call the Saint. DeSales."

"He's downtown. Violence Task Force. Here, I give you the address."

Merry shook her head. "No, I'll wait here."

"Okay, sweetie. Why don't you sit on the bench over there and as soon as a detective is available, I'll have him see you."

Merry headed for the bench but never made it. She was distracted by the photos of wanted criminals on the wall, and lingered there, seeing if there was anyone she knew.

·   ·   ·

Megan Moore emerged slowly from her Seconal-induced sleep and had a little trouble orienting herself. There was the sawdust, the grimy walls in the half-light from the dirt-encrusted skylight. It must be daytime. It was Tomorrow. Brave New World time. Randy or the police were coming to get her.

This was the sort of thing that was not supposed to happen to people like Megan Bradford Moore. She had been raised to be protected and surrounded by gentility. Had she simply stayed in the suburbs or moved back into her parents' milieu, she would have married again; conceivably she would have only good things to look forward to. Like her mother, who had preceded her in all other life experiences—at Miss Porter's and Vassar, married at St. Bartholomew's to a Wall Street man. She might even have had children. By now, nearing forty, she would have every expectation that the kids would be off to boarding school and visits abroad. She, Megan, could look happily forward, like her mother again, to a peaceful existence divided between an Upper East Side pied-à-terre and the condo on the Gulf Coast of Florida, fawned over by closet fags, with a closetful of Lily Pulitzers. But instead she had wanted independence. She had chosen the excitement of the electronic media. At least something exciting could have happened on the job, with her boots on, as it were—like crashing the traffic helicopter in the East River and becoming a martyr to the cause of Drive Time. But instead she was lying in a disused butcher shop, in her underwear, no boots at all but cuts on her naked soles, waiting for the original Polish Prince to return and induce her to beg him to put—as she was sure he would put it—the *meat* to her, to *pork* her, not to mention numerous illegal substances that she was sure were capable of leaving her something like demented. Like her mother again. Full circle.

Sometimes sardonic thoughts gave Megan ease, but these were not working. The fact was that she was cold, scared, alone, and enormously resentful. She had been abandoned by every man—and not a few of the women—she had ever trusted. She had worked her way through that—in her therapy and her career—and she had come up empty.

Then she heard the shuffling sound outside and she even forgot that she had to go to the bathroom. There was the tinkle of broken glass, then voices. Her teeth began to chatter.

She heard for an extended period of time from the outer room a sound that resembled heavy furniture being moved around. There were some yips of elation, then deep masculine laughter. Then there were hands on the locker door, and the long tantalizing creak it made as it swung open. She turned her head, forcing herself to directly confront the visitor. If it was Rand, she would intimidate him with threats; if the police, she would squawk for DeSales's scalp.

But it was neither. In the doorway stood two very black men wearing the sort of velveteen suits she had always associated with pimps and other unsavory characters of the night. One of them, who appeared to have the authority, was an extraordinarily large fellow with a shaven head and fingers full of rings. The other had a haircut that looked like a block of steel wool, a ring in his nose, and a semiautomatic pistol in his hand. This second fellow said, "Oh, my. Looks like our boy Randy fixin' to sweeten the pot."

CHAPTER 30

THE WITCH WAS WORKING the crowd. She wore a tall pointed hat and a black gown. Her face was gray, the nose shading to green, and there were red crosses on her cheeks. She flourished her broom and from time to time made a foray into the line to menace some particularly eager-looking child. The miniature devils and spacemen standing around the barrel-stave fence in the Nethermead crossed their fingers and shrieked with panic-ridden delight. The witch spotted Nick Desmond and approached him, wiggling her fingers in front of her. Her voice had an eerie, nasal pitch. "Here is a little boy who thinks that he will not be eaten because he is made of nuts and bolts and can transform himself into a Mighty Vehicle!"

Nick nodded, not without hesitation.

She loomed over him. "Still you must beware the Haunted Ravine! No one returns whole from the Haunted Ravine!" She cackled maniacally, pointing a blackened finger at another child farther along.

Tim knelt so he and Nick were level, and put his arm around his shoulder. They resumed their precautionary rap:

If there's somethin' weird,
And it don't look good,
Who ya gonna call?
Ghostbusters!

Then there was the thundering of heavy hoofbeats and the Headless Horseman materialized from the forest. The horse whinnied, standing almost erect on his back legs, then charged for the crowd. Crossing his fingers and laughing, Nick ran out to head off the interloper. Desmond experienced a moment of indecision, torn between admiration for his son's bravery and his paternal instinct to protect him. Just as he poised himself to dive and sweep Nick out of harm's way, the rider pulled back on the reins and the stallion swerved away from the crowd and back in the direction of the ravine. Desmond watched the disappearing horse intently, then his eye caught the movement at the top of the far hill where a solitary ranger on a white horse, armed, looked them over. Then he noticed the pumpkin-colored sign that had been posted near the head of the line, decorated with clumsy drawings of bats and jack-o'-lanterns:

THE HISTORY OF HALLOWEEN

Organized as a Pagan feast on October 31. The Pagan celebration honoring the dead Druids marked the day by inviting souls of dead evil people to find out if these dead had redeemed themselves. But the name Halloween comes from the Christian feast day of All Hallow's Eve celebrated on May 13. Eighth-Century pope Gregory IV changed the Christian feast from May to October to counteract the Pagan celebration. Dressing in costume and Trick-or-Treating became popular in the 17th Century as people went from house to house singing and dancing to keep evil spirits at bay. . . .

The juxtaposition of the law-enforcement officer and the printed historical word—printed words with an affinity to his own studies— induced in Desmond a sense of ease that he rarely ever felt, particularly in a situation like this. He had asserted himself with Mona about bringing Nick to the park and ever since he had felt deep in his subconscious a kind of guilty dread that doing what *he* wanted, getting *his* own way, would inevitably end in some disaster. Because he had taken responsibility.

Nick was wrestling with a werewolf about his own size and a larger girl dressed in pink taffeta. The line lurched forward and Desmond called, "Let's go, Nick, we're in the next group."

Nick ran up, beaming, pushing forward so energetically that Desmond had to restrain him from knocking into the people in front.

"Oh, Daddy," he piped, "I can't *wait!*"

DeSales, wearing the ten-gallon hat, Reagan mask, and chaps, cut in line as prearranged. He was only about ten yards ahead of Desmond, but the mask severely limited his peripheral vision and he didn't notice the professor and his son. Instead, he concentrated on keeping just behind the curly brilliantine gloss of Colon's head, and making sure that Jackson, dressed in a baggy old Brooklyn Dodgers uniform, gabbing with a black woman and children as if they were his own, was just behind him. They passed through the dark tunnel under the Central Drive, fending off the various ghouls and goblins who reached out to harass them. On the other end, the sunlight, through the drying leaves and defoliated branches, was painfully bright. The ravine appeared on the right. There was a shallow stream that meandered through its depths occasionally marked by a Coca-Cola can or a Big Mac wrapper. Then the brightness dimmed as the forest became thicker and the sun fell behind a hill. They were entering the Zone of Dead Souls. Hooded figures rocked and shuffled like asylum inmates in the crepuscular gloom, making low moans. It reminded DeSales of the last time that he had visited his mother at the state hospital ward. It also called up to him, equally vividly, the word pictures conjured from the pulpit by Father Angelini at Our Lady of Peace. In badly broken English. On All Souls' Day, the Day of the Dead.

Then the familiar voice from Megan Moore's answering machine was speaking into his ear: "Mr. President, I've got a *very* heavy drug problem. I wish you would have brought Nancy along. She's done so much good fighting that nasty old substance abuse."

The costumed detective turned his head slowly so he could look at the guy straight on. He was, like DeSales, about five-ten. He had a uniform that was a size or two too small and a real badge and long sideburns and a mustache. He had an official-looking .38 in his holster. He had the kind of eyes that suggested he'd been scared shitless more than a few times and had taken on a certain capacity for pitiless retribution as a result. In short, he looked like a cop. A Polish cop, confirmed by the name on the tag: Pulaski.

"I'm a busy man," snapped DeSales, "so can the fuckin' jokes. Where do we deal?"

"No offense, *hombre*. They got some coffins a way up the trail here. On the left. Dead witches and a midget vampire come back to life and rise out of them one by one. Every ten minutes or so. It gets the audience real turned on, real distracted by there. There's a bunch of trees right behind the coffins. You wander on up when the folks on line are going bullshit and we can play show-and-tell."

DeSales was working to sound like a vaguely Latin punk with no peripheral vision. It wasn't hard. "Hey, man, there's pigs all over the place. Even these ranger fucks. How I know they don't catch our act?"

"I've been here all morning. It's like a protected glade. They don't really see it. Besides, *I'm* in charge of covering the area. Helping citizens in distress. Like you."

"Timing?"

"You'll get there in about five minutes. Like I said, when the monsters come out of the coffins and everybody starts to scream, you just slip up the hill behind the trees."

"Check." DeSales and Colon had anticipated this dilemma. Did they just bust the guy right now or wait until they got to his selected rendezvous? They had made the right choice. There were too many kids around the pathway to take a chance on anybody getting hurt. In a secluded spot, there would be just DeSales and the perp and the close-tail detectives with weapons trained on the bad guy's head. And no civilians up close. They could wait.

The Ghost of America Past lay in the plywood box, regretting only that he had left his long knife sticking between the shoulder blades of the short teenager they had dressed up as Dracula. He wished he didn't have to jump out, make his point. There was something about being in the damp dark container there, about being sealed off, secure, that had something of the sweetness about it. It all but erased the bad days in Ono, Pennsylvania, and brought back instead the deep, warm vibrations of his grandmother's kitchen in the days before he was old enough to get into trouble. It was New Year's Day, Jack Frost on the drain pipes, pork-and-sauerkraut in the coal stove. And the woman was there he sometimes dreamed of who might have been his mother. There were no bad boys in the room. Only the women, the stove, the pretty curtains, and the bright patterned linoleum. But although it was sunny daylight it was also dark. Like the coffin.

The Desmonds were into it, along with the rest of the crowd. Nick leaped forward and backward like a bullfighter, moving with the bolder children as they repelled the repeated onslaughts of trolls and werewolves and zombis along the trail. Desmond smiled broadly. The performers weren't half bad, and his son's bravado tickled him. Then there was the woman some yards off the path with the bloated head and the housedress stained scarlet on the front who, after attracting their attention, turned slowly to full profile, revealing that she had been stuck through by a vicious-looking scimitar. At the same time, a figure swathed in bandages emerged from an upright coffin like he was coming out a phone booth and walked with arms thrust out before him straight for the unsuspecting Nick, who was still keeping a wary eye on the woman. He grabbed Nick by the shoulder. The child started, turned, and his face contorted with fear. But before he could cry out, the man pulled a section of bandage from his face and revealed that he was Bill Taylor, their next-door neighbor, who happened to be on the board of the Prospect Park Foundation. He winked, giving Nick a hug. "It's just me, kid." Nick shrugged off the scare, hugged Taylor's leg, then gave him a punch just to show even a monster doesn't mess with the leader of the Autobots.

At the next turning there were three gravestones set up at the heads of three long wooden boxes, painted gray. Each headstone had the name of a witch and a set of dates: Broomhilda, Cruela, Witch Hazel: 1530–1920, and so forth. The first coffin creaked and began to open. The children screamed, fell back, then the tiny leaders charged.

DeSales trudged up the hill. The rubber mask was hot and confining. The chaps made his legs itch. The loaded Colt .45 he had borrowed from the force's weapons collection hung heavy from his gunbelt. The mixture of shrieks and nervous laughter was behind him as he felt, rather than saw, the first coffin open. The phony cop was waiting for him in the clearing among the trees where even the dead grass on the ground appeared to have been sprayed yellow.

"You got another name besides Hector?" the cop asked DeSales.

The detective imagined his backups, weapons drawn, crawling toward them up the hillside. There was more noise from the crowd on the path. He slurred, "This ain't a business you want all your names known in."

The cop had an abrasive chuckle. "Know what I think? I think this is a leveraged buyout."

"Whassat?"

"Stock-market talk. I made a couple of fortunes downtown

235

before I decided to diversify into other areas. Means I think you're
the front man for someone else, someone much bigger. Like, I hear
the Archdioceses, the universities, the corporations are all over the
place looking for sound investments now they got to divest their
South African holdings.''

DeSales grunted. "So call me Cardinal O'Connor. If the
smart guys on top are buying in, why you selling out?''

"On Wall Street, we got another expression: the triple
witching hour. Ever heard it?''

DeSales shook his head. Or mask. The uniformed cop
smirked. "Didn't think so. It's the time when all your options and
futures expire at once. This happens to be my personal witching
hour. Time to move on.''

"Let's move it *on* then. I need a taste.''

The man who usually called himself Rand Furlong removed
three packets of powder and pills and an official-looking sheet of
paper from his pocket. "Here's samples of the dope and the
delivery invoice from the pharmaceutical company. The address
has been covered until I see the color of your money and we
finalize the details.''

DeSales took the packets in one hand, producing the envelope
with the twenty-five thousand in the other. Rand eagerly began to
count the money. At the same time DeSales felt himself go numb.
They had fucked up; he would have to take off the mask to taste and
this guy Pulaski might well recognize him and bolt before Colon
and Jackson had him properly covered. He tried to formulate a
delaying strategy.

Then all hell broke loose.

Dutch Shultz left the van that served as communications center on
the bridle path near the Old Elephant House and tried to find some
bushes in which to take a leak, leaving behind his buddies howling
with laughter at the Road Runner cartoon they were watching on
the portable TV. He found himself a convenient tree that sheltered
him from the ravine crowd and unzipped his fly. This was no easy

matter, as some of the most severe blistering from the sunburn had occurred there, and where it didn't hurt it was unbearably itchy. He finished and zipped up again gingerly, but hurt himself anyway at the last notch for he had seen something that distracted him. There was a body hanging from a tree along the bridge where the horse trail turned back on itself and away from the Halloween Extravaganza. This body had been there all morning and, in fact, Shultz had personally inspected it on his first reconnaissance of the area. It had a balloon for a head and a stuffed long pillow inside an old suit of clothes for a torso. But now it looked different, more weighty, not hanging from the branch so much as leaning against the tree trunk with the rope around its neck. He approached from the side and tapped it. It was heavier now, swung away from him, then back. The clothesline snapped and the thing fell into the blanket of leaves, sprawling at his feet. It was no longer a balloon and a stuffed pillow, but a real body. Made up as a vampire. On closer inspection, the Vampire was a male adolescent, unusually short and small-boned, with white paint on his face and his blond hair charcoaled and greased and brushed back into a kind of D.A. He was very dead. Shultz turned the body over with the toe of his shoe and saw that there was a butcher knife sticking out of its back.

The fat, sunburned detective staggered down the steep slope to the van. "There's a fucking corpse up there," he said.

"So what else is new?" asked Caruso, intent on the TV as Wile E. Coyote set an elaborate trap designed to ignite a quantity of Ace gunpowder when the Road Runner, on his merry way down the canyon, would trip it.

Shultz switched on the bank of two-ways. "Ten eighty-five to Sergeant! Ten eighty-five! Corpse on Hill 13!" he shouted into the mike.

Desmond watched the first witch crawl out of her coffin, then the second. He heard the crackling calls from the walkie-talkies and saw the armed men surrounding the thicket. Then a uniformed cop burst from the thicket at the top of the hill trailing greenbacks with a man dressed as Ronald Reagan in a cowboy suit, gun drawn, on his heels. He checked for Nick and saw him hanging out with the same gang of kids, now approaching the third coffin from which, apparently, Witch Hazel was delaying her appearance. He heard a gunshot, looked back up the hill, and saw the cowboy and the uniformed cop wrestle one another to the ground. One of the walkie-talkies was nearby now, and he heard the thick voice calling, "Ten eighty-five to Sergeant!" Cops and rangers were racing now from all over in the direction of the struggling men. The cop was pulled off the cowboy and knocked to the ground. He lay there, deep in the leaves, surrounded by a dozen angry men. There was a scream, this time a woman's, to the right, and Desmond, still fascinated by the scene being enacted on the ridge, turned slowly. Witch Hazel's coffin was open now, empty, and there was no sign of its former occupant. The second witch was trying to say something, a kind of gurgling in the throat, but was being ignored by the horde of children and adults who were running both toward and away from the melee on the hill.

Timothy Desmond looked for his son and couldn't find him. He dashed up to the second witch. "Somebody stole a kid," she was crying. "There was an impostor in Witch Hazel, an impostor in Witch Hazel." Desmond felt as if someone had kicked him in the chest. He ran as far as the last tombstone and found a sneaker there, one of Nick's red-and-white Pumas, the one he had forgotten to tie. He looked up toward the policemen and realized that before he could get through to them, it might be too late. He grabbed the witch by the shoulders. "It was my son," he gasped. "Who took him?"

"A nut. A nut with long hair and an Uncle Sam outfit."

"Where?" She looked dazed behind the makeup. He shook harder. *"Where?"*

Feebly, she pointed the false fingernail in the direction of the peak where not too long before the ranger astride the white horse had radiated confidence, warming the hearts of worried parents, the same ranger who was now huddled with the others around the fallen cop on the facing ridge. His horse was tied to a tree.

Desmond saw, or thought he saw, a man disappearing over this peak. A man carrying what looked like a shiny piece of machinery.

Optimus Prime.

There was no time to waste. Desmond began to run after them.

CHAPTER 31

BIG BIRD HAD NOT lifted a finger to help, but he was the one who made the gesture of wiping his hands as the last case was carried out of the storefront by the driver of the truck. "Well," he said, "there goes the last of Rand's Golden Parachute, Brother Sam."

Brother Sam, the tall man with the gun and the cubic haircut, nodded. "I'd like to be the fly on the wall when he bring the buyer here and the cupboard is *bare.*"

"Not exactly *bare.*" Bird leaned in the direction of Megan. "He still got the blushin' bride in there."

"No, sir," said Sam. "She's mine. I get the use of her for a while . . ."

"And then what?"

"What? She seen us already. Could be a host*ile* witness. Maybe we bring her around to our way of thinkin'. I done it before."

With their soft Caribbean lilt, they might have been discussing the weather instead of drug heists, abduction, rape, even murder.

Megan, who could not remember having ever been anything but alert and inquisitive, suddenly felt faint. She was trying to will unconsciousness on herself. Then, fighting against giving in, she squirmed on the bench to keep up the circulation, particularly in her lower legs.

Big Bird shook his head emphatically. "We in the pharmaceuticals business right now. You want women, you get them on the street, wherever. White women a dime a dozen these days. She, in there, is part of the merchandise here and as such must be accounted for."

"I do the accountin'; you better believe me, Brother Bird." He scratched his nose with the gun barrel. "Seem to me I'm *owed* a bonus."

"Tell you what," Bird said. "I got a fair solution. You go by the book?"

Sam made an uncooperative face, then gave in. "Sure thing."

"Then hand it over."

Sam removed a green pamphlet entitled *Old and New Black and White Magic* from his pocket and passed it to Big Bird, leaning in the entrance to the locker.

"Miss," asked Big Bird with the utmost gravity, "your sign, please?"

Megan stared at him, wide-eyed and speechless.

"I mean," he said, "can you tell me your birthday?"

She swallowed hard. "March seventeenth, St. Patrick's Day. Do you need to know the year?"

He waved off the question and turned the pages of the little book with his fat fingers. Brother Sam did not look hopeful. He sat on the floor with the weapon resting on his forehead and his face in his hands. The highly polished barrel and his flesh exuded the same ebony glow. "Ah, Pisces," said Big Bird, knowingly. "Here it is, the Fishes." He scanned the lines on the page, moving his lips, then marked a place with his thumb. "You hearin' me, Sam?"

Sam moved his head, but just barely.

Big Bird began to read: " 'Many Pisces people are inclined to be careless, and will lose and misplace articles. The women are careless housekeepers . . .' " He paused, obviously skipping over something he considered irrelevant, then went on. " '. . . Advice to them is useless, and they will listen to no one. The more they are talked to the more obstinate they become. They talk too much and ask all kinds of unreasonable questions . . .' " Big Bird had heavy-lidded, almond-shaped eyes. He lifted them slowly now, focusing on the wall above Sam's head. "Had enough? She's bad *karma*."

"Not fair," said Sam. "You only read the part about the lower plane of life. How about the lucky gem, the numbers?"

This, apparently, was the clincher. Big Bird glanced again at the page and said with finality: "*Blood*stone. Blue and *green* candles. Twenty-nine, seventy-three . . ."

Sam waved the semiautomatic 9 mm in a gesture of surrender. "I give up. What do we do with her?"

Big Bird looked long and hard at the mostly naked woman on the bench. "Not much when she's dressed like that. Might attract the wrong attention." He walked to the street door and hissed to the lookout on the sidewalk. "Get a tarpaulin out of the truck and bring it here." He turned back to Sam. "I'm sorry to say we'll have to wrap her up and dump her at the first opportunity."

Sam was resigned, coolly professional. "May I suggest the Rockaway Inlet?"

Megan began to shiver uncontrollably.

"Taste it," DeSales ordered Colon.

Colon opened the packet of white powder. He inserted his index finger, got some powder on the tip, and gingerly placed it on his tongue. After allowing his taste buds to savor it a while, he breathed, "Good shit."

Rand Furlong lay on the ground. He was outnumbered but

unvanquished. "You bet your fucking ass," he said. "It's better coke than what Merck used to make."

DeSales pulled the mask off his face and leaned over Rand, grabbing his ears, pulling him rudely into a sitting position. "Good enough to put you away for a long time," his eyes wandered to the name tag, "Officer Polack Pulaski. Or do you have another name?"

Rand blinked, his eyes showed recognition, then pure hatred. "Fuck you, Superwopcop, I got your girlfriend, Megan. I played with her tits already. Saw that big bush. You don't let me walk now, her pussy is chopped liver."

DeSales had, at least in part, built his career on his level-headedness. Few cops had managed to resist the inevitable violent impulses that come with the job as consistently as he had. He also realized that this was *precisely* not the moment to commit an indiscretion, as he was under extensive public and collegial scrutiny. But he no longer cared. A scumbag is a scumbag, he thought. He took the Colt .45 out of the holster, spun the chamber for a moment, and suddenly, without warning, whipped Rand across the cheek with the long barrel, tearing flesh and knocking away the false mustache.

Rand put his hand to his cheek, felt the blood, the deep gash. Now he was popeyed with fear. DeSales leaned forward, gun poised to strike again, and bared his teeth. "You don't talk right now, Officer Krumpki—where your stash is, who you are, where you got Megan Moore—and I'm going to make sure you bear a close resemblance to the guy who's been riding around here on the horse, the one who's got a pizza pie where his head ought to be."

Rand looked around in disbelief, searching for some humane, at least ceremonial, gesture of cautious intervention from one of the men who surrounded him. Nobody batted an eye or made a move. He sighed, felt his cheek again, and said, "The broad and the dope are in the same place. On Brighton Seventh Street. Off Brighton Beach Avenue." He gave them the number.

"Take him and get some squad cars to that address right away," DeSales said. "We'll finish this guy later. We've got a hostage situation out there, and that's the priority." He looked about, mentally ticking off the men he would take with him, the message he would send to the nearest precinct. Then the thought struck him: "Hey," he asked, "who the fuck was that yelling a ten eighty-five on the walkie-talkie when we were all set to make a nice quiet private collar."

"It sounded like Shultz," said Colon.

"Where is he?"

"In the communications van."

DeSales took the walkie-talkie and barked, "Shultz?"

The voice crackled back: "Yeah?"

"Where are you?"

"Over the hill here with the corpse."

"What corpse?"

"The corpse of the kid who was supposed to come out of the third coffin."

"What does that mean?"

"It means that the kid got stabbed in the back and was set up to look like the dummy they had hanging from a tree here."

"But . . ." DeSales couldn't finish. A woman, panting, burst through the circle of onlookers. Her hair was messed from the witch's hat she had tossed off and the white, gray, and green makeup was smudged together. Her nose was clean because she had been wearing a false one.

"Someone else was in the third coffin," she gasped. "He came out raving about American history and grabbed the nearest kid, a kid dressed like one of those Transformer toys, a robot, and just picked him up and took off with him."

"Nobody else saw this?" DeSales was incredulous. "We had half the force here to prevent something like this from happening." He threw the mask down on the ground, then the gunbelt. "The kid doesn't have a family?"

A number of people began talking at once. One of the rangers said, "Everybody heard the walkie-talkie alarm and gunshot and saw you wrestling with the guy and we headed this way."

The witch caught her breath. She said, "The kid had a father. He chased them. That way." She pointed easterly, toward the zoo, and the Vale of Cashmere. "Everybody thought it was part of the act; they laughed. Then they were distracted by what was happening up here."

A man completely wrapped in bandages spoke with authority. "I know who it was. A neighbor of mine, Tim Desmond, is the father. The kid in the Transformer suit is his son, Nick. He's four years old."

"The kid was singing 'Ghostbusters' and the man who grabbed him was dressed like Uncle Sam in the 'I Want You' poster," said another man, defensively, as if that excused everything that had happened.

"Jesus Christ," said DeSales under his breath. Suddenly he was conscious of how foolish he must look, standing in a cowboy suit in the middle of the woods with a woman dressed like a witch continuing to point and say, "They went thataway." He also knew he had some very big, very quick, decisions to make.

Hector Colon was leaning over him. "C'mon Frank, where do we go?"

"Split it up." He hesitated, then picked up the speaker again and told the communications van to radio the adjoining precincts with an APB for the Uncle Sam guy with the little robot. Then he ordered the highest-ranking ranger to take charge of the corpse that had been hanging from the tree. It was his jurisdiction and the M.E. team and ambulance would be there in a minute anyway. "Half of us will go to Brighton Beach. The other half, plus whatever rangers you can spare, fan out through the park and also try to seal off at Flatbush and Eastern Parkway and Prospect Park West."

Colon said, "And me and you? Who goes where?"

DeSales hesitated. He had to make a choice. The little boy or Megan. He tried, as he had been doing since Roz turned him out, to play the Jesuit. That would mean he had to attend to the area where he had personal responsibility. And guilt. And, if you wanted to go that far, desire. The kid would live or he wouldn't live. The guy who had him was paranoid schizoid, not responsible for his actions. But Megan deserved special treatment. DeSales knew he himself was the guy directly responsible for her being taken by that Polack who made him feel like something out of the Spanish Inquisition. Jesuits again.

Shultz's voice was on the walkie-talkie again. Anyone within twenty yards could hear his crackling hoarseness: "Frank, we just got two emergency calls from Headquarters!"

"Yeah?"

"First, there's a woman—the one from the suntan parlor—says she knows where the Moore broad is. In Brighton Beach." He read the address.

"We got it already, Dutch. People heading there right now. I'm a little pressed myself. What else?"

"Some guy named Frick. From the Botanic Gardens?"

DeSales made a plaintive gesture skyward. "Yeah?"

"He says he's got the medicine you were desperate for."

"Which medicine was that?"

"Black snakeroot. Says you were going to give him a badge if he found out what it was used for. Thinks he's broken the case."

"He should have his neck broken."

"It's used for menstrual problems, hypertension, and schizophrenia. In tropical rain forests."

DeSales was silent, counting his troops.

"Frank," croaked Shultz, "why didn't you confide in us? About your monthlies. We coulda formed a support group."

The officers ranged around DeSales began to titter. Colon laughed out loud.

DeSales threw the receiver to the ground. "Colon," he said,

"you and Jackson laugh your brown asses over to Crown Heights. Try not to shoot too many innocent bystanders while you're saving Desmond's kid. I'll be at Brighton Beach."

Brother Sam cut Megan's bonds with a switchblade knife and stood her up. He held the blade at her throat with his right hand while patting her ass with the other. Megan tried to fight off the shakes. She clenched her fists and pictured herself as a nothing: a piece of merchandise at a fire sale. It took the emphasis off the tenderness of her corporal being. There was Method acting. This was Method captivity. Sam led her into the front room. She could now see the truck they had loaded parked at the curb, and the third black man, the laborer, leaning against it looking up and down the street. Big Bird was heading back in with a large, dark green cloth under his arm. There was a sound, indistinct, official, and the heavyset man with the rings stopped in his tracks and looked up the street to his right, Megan's left. He made a surreptitious gesture with his hand, as if he were scratching a cat under the chin. Otherwise he remained still, expressionless.

Sam pricked Megan's neck with the knife. "One move, you dead," he whispered and walked alone to the door. Bird made the scratching motion again and the taller man slipped the knife into his pocket, showed Megan where the gun was in the other pocket, how he could point it at her without it being seen. Then he joined his colleagues on the pavement. Megan recognized the sound now: a police bullhorn. The disembodied voice was saying something about alternate side of the street parking, about clearing the street. Then she heard the car-wash noise of the sweeper. Big Bird cupped his hands, calling out, "Delivery, officer." He indicated the other two men. "We's leavin' just now. One more package for the truck." Now he held out the fat palms in supplication. Sam looked sideways through the window, hand moving in the pocket.

Megan gulped, holding back nausea. She had to make a move. She could run out into the street and get the cop's attention. And get shot, to boot. A WASP sacrifice to the democraticization of big business. Or she could go for the trapdoor she had spotted in the meat locker and hope for the best.

The driver got behind the wheel of the truck. Big Bird cupped his hands again to continue his dialogue with the bullhorn, and she saw Sam's hand touching each weapon from outside his pockets now, shifting his weight, as if he were about to reenter the store. She spun around and made it into the locker, pulling the big door shut behind her. With all the strength she could manage, she pulled the heavy bench on which she had slept the night before up against the door. She bent over and, after a brief struggle with the handle, breaking three fingernails off at the quick, pulled open the trap. She heard a shout from outside. There was no time to determine whether this was merely a continuation of the conversation between Big Bird and the cop or whether Sam was already after her, on her tail.

An unhappy turn of phrase, she thought, that latter one, and dropped into the cellar, just managing to pull the door back into place above her.

She tried to suppress the part of her mind that was calling up dark fantasies of a floor teeming with vermin, soaked with poison to counteract the vermin, littered with nasty fragments of broken glass and rusty metal. Her feet ached in anticipation before she landed.

But the cement floor of the furnace room felt clean and her landing was smooth. She touched a wall, found some peeling whitewash, and followed it until she encountered a steel door. But she could not get the door open. She heard noise overhead: someone was trying to pry open the trapdoor.

She found the bolt, pushing it with one thumb and then the other until she was sure they were both bleeding. The trapdoor began to open. In one last desperate effort, she hit the bolt as hard as she could with her elbow. It gave. She was quietly closing the door behind her, left arm quite numb, as the light from the floor above spilled into the furnace room.

She was in the rear of the basement now, and there was light from a space where a window had been. She sprinted for it and barely pulled herself through, dusty now, knees bleeding from contact with the broken glass. She emerged into a well-tended garden of winter vegetables, confident that neither Sam nor Big Bird would be able to squeeze through the same space she had. Now she had only to find the civilized souls who tended the garden. From the fire escape over her head someone hollered. In a strange language, something Slavic. She looked up, smiling. The old wrinkled woman in the babushka was clearly furious. She hollered again, a word that Megan imagined was something like Russian for ''whore.'' The woman pointed at her with indignation, made a menacing gesture with her broom, then called across to the adjoining building. Another old woman appeared, looked at Megan with shock, and began babbling to her friend, fire escape to fire escape.

Megan cried: ''Please! I've been abducted.'' She pointed at her state of undress. ''Molested! Help me.''

The women showed no sign of comprehension. Their only response was a pair of icy stares. Then the second woman climbed in her kitchen window, reappearing on the landing with what looked like a softball. She reared back and released it. The cabbage landed at Megan's feet with a dull thud. There was cursing from the cellar now, then what sounded like a sledgehammer pounding on the crumbling walls. She passed under a grapevine, found a dark, dirty passageway between the buildings, and headed back to the street. When she tilted her head and peered out, she saw Big Bird and the driver still on the pavement, and Sam reemerging from the shop, his suit rent and filthy. She broke to the right, away from the direction of the cop and what she now saw was an avenue with an elevated subway running over it. Civilization. But civilization was blocked off by her captors. Instead she seemed to be dashing into nowhere, a horizonless cul-de-sac. She heard another shout and the pounding of heavy feet behind her. In front the wind was cold and stinging. She realized that the smell she had isolated from the cooking cabbage that permeated the backyard was the sea.

And then the buildings were no longer old-law tenements, but modern high-rises and she was on a clean, sandy beach. She was hallucinating: San Juan perhaps, or Rio. Winded, she slowed down and looked over her shoulder. Sam and the driver were legging it after her now. Perhaps it was Montego Bay. They had brought her home with them. But the wind was too cold and the beach too empty and the sense of commercial void and the Slavic voices of the women ringing in her ears suggested that instead she had slept for years and awakened in some totalitarian Eastern European holiday nightmare. The sand in the ocean breeze burned her eyes and nostrils and lips. She was about to give a last gasp, collapse on the sand, surrender herself to the black hoodlums, when she had a vision.

In this vision, a flying column of men and women, mostly aged, seminaked like herself, emerged from between two of the high-rises. The women ran hunched over, fists clenched. A few of the men rotated their arms and fell to the sand to do quick pushups. All of the women and some of the men wore bathing caps. Although wrinkled, their bodies radiated healthy exposure to sun and surf. One of the men carried a banner, reading, BRIGHTON BEACH POLAR BEARS CLUB.

Megan went down on her knees. The detachment of swim-suited senior citizens veered toward her. One of the women shouted, "It's Megan Moore from 'New York Live!' "

A laughing man called out, "Smile, you're on 'Candid Camera.' "

"Schmuck," said another. "This is no TV show. She's the one who was kidnapped. And she's *bleeding*! I heard it on CBS Radio. On Mary Gay Taylor's 'Crime Blotter' segment."

"In her step-ins," cried a shocked woman.

This was the first person to reach her. The woman threw a

towel over Megan's shoulders and cradled her to her warmth. "Poor dollink," she said. "Wha hoppen? Who *did* this?"

Soon Megan was completely surrounded by concerned Polar Bears forming a protective tent against hostile human and natural elements. The biting wind was gone. Through a man's hairy bowlegs, she saw that her pursuers had disappeared. Then their truck hit the street running along the beach on two wheels and sped away.

That was when she first heard the police sirens.

CHAPTER 32

LUNGS AND LEG MUSCLES burning, Timothy Desmond struggled up the grassy knoll near the main entrance to Prospect Park. For the third time, he had lost sight of Nick, and had only come here because a Chinese bicyclist, when questioned about a man dressed as Uncle Sam and a child as a robot, had pointed vaguely in this direction. Now Desmond looked over the Plaza and it seemed as if half the borough's four million residents had turned out here at once. The stoplight changed in front of the library, and masses of people, many costumed, poured into crosswalks on Flatbush and Eastern Parkway. Desmond's glasses were stained with sweat and tears so he wiped them frantically on his shirttails and then squinted into the throngs a hundred yards away. For a moment, he caught a glimpse of something, the metallic tinny sheen of Nick's costume—the child limping as if he had only one shoe—being dragged along by a man who himself had an unusual gait. It was the idiosyncratic pained shuffle of the Amish wanderer. As Desmond had suspected, and dreaded, Nick was in the hands of the same character his son had called "Zorro." Desmond was running down the hill and trying to cut across the Plaza and head them off when the police sirens started up and patrol cars came racing up Flatbush, around the monument, and spilled into the park and Eastern Parkway. Desmond flagged one down, shouting over the oscillating disharmony of the alarms: "I've lost my kid, he's . . ." The cop riding shotgun had his elbow sticking out the window. "That's who we're looking for," he said. "Relax and go home." They burned rubber pulling out. Then the Plaza was empty of cars for a moment and Desmond was able to sprint across to the corner of Underhill where Nick and the man had been headed.

But they were nowhere in sight.

The kid kept asking questions. Being a nuisance.

"When are we gonna meet my daddy?" he would whine. "Where's the toy you promised me?"

Then he would try to wriggle free. Swartz tightened his grip on the boy's wrist and yanked as hard as he could. Just as he used to do with his own kid when he bugged him. It was kind of a good feeling. So was being back on St. John's Place, what with the sirens on the parkway. St. John's, devoid of pedestrians or traffic, felt like a sanctuary. And it didn't hurt that he had come from the opposite direction this time. If there were spies, they would be fooled.

"This is it," he said, now soothing, as they approached St. Brownstone's. "Now you get your prize."

"And my daddy?"

"*And* your daddy."

Once again, Swartz regretted leaving the long knife behind. The short one he had concealed in his boot would have to do. Then the soothing thought of the gleaming new bath erased any concern he was feeling about sharp instruments. In his new home, there was the chance for a new start. The sinner—sinners—would be cleansed. He remembered the clean peaceful pallor beneath the layers of rouge on his grandfather's cheeks in the casket, the tub-shaped box. Swartz put his hand on the doorknob, but it didn't turn. He was about to thrust himself angrily against the door, when he saw through the window the four people standing around the coffee table in the living room. One of them was flourishing a brochure and talking rapidly. Buying and selling. Real estate. Invading the domain of the man who chose to be Plain, to wash away the sins of the world. He felt the rage swell within him and the inevitable terror following closely behind, rising into his eyes and ears and brain. "Mistake, mistake," he began to mutter and yanked the child again by the arm, desperate to get back into the Plaza. In spite of the sirens. There, the two of them could get lost in the crowd. The quiet street now made him feel undressed. His charge was defiant this time, pulling back as hard as he could. Swartz almost lost his grip on the tiny arm.

"*Daddy* . . ." the boy began to scream and Swartz shoved him against the wall and backhanded him across the mouth. The kid slumped to the pavement, lifeless. Sirens ringing in his ears, Swartz considered abandoning him, saving his own ass, but he had never had his own guest, never felt the sweetness except almost that time in Greenpoint. But the locker room had been too dirty and the showers didn't work in Greenpoint. So they weren't going to take it away from him now. He felt the boy's pulse. It was beating, if rapidly, and the flesh was warm. He picked up his burden and threw him over his shoulder, making as close an approximation as he could to the way a parent carries a sleeping child out of a car and into his bed. There were cops under the arch in great numbers but the sidewalk to the Botanic Gardens looked safe. In the Botanic Gardens, *if* they let you in, you could find time to think.

Desmond pressed forward, more and more aware that he was forcing himself into nothingness. Or forcing a nothingness into himself. The police were on the job; his responsibility was to find Mona, share the pain of waiting with her. But he could feel no possibility of sharing with her now. He had lost their son. He had taken a chance, against her counsel, and lost everything. So he followed a hunch. He ran up the stairs into Mount Prospect Park, where there was a playground, between the library and the Botanic

Gardens. It was a bad hunch. Neither white children, nor white men, apparently, used Mount Prospect Park. For he was the only one there. So, drawn to the gardens anyway, Desmond began to scout the hilly wooded ground that was separated from the sidewalk and the street only by a cast-iron fence with ugly spikes on top. The Botanic Gardens was where it had all started, where he had seen the strange corpse in the Japanese Temple, where he had felt so all-knowing about voodoo and superstition and Death-in-Life and Life-in-Death, where now in his mind's eye, he saw feet protruding once again from the shrine. And the feet were Nick's, wearing only one sneaker. Desmond, still carrying the other shoe, continued to rush along the steep terrain, through dogshit and rat-poison warnings, balancing himself by clutching at the saplings that studded the slope.

A montage of images clicked through his consciousness, a family holiday slide show composed of the photos Mona kept on her dresser: Nick, sleeping peacefully—for perhaps the last time in his life, they had often joked—half-a-day old in his father's lap in the hospital room. Tim, in the grainy black-and-white print, showing the strain of the twelve-hour labor at which he had ineffectually assisted.

Nick, now in color, still bald and diapered, astride one of his father's broad shoulders, sticking out his tongue.

Nick, three years old, curls tamped down, freckles vivid on a pink nose, swimming at the country house with yellow floats on his arms.

Nick, grinning broadly and cuddling a cardboard dinosaur in his arms . . . his official pre-school portrait.

Then Desmond began to go over the things he had missed. The weekends when he was writing and didn't want to go out to the park and play. The conference he attended rather than go to Nick's fourth birthday party. The . . .

He shook it off. Something had caught his attention, erasing the self-pity. Fifty feet away, across the unscalable spikes of the fence, Nick was being carried down Eastern Parkway, his chin resting on the man's scruffy shoulder, eyes shut, mask knocked askew. Blood seeped from the corner of his mouth. Lover's lips. Lips that pouted. Lips that were jolly. Lips that spoke his parents' names.

Desmond clasped the iron fence, standing stock-still, mute. He had, after all, foreseen this moment, anticipated a strategy. He had, it seemed a lifetime ago, decided that, when and if he caught up with his quarry, he would not alert him to his presence if possible. This would only endanger Nick: the sick abductor becoming the cornered animal, even more lethal. Desmond wanted to wait until the right moment, as he had seen hostage rescue teams do on TV a dozen times. Perhaps by that time, he would have the support of such a team, a cool character like DeSales to lead the way. But he could not have predicted the fence, the sense of impotence he felt behind it. He could not have predicted Nick's condition, which might be critical. And he could not have predicted the human surroundings in which he had discovered his son. This last item tilted the balance.

The formerly Amish lunatic was carrying Nick through a crowd issuing into and out of the Brooklyn Botanic Gardens and Brooklyn Museum. These were their, the Desmonds', own *people*. They were predominantly white, interested in gardening and natural beauty and the arts. They were educated. They were homeowners. They skied, jogged, played tennis. They were the new gentry, the people who had turned Brooklyn around, had made the streets of the old brownstone neighborhoods safe to raise children in again. It was easy for Desmond to make his choice. He yelled from behind the fence at the top of his lungs: "Kidnapper! That man stole my son! Grab him!"

Swartz heard the voice, saw the father pointing from behind the fence, and felt the old darkness begin to fall. He was trapped again. But he had the warm, tainted sweetness on his shoulder and would not relinquish it without a fight. He began to run, straight into his adversaries, head up to detect and ward off any blows. But, to his amazement, the people parted before him like the Red Sea before the Chosen People. The tormentors of his lifetime were routed. A woman with the hair and eyes of his first-grade teacher, the one who had sent home the first bad report, ducked, cradling her camera. A man with the beard of the psychiatrist in D.C. jumped sideways and made sure his wallet was secure. A host of them, like a chorus of angels in Easter-egg-colored sporting gear, merely stepped back with looks ranging from indifference to distaste. Swartz felt, as if for the first time, he had broken free.

It was a Sign. He was one with the Almighty. Better than Plain. Fearless now, he carried the boy at a slow trot down into the subway, the father's cries feeble echoes in his ear. At the turnstile, he barely paused, projecting the child's body across and jumping after it, gathering it up again, and darting into the idling train at the platform just as the doors slid shut.

The token clerk watched this without expression.

Desmond leaped the fence, tearing his corduroys and cutting his leg in the process. He followed the path of Uncle Sam and Optimus Prime through all the people who were minding their own business. This was, after all, *Brooklyn.* He passed close to the man who had jumped out of the way, protecting his wallet, put the heel of his palm into the man's beard and shoved. He didn't tarry to watch the man tumble into the gutter. He leaped to the bottom of the stairs, found a token, and inserted it and made it down to the platform. Nothing. No lunatic. No Optimus Prime. He ran back up to the token booth.

"Did you see . . ." He was speechless. He tried sign language, the man with the hat, the little boy.

The clerk peered out at him from heavy-lidded eyes, a polyglot man, the essence of Brooklyn, neither black, brown, white, nor yellow. Expressionless to boot. But he spoke before Desmond had completed his charade. "Yup. Took the Three train to New Lots. Just left. Didn't pay. I got a call in now. They's a cop gonna pick 'em up." He looked at his watch. "Maybe Franklin.

Nostrand for sure.'' He raised the eyelids. ''Of course, that's assumin' they don't change at Franklin. Could get on the Flatbush train there. Could go to the other platform and go back uptown, to the City.''

''Then what?'' asked Desmond.

''Then we lost 'em.''

''When's the next New Lots Train?''

''Here she is now.''

Desmond could do nothing but hope. The clerk buzzed him through the gate and he headed in a direction he had never taken before.

In the squad car, Hector Colon picked up the message from the Transit Authority Police. Suspect and victim had been spotted boarding the IRT number 3 train, bound for New Lots, at the Eastern Parkway–Brooklyn Museum stop.

''Any cops on the train?'' Colon squinted at the crowd in the Plaza.

''Nope.''

''They got somebody on the Franklin platform?'' Colon looked directly over at Jackson. Jackson held the map in one hand and the mike in the other.

''Someone going in now. Wait a minute . . . *Maybe* someone going in now.''

''Shit.''

''And what's after Franklin, if he stays on the number Three?''

''Nostrand, Kingston, Utica . . .''

''No-man's-land after that,'' Colon interrupted. He hit the accelerator and turned on the siren. ''I won't get to Franklin or Nostrand in time, but we can stop the train at Kingston. Dig?''

''I'm with you,'' Jackson concurred, still staring at the map.

Swartz felt the courage draining out of him—drip, drip drip, like the IV they had put in the last time they had him in a hospital. The black faces stared and stared, like they had at the trade school, figuring out ways to get to him. The kid began to revive. He squeezed him hard against his shoulder to stop the squirming, but a whimper, then a bleat, emitted from his throat. The black faces, they were all black, became suspicious. Swartz lifted the boy up, trying to stifle him without anyone seeing it, and checked out the subway map. He had no idea where he was going. New Lots Avenue conjured up for him an empty space where they might put a development, then some blacktop parking lots with churches on them. Something not like Brooklyn at all. Something worse. The glass over the map was cracked and splattered with graffiti. He was too frantic to read anyway. All he could tell was that he was headed somewhere only black people went. His luck had deserted him already. The train stopped at Franklin, the doors opened and stayed that way while another train entered the station, took on new passengers, and left. In the same direction, only it was a number 2. No matter; Swartz couldn't move. There was a fat nurse with a face like a gorilla on one side and a man in black leather on the other who looked like one of those giant warriors in *King Solomon's Mines*. With Stewart Granger. That had been the first movie he had ever seen. And the last, for a long time. After Grandpa found out and Daddy said, "Okay, you want to run his life, you keep him!" He now half expected drums to start beating and the warriors with the lips twisted up and coils around their necks to march in and string him up right there. The doors closed. The child began to cry. Swartz tried to smile apologetically and edge his way past the wary tribesman toward the door. He was more afraid of the nurse. He felt this humming in his brain, like he was surrounded by a cloud of stinging flies.

And the child was wailing louder and louder and the doors opened and he slipped out onto the platform and took the kid over to a bench where he pretended to be ministering to a sickness and then the other people that got off at Nostrand Avenue, for that was where they were, decided it was okay and headed up to the street. He wanted to throttle the boy. But he looked at the tear-swollen eyes, the split lip, and could not do it. He had lost the Shmoo, the soapbox-derby car, the boy the papers called Noah. He wanted to keep one, take him home.

Another train was about to pull into the station. He had no idea now whether he might be followed. To be on the safe side, he whisked the boy up again, climbed to the street, and saw the incredible blackness of Nostrand Avenue. The faces were African; the language of the signs was often not English; the most common sign he could read said: MONEY EXPRESS TO KINGSTON IN ONE HOUR. Where was Kingston? He headed in the other direction, began to run, head down, thinking that he would not look up until he could run no more. Then the Lord would deliver another Sign. Clearly he had descended into some infernal region and had to get away from it. He could now hear only the sound of his own breath, of his own heart beating.

After a while, he looked up and saw that he had entered another country. There were school buses and ambulances and buildings with signs that were not only not in English, they were not even written in the same script. Then he heard voices: the voices spoke a kind of version of the Pennsylvania Dutch Low German he had first heard in his grandfather's church, but here the accent was different, something about the phrasing too. He paused, trying to comprehend. He was surrounded now, by another strange tribe. These were white, could only be Devils, a final visitation of torment upon him. They were Jews, he knew; he had seen them before, but only one or two at a time. But here was the broadest of city sidewalks and the broadest of city avenues, completely full of them. There was not an inch to move. Instead of a massed brigade of naked Watusi warriors against him, it had been decreed that he should suffocate among the black coats and beards and black hats, and hawk eyes of these Jews speaking something like the language with which he had been shunned, having the same faces as those who shunned him. It was as if all the smothering rejection in the world had been gathered onto one street corner full of disapproving, alien eyes.

He had forgotten about the kid, who now cried out: "Help! He's not my daddy! He stealed me, he *stealed* me."

The horde of Jew-Devils, as if controlled by one simultaneous instinct, furrowed their brows in outrage, pointed the collective finger at him, and, as he turned away to run again, began their pursuit. Out of Israel, back to Africa.

When the train stopped at Franklin, Desmond yelled out to people waiting, asking if a man and boy in costume had gotten off the last train, any white man and boy, and received silent, negative shakes of the head. At Nostrand, there was only an old wrinkled woman huddled in a corner of a bench with her shopping bags. From her he received an enthusiastic, if possibly deluded, affirmative. Her finger pointed toward the street. He climbed the stairs to the open air. He looked up and down and saw nothing. He began to distrust the woman. He began to lose faith. The transplanted tropical environment invoked a kind of lassitude and, suddenly, he wanted to sit down, cry, wait for someone to take care of him as he had not been able to take care of his only begotten child. Disoriented, he strolled south on Nostrand like a window shopper. He looked into a coffee shop with a Codfish and Banana Breakfast Special; into a record store with a Bob Marley song playing over a poster in which were juxtaposed primitive portraits of Martin Luther King, Christ crucified, Haile Selassie (with dreadlocks), the Statue of Liberty. On the periphery, drug bottles full of grinning little skulls looked on at some particularly nasty-looking snakes. Ones that Nick would have loved. The painful present was forcing itself back into the center of Desmond's awareness. About to give up, he realized he would have to call Mona. But he dreaded that moment. He leaned against the Jamaica travel agent's window full of pictures of "*Rear* Tropical Birds": a lineup of naked buttocks, multiracial sunbathers basking in Caribbean glory.

Give up, he thought. Admit Nick is gone. Go home and face the music.

Then he heard the roar.

He turned toward Eastern Parkway, saw Uncle Sam carrying Nick like a broken doll across Nostrand with dozens of Hasids in hot pursuit. Abruptly, having reached the curb, the bearded men stopped. Desmond pushed through them, crossed the street in a couple of strides, and watched the man drag his son into a marqueed building with a façade that suggested a jazz-age Taj Mahal. Rushing in their wake, he looked back fleetingly and saw the Jews still standing by the curb as if held back by some invisible shield, ruefully shaking heads and prayer books.

Swartz ran through what had once been a lobby, knocking over the card tables with the Bible-study pamphlets on them. He opened a door that was little more than a sheet of unfinished plywood, the child swinging almost free of his grasp, and another miracle occurred. Having suffered so on earth, he had earned his place in heaven. Above him the sky was the brightest blue he had ever seen, peopled by a host of celestial bodies: scantily clad angels and naked infants with pink flesh. From the Scriptures. They were singing and the music had a harmony that was thick and slow and sweet, like the syrup on his grandma's waffles, a hymn that he had not heard in all these years. Then there was a shout and he was taken up by powerful hands. He was separated from the boy. He was knocked to the ground. There was a great weight upon him. The hands that held him down were black, black as hellfire. It was a test, had to be, a last ordeal at Saint Peter's Gates. So he submitted himself, lay back and warmed himself in the divine rays from the ceiling and the soothing sounds of the choir. Now the strong hands picked him up and carried him across a kind of stage to a large, deep, stone basin. Another ordeal. The hands released him and he plunged into the womb of water. It was his baptism, his true one. Here was a clean pool, no waterbugs, no apples bobbing. He closed his eyes, allowing himself to sink submissively to the bottom; then, inspired, he bounced back, began to rise to the top. He imagined himself climbing, climbing, until he burst through the surface, ascending beyond the black hands into the firmament, where he would become one with the pale, lustrous, melodic instruments of peace, of Plainness.

Instead he found himself confined to the font, his head just above water, supported by his knees on the bottom, his elbows brushing the sides. A mural had been painted on the marble above the waterline. Gray and burnt-orange and aquamarine, the souls of the dead wandered through an infernal landscape of smoke.

It was Resurrection Day, no doubt. Someone, a man, was speaking, a voice of timbre and authority. He spoke of the complete extinction of the unrighteous, the denial of rebirth to the wicked.

The men with the strong black hands had dark wooden faces and eyes of stone, the hands and faces and eyes of the boys at the orphans' trade school. Swartz felt more at home among the dead souls in the painting, however unforgiving and pious in their incumbent sainthood. He nodded his head slowly at the men with the stone eyes and showed his bare hands out of the water, an act of submission, an unspoken obeisance he had learned, it seemed, at birth. The men looked at one another, back at him, nodded their heads, and turned in the direction of the speaker, hands clasped behind their backs.

Swartz began to move his hand slowly toward the blade concealed in his boot.

"Why they got these huts around. With the bamboo roofs?"

"Succot," said Colon, the new expert. "Reminds them of the Exodus to the Promised Land. Out in the desert, under the sky, get it?"

Colon and Jackson sat in the car outside the Kingston Avenue Station. Discouraged. The kidnapper and boy had not been on the train.

A woman came running over to them. Colon knew she was a Hasid because of her wig. And because she was dressed like somebody in an old James Stewart rerun on "The Late Show." He thought of DeSales and almost smiled.

"A crazy man has stolen a little boy," she said. There were tears in her eyes.

"Where are they?" Jackson asked.

She pointed. "Our men chased them. The rebbe too. Back toward Nostrand."

Colon turned on the ignition and siren again. He ran a light at Brooklyn Avenue and then another at New York Avenue. At Nostrand he hit the brakes. They saw Desmond entering the building and the throng of Jews poised on the curb, pointing excitedly.

"Why did they stop running? Why are they just standing there?" exclaimed Jackson.

Colon's laugh was almost maniacal. "It's the fucking *string*," he said. "They all got their prayer books. They can't drop them, and they can't carry them out of their designated property."

He hit the gas again and swerved into Nostrand, effectively cutting off the Lubavitchers just as the aged, white-bearded rebbe came panting from the rear and shouted a dispensation, that the child's life overruled the Sabbath regulation.

But Colon was there first, waving badge and pistol at once. "Police," he barked. "You gentlemen stay put. This is *our* jurisdiction now."

There was muttering among the Jews and a couple made moves to cross the street, but Colon flagged them down.

Inside the car, Jackson was calling into the mike: "Ten-thirteen! Ten-thirteen! Send everything we got. Eastern Parkway and Nostrand. They're in that Seventh-Day Adventist Church that used to be a movie house!" Then he was out on the sidewalk with Colon and the two armed officers proceeded to the swinging door under the old marquee.

Desmond was in such a rush that he had first entered by mistake the Heavenly Bodies Health Club that adjoined the old cinema. He stepped back onto the sidewalk, saw the patrol car cut off the Hasids, then dashed into the dilapidated lobby. At an inner door, he hesitated briefly, then plunged through. He was almost blinded by the dome of brilliant blue sky over the center of the theater. Then he felt the viselike grip of two men, one on each arm. He looked at them, sputtering, "My son . . ."

The man on his right, whose skin was a hue somewhere between the color of his chocolate suit and black tie, raised a finger, smiling gently, to his steel-wool mustache and slightly parted lips.

Desmond couldn't move. He opened his mouth again.

"Be cool," the man said. "Everything's gonna be all right. Service almost over."

Desmond realized there was a preacher on the stage. The preacher was pointing around the building, at the disintegrating walls and ripped-out seats in the side aisles and the holes in the parts of the ceiling that had not been restored. Then his attention rested on the glitter of the brocaded cherubim and seraphim and angels in the azure sky. The speaker intoned, "Once again we are reminded of our earthly chores, even as we worship in our celestial retreat. We found this building in ruin, a pagan picture palace that had been sacked by the Huns, a testament to the crime and iniquity, the economic and moral inequity, which surrounds us."

The congregation, filling most of the center aisle, demarcated by glowing space heaters, chimed in a vigorous chorus of amens. Desmond heard an odd discordant note from the electric organ on the side of the stage and saw Nick, smiling through tears, sitting comfortably on the lap of the woman organist. Nick pulled at the flowers on her hat, then hit another note. The woman chuckled; the congregation uttered another, unsolicited amen.

The preacher went on: "Like I said before many times, this building is a symbol of our predestined role. On earth before heaven. Such as Jesus Christ the Son of God had *His* role on earth. We saved our money to paint the ceiling; the Greek man comes, uncovers the original, and he says 'This theater *meant* to be a church!' So we have above us the original ceiling, the true ceiling,

the heaven we aspire to. Time will pass and our house of worship
will be all over as beautiful as the sky. But what we gotta do first,
in this world of crack and rape and muggings we been forced to live
in? What we gotta do first?'' He made a dramatic gesture in Nick's
direction. Nick ran his hands over the lowest keys, effecting a
thunderous rumble through the room.

The congregation cried, "Save the children! Save the children!''

"Right! And the world will be *ree*-stored like our church. A
celestial retreat. Heaven on earth!'' The preacher nodded to the
organist. The men released Desmond's arms.

"You can go now," said the man on his left, complacent,
West Indian. Desmond first walked, then began to run down the
aisle toward Nick. Nick saw him, slid off the woman's lap, and
rushed to greet his father. The organist began to play. The
congregation sang:

> *Swing low, sweet chariot,*
> *Comin' for to carry me home.*

Nick and Timothy Desmond were embracing in mid-aisle. The
eyes of the parishioners danced over them as they raised their
voices in sweeter and sweeter harmony:

> *I looked over Jordan*
> *And what did I see*
> *Comin' for to carry me home?*
> *There was a band of angels*
> *Comin' after me,*
> *Comin' for to carry me home.*

As one, the churchgoers, already standing, raised their hands
worshipfully toward the domed ceiling. Then the musicians, the
ushers, the strong men in the back, followed suit. Finally, the

Desmonds did the same. Everyone stood still, in silent witness to the miracle, the miracle that was ongoing.

Colon and Jackson burst through the doors, one to each aisle, knelt, and assumed the position.

"Lift 'em to the skies," shouted Colon before he had a chance to take in the situation.

"We already are, gentlemen," said the preacher, smiling.

Colon felt a flush in his cheeks. He saw Desmond holding his son. The professor waved to him, giving him the A-OK sign. Colon and Jackson stood slowly.

Colon nodded his head, looking with embarrassment at his gun. Then he remembered: "Where's the loony? Who took the kid?"

The preacher looked to the rear of the stage. A shiny-new marble font stood there, ornate and overstated in contrast to all but the central ceiling. Two large men the size of professional football linemen stood about ten feet in front of the stone basin, arms folded, facing the congregation.

"The man is in the baptistry," the preacher intoned, "subdued but unharmed." He chuckled. "We thought we'd just dunk him to cool him off for a moment, but he seems to *like* it in there. He's sort of kneeling with his head just out of the water. Maybe," he continued with greater resonance, so he could be heard throughout the church, "he's praying for forgiveness. There is, you know, always the possibility of Salvation through Faith."

The two detectives stepped forward. They looked at one another, shook their heads, and holstered their weapons. Colon showed the preacher his badge. "Sorry for the bother, Reverend. And thank you." Colon gestured for Jackson to follow him. They edged past the impervious guards and slowly approached the font. There was a ripple, then a gurgling sound from the surface of the water. Jackson started, then gripped Colon's arm. "Oh, *shit!*" he breathed.

Colon took a quick step forward so he, too, could see over the edge of the marble wall.

Livid swirls of crimson rose with a kind of urgency to the surface of the water. For a moment, the policemen could make out the self-inflicted wounds on Swartz's wrists, then the color was deeper, more viscous, unpenetrable to the eye. A bloodbath.

"He's empty," Jackson said and, rolling up his sleeves, fished around in the pool until he came up with a short paring knife. He held it up for Colon to see, gave a knowing look, and dropped it in the plastic bag he had taken out of his pocket.

Colon twitched. "That must've been rough," he said. "Not exactly state-of-the-art surgical equipment." Jackson nodded. Colon tried to concentrate on the saints and rehabilitated sinners painted on the marble exterior. Then he put back his head and contemplated the bright dome of hope above them. He was thinking of DeSales. He poked Jackson in the arm, prodding him to initiate their professional duties. He coughed, then took a deep breath and said, "At his most cynical, the Saint couldn't have written a better scenario than this one."

"We got the kid back, didn't we?" Jackson sounded almost defensive. "Listen, you call the morgue and get this cleaned up. I'll take care of the congregation. These are *my* people."

"Daddy," said Nick Desmond with enthusiasm, unaware of what had taken place on the other side of the altar, "this is *fun*! Why don't *we* go to church? I want to be an organism when I grow up."

Desmond was rocking his son in his lap, oblivious to all but the salvation of his family.

"Organ*ist*," he corrected. "Organ*ist*."

CHAPTER 33

MEGAN MOORE SAT PROPPED against an upended lifeguard's boat, a sad vestige of lost summers. She shivered uncontrollably. She adjusted with shaky fingers one part or another of the outsized lime-green sweat suit Mildred Pearl had loaned her and she had changed into under the blanket. She sipped chicken soup from the thermos. She breathed more easily, nodding agreement—without much comprehension—to the solicitous questions of the Polar Bears. To the crew from her station that had arrived so uncannily soon in the wake of the first cop cars, she shook her head: no, she was not yet ready to go on camera; and double no, she was not speaking to the authorities until her lawyer arrived. She watched the mild surf trickle onto the sand, which grew pinker as the day wore on. Her face reddened at the thought of them all: Rand, Merry, Big Bird, Brother Sam. But especially the NYPD and Francis DeSales. She was taking them to court. After she managed the energy to scorch their asses on live TV, before the American public.

And then the warmth would go cold, as if a cloud had passed over, and Megan would shiver and fidget again, pulling at the waistband of the pastel cotton leisure togs, tucking the blanket up under her chin.

Allen Pearl let out a low whistle. "Catch this one," he exclaimed.

Megan tipped her head against the hull of the long lifeboat and watched Allen flip the dark lenses down over his regular spectacles and push back the yachting cap on his head. She followed her rescuer's gaze, and was sure she was hallucinating.

A man in a Hopalong Cassidy outfit had climbed out of a blue-and-white police cruiser on Brightwater Avenue and was sprinting across the beach in their direction.

"Another nut," said Mildred. "They must've sent all the carny types from Coney Island over here."

Allen chuckled. "Remember the old days? When we'd go in the fun house at Luna Park and call it Loony Park and think we were the greatest wits that ever hit the seashore?"

The cowboy's hat blew off. The man didn't bother to chase it. He stumbled. While he drew himself back up, Megan saw he wore sheepskin chaps. And even when running a fairly smooth course he had a strange gait.

"Looks like he's got a chapped ass," chortled another of the Polar Bears from behind the hull. There were titters from some of the women.

But Megan Moore was not amused. The costume and the impending sense of Halloween doom she had felt since DeSales had abandoned her reminded her of the missing child everyone had been talking about. Spirited out of Prospect Park under the eyes of the cops and, it was reported, the kid's own parents. Truth be told, Megan felt jealous, like an orphaned child herself. And the one kidnapped from the park was being retrieved by the collective force of DeSales and the entire city while she had been shunted aside, left out in the cold in the periphery of the outer boroughs, surrounded by mere patrolmen and a motley collection of garment manufacturers and their bridge-clubbing wives. She felt the heat return to her cheeks. Vengeance would be hers.

Then she saw the cowboy approach, saw the long pistol in the holster dangling between his legs, slapping from thigh to thigh. This was what was impeding his stride. But she was still thinking angrily of DeSales as the man pulled up and adjusted the gunbelt so that he could run freely. And then she saw it *was* DeSales.

"Oh my God," screamed Mildred Pearl. "He's *armed!*"

Megan's protectors began ducking for cover. She laughed. "Don't worry. It's only that *cop*. The one who got me into this." And then her voice cracked and she was afraid she was going to cry.

She swallowed hard, sipped some chicken soup, squinted away from DeSales, down the stretch of pink sand, past the salt spray and whitecaps and pleasure boats. Toward Europe. When she turned back, she wore a nasty smile that cut creases into the corners of her eyes. "Ready, boys," she called to the crew. "Let's get this guy in all his glory!"

The Polar Bears were back on their feet. "I'd love to see him *swim*," called one. "On top of the way he *runs*."

Then he was standing there, panting. Megan stood up, dropping the blanket with which she had infantilized herself, and looked him over with scorn. She had been chased across the same expanse by a couple of killers and hadn't been so out of breath, so out of shape, so lathered up. He spread his arms and attempted to speak, but couldn't get the words out. Where his hair was always neatly parted and slicked down, it was standing on end, revealing bald spots and a general sense of oiliness. Sweat oozed from his forehead.

Her stomach went into a tailspin. The man against whom she had sworn revenge was nothing but a child dressed up like a grown-up hero. And an aging, foolish, clumsy child at that.

Finally, DeSales got his jaws working in synch and he croaked: "Megan, I'm sorry."

He was in her power now, but the same something that had snapped her resolve refused to allow her to act on the concession.

She had had her arm raised, poised to signal the crew to start shooting, but she faltered.

There was a glint of recognition in his eye, one she should have mightily resented, but she didn't. She couldn't.

"I mean it. I'm sorry. I made a mistake." He took a tentative step forward. "I *owe* you one."

Raising an eyebrow, Megan Moore looked back at the Polar Bears. They were watching the little scene as intently as if it were an episode from "As The World Turns." Mildred Pearl winked, nodding her head vigorously. Megan's voice was harsh; she began giving orders to the crew: "Cut, already, you guys. We're not ready for pictures yet. I don't even have on my *makeup*." The men lowered their cameras. Then she turned back to DeSales, seeing him whole for the first time: not just a little boy; a man who had lived to middle age bound up by his defenses, his uniforms, his guns, his assorted toys. He had never before had the strength to give in. And now he was repeating himself.

"I said I owe you one, Megan."

She took his hands in hers. They were smaller, softer, than she remembered.

"You sure do," she said.